CHRIST
THE
LORD

CHRIST THE LORD

Out of Egypt

A Novel

ANNE RICE

Chatto & Windus
LONDON

Published by Chatto & Windus 2005
First published in the United States of America by Knopf in 2005

2 4 6 8 10 9 7 5 3 1

Copyright © 2005 by Anne O'Brien Rice

Anne O'Brien Rice has asserted her right under the Copyright, Designs
and Patents Act 1988 to be identified as the author of this work

First published in Great Britain in 2005 by
Chatto & Windus
Random House, 20 Vauxhall Bridge Road,
London SW1V 2SA

Random House Australia (Pty) Limited
20 Alfred Street, Milsons Point, Sydney,
New South Wales 2061, Australia

Random House New Zealand Limited
18 Poland Road, Glenfield,
Auckland 10, New Zealand

Random House (Pty) Limited
Isle of Houghton, Corner Boundary Road & Carse O'Gowrie,
Houghton, 2198, South Africa

The Random House Group Limited Reg. No. 954009
www.randomhouse.co.uk

A CIP catalogue record for this book
is available from the British Library

ISBN 0 7011 7692 X

Papers used by Random House are natural,
recyclable products made from wood grown in sustainable forests;
the manufacturing processes conform to the environmental
regulations of the country of origin

Printed and bound in Australia by
Griffin Press

FOR

Christopher

When Israel went out of Egypt, the house of Jacob from a
    people of strange language;
Judah was his sanctuary, and Israel his dominion.
The sea saw it, and fled: Jordan was driven back.
The mountains skipped like rams, and the little hills like
    lambs.
What ailed thee, O thou sea, that thou fleddest? thou
    Jordan, that thou wast driven back?
Ye mountains, that ye skipped like rams; and ye little hills,
    like lambs?
Tremble, thou earth, at the presence of the Lord, at the
    presence of the God of Jacob;
Which turned the rock into a standing water, the flint into a
    fountain of waters.

—Psalm 114. King James Version

CHRIST
THE
LORD

I

I WAS SEVEN YEARS OLD. What do you know when you're seven years old? All my life, or so I thought, we'd been in the city of Alexandria, in the Street of the Carpenters, with the other Galileans, and sooner or later we were going home.

Late afternoon. We were playing, my gang against his, and when he ran at me again, bully that he was, bigger than me, and catching me off balance, I felt the power go out of me as I shouted: "You'll never get where you're going."

He fell down white in the sandy earth, and they all crowded around him. The sun was hot and my chest was heaving as I looked at him. He was so limp.

In the snap of two fingers everyone drew back. It seemed the whole street went quiet except for the carpenters' hammers. I'd never heard such a quiet.

"He's dead!" Little Joses said. And then they all took it up. "He's dead, he's dead, he's dead."

I knew it was true. He was a bundle of arms and legs in the beaten dust.

And I was empty. The power had taken everything with it, all gone.

His mother came out of the house, and her scream went

up the walls into a howl. From everywhere the women came running.

My mother lifted me off my feet. She carried me down the street and through the courtyard and into the dark of our house. All my cousins crowded in with us, and James, my big brother, pulled the curtain shut. He turned his back on the light. He said:

"Jesus did it. He killed him." He was afraid.

"Don't you say such a thing!" said my mother. She clutched me so close to her, I could scarcely breathe.

Big Joseph woke up.

Now Big Joseph was my father, because he was married to my mother, but I'd never called him Father. I'd been taught to call him Joseph. I didn't know why.

He'd been asleep on the mat. We'd worked all day on a job in Philo's house, and he and the rest of the men had lain down in the heat of the afternoon to sleep. He climbed to his feet.

"What's that shouting outside?" he asked. "What's happened?"

He looked to James. James was his eldest son. James was the son of a wife who had died before Joseph married my mother.

James said it again.

"Jesus killed Eleazer. Jesus cursed him and he fell down dead."

Joseph stared at me, his face still blank from sleep. There was more and more shouting in the street. He rose to his feet, and ran his hands back through his thick curly hair.

My little cousins were slipping through the door one by one and crowding around us.

My mother was trembling. "He couldn't have done it," she said. "He wouldn't do such a thing."

"I saw it," said James. "I saw it when he made the spar-rows out of clay on the Sabbath. The teacher told him he shouldn't do such things on the Sabbath. Jesus looked at the birds and they turned into real birds. They flew away. You saw it too. He killed Eleazer, Mother, I saw it."

My cousins made a ring of white faces in the shadows: Little Joses, Judas, and Little Symeon and Salome, watching anxiously, afraid of being sent out. Salome was my age, and my dearest and closest. Salome was like my sister.

Then in came my mother's brother Cleopas, always the talker, who was the father of these cousins, except for Big Silas who came in now, a boy older than James. He went into the corner, and then came his brother, Levi, and both wanted to see what was going on.

"Joseph, they're all out there," said Cleopas, "Jonathan bar Zakkai, and his brothers, they're saying Jesus killed their boy. They're envious that we got that job at Philo's house, they're envious that we got the other job before that, they're envious that we're getting more and more jobs, they're so sure they do things better than we do——."

"Is the boy dead?" Joseph said. "Or is the boy alive?"

Salome shot forward and whispered in my ear. "Just make him come alive, Jesus, the way you made the birds come alive!"

Little Symeon was giggling. He was too little to know what was going on. Little Judas knew, but he was quiet.

"Stop," said James, the little boss of the children. "Salome, be quiet."

I could hear them shouting in the street. I heard other noises. Stones were hitting the walls of the house. My mother started to cry.

"You dare do that!" shouted my uncle Cleopas and he rushed back out through the door. Joseph went after him.

I wriggled out of my mother's grasp and darted out before she could catch me, and past my uncle and Joseph and right into the crowd as they were all waving and hollering and shaking their fists. I went so fast, they didn't even see me. I was like a fish in the river. I moved in and out through people who were shouting over my head until I got to Eleazer's house.

The women all had their backs to the door, and they didn't see me as I went around the edge of the room.

I went right into the dark room, where they'd laid him on the mat. His mother was there leaning on her sister and sobbing.

There was only one lamp, very weak.

Eleazer was pale with his arms at his sides, same soiled tunic, and the soles of his feet very black. He was dead. His mouth was open and his white teeth showed over his lip.

The Greek physician came in—he was really a Jew—and he knelt down, and he looked at Eleazer and he shook his head.

Then he saw me and said:

"Out."

His mother turned and she saw it was me and she screamed.

I bent over him:

"Wake up, Eleazer," I said. "Wake up now."

I reached out and laid my hand on his forehead.

The power went out. My eyes closed. I was dizzy. But I heard him draw in his breath.

His mother screamed over and over and it hurt my ears. Her sister screamed. All the women were screaming.

I fell back on the floor. I was weak. The Greek physician was staring down at me. I was sick. The room was dim. Other people had rushed in.

Eleazer came up, and he was up all knees and fists before anyone could get to him, and he set on me and punched me and hit me, and knocked my head back against the ground, and kicked me again and again:

"Son of David, Son of David!" he shouted, mocking me, "Son of David, Son of David!" kicking me in the face, and in the ribs, until his father grabbed him around the waist and picked him up in the air.

I ached all over, couldn't breathe.

"Son of David!" Eleazer kept shouting.

Someone lifted me and carried me out of the house and into the crowd in the street. I was still gasping. I hurt all over. It seemed the whole street was screaming, worse than before, and someone said the Teacher was coming, and my uncle Cleopas was yelling in Greek at Jonathan, Eleazer's father, and Jonathan was yelling back, and Eleazer was shouting, "Son of David, Son of David!"

I was in Joseph's arms. He was trying to move, but the crowd wouldn't let him. Cleopas was pushing at Eleazer's father. Eleazer's father was trying to get at Cleopas, but other men took hold of his arms. I heard Eleazer shouting far away.

There was the Teacher declaring: "That child's not dead, you hush up, Eleazer, who said he was dead? Eleazer, stop shouting! Whoever could think this child is dead?"

"Brought him back to life, that's what he did," said one of theirs.

We were in our courtyard, the entire crowd had pushed in with us, my uncle and Eleazer's people still screaming at each other, and the Teacher demanding order.

Now my uncles, Alphaeus and Simon, had come. These were Joseph's brothers. And they'd just woken up. They put up their hands against the crowd. Their mouths were hard and their eyes were big.

My aunts, Salome and Esther and Mary, were there, with all the cousins running and jumping as if this were a festival, except for Silas and Levi and James who stood with the men.

Then I couldn't see anymore.

I was in my mother's arms, and she had taken me into the front room. It was dark. Aunt Esther and Aunt Salome came in with her. I could hear stones hitting the house again. The Teacher raised his voice in Greek.

"There's blood on your face!" my mother whispered. "Your eye, there's blood. Your face is cut!" She was crying. "Oh, look what's happened to you," she said. She spoke in Aramaic, our tongue which we didn't speak very much.

"I'm not hurt," I said. I meant to say it didn't matter. Again my cousins pressed close, Salome smiling as if to say she knew I could bring him back to life, and I took her hand and squeezed it.

But there was James with his hard look.

The Teacher came into the room backwards with his hands up. Someone ripped the curtain away and the light was very bright. Joseph and his brothers came in. And so did Cleopas. All of us had to move to make room.

"You're talking about Joseph and Cleopas and Alphaeus, what do you mean drive them out!" said the Teacher to the whole crowd. "They've been with us for seven years!"

The angry family of Eleazer came almost into the room. The father himself did come into the room.

"Yes, seven years and why don't they go back to Galilee, all of them!" Eleazer's father shouted. "Seven years is too long! That boy is possessed of a demon and I tell you my son was dead!"

"Are you complaining that he's alive now! What's the matter with you!" demanded my uncle Cleopas.

"You sound like a madman!" added my uncle Alphaeus.

And thus and so it went, with them shouting back and forth, and making fists at each other, and the women nodding and throwing glances to one another, and far off others joining in.

"Oh, that you say such things!" said the Teacher, saying every word as if we were in the House of Study. "Jesus and James are my finest pupils. And these men are your neighbors, what's happened to make you turn against them like this! Listen to your own words!"

"Oh, your pupils, your pupils!" cried Eleazer's father. "But we have to live and work, and there's more to life than being a pupil!" More of them came into the room.

My mother backed up against the wall, holding me close. I wanted to get away, but I couldn't. She was too afraid.

"Yes, work, that's it," my uncle Cleopas said, "and who's to say we can't live here, what do you mean drive us out, just because more of the work goes to us, because we're better and better at giving people what they want—."

Suddenly Joseph put up his hands and he roared out the word: "Quiet!"

And they all went quiet.

The whole mob of them fell quiet.

Never had Joseph raised his voice before.

"The Lord made shame for an argument such as this!" Joseph said. "You break the walls of my house."

No one said anything. Everyone looked at him. Even Eleazer was there and he looked up at him.

Not even the Teacher spoke.

"Now Eleazer is alive," Joseph said. "And as it happens, we are going home to Galilee."

Again no one spoke.

"We will leave for the Holy Land as soon as our few jobs are finished here. We'll bid you farewell, and those jobs that come to us as we prepare to go we'll send to you by your leave."

Eleazer's father stretched his neck, then nodded and opened his hands. He shrugged. He bowed his head, and then he turned. His men turned. Eleazer stared at me, and then all of them went out of the room.

The crowd left the courtyard, and my aunt Mary, the Egyptian, who was Cleopas' wife, came in and closed the curtain partway.

What was left now was all our people, and the Teacher. The Teacher was not happy. He looked at Joseph. He frowned.

My mother wiped her eyes, and looked to my face, but then the Teacher began to talk. She held me close, her hands shaking violently.

"Leaving to go home?" said the Teacher. "And taking my fine students with you? Taking my fine Jesus? And what will you go home to, may I ask? To the land of milk and honey?"

"You mock our forefathers?" asked my uncle Cleopas.

"Or you mock the Lord Himself?" asked my uncle Alphaeus, whose Greek was as good as the Teacher's Greek.

"I don't mock anyone," said the Teacher, looking at me as he spoke, "but I marvel you can leave Egypt behind so easily over a little hubbub in the street."

"That has nothing to do with it," said Joseph.

"Then why go? Jesus is coming along wonderfully here. Why, Philo is so impressed with his learning and James here is a marvel, and . . ."

"Yes, and this isn't Israel, is it?" asked Cleopas. "And it isn't our home."

"No, and it's Greek that you're teaching them, Scripture in Greek!" said Alphaeus. "And we teach them here at home in Hebrew because you don't even know Hebrew and you are the Teacher, and this is what the House of Study is here, Greek, and you call it the Torah, and Philo, yes, the great Philo, he gives us work to do, and so do his friends, and all this is very fine, and we've done well, and we're grateful, yes, but he too speaks Greek and reads the Scriptures in Greek, and marvels at what these boys know in Greek—."

"All the world speaks Greek now," said the Teacher. "The Jews in every city of the Empire speak Greek and read the Scripture in Greek—."

"Jerusalem does not speak Greek!" said Alphaeus.

"In Galilee we read the Scripture in Hebrew," said Cleopas. "Do you even understand Hebrew, and you call yourself a Teacher!"

"Oh, I'm weary of your attacks, why do I put up with you, where are you taking yourselves and these boys, back to some dirt village! You leave Alexandria for that."

"Yes," said Uncle Cleopas, "and it's no dirt village, it's my father's house. Do you know one word of Hebrew?" He then sang out in Hebrew the psalm that he loved and had long taught to us. "The Lord shall preserve my going out and my coming in from this time forth, and even for evermore." Following it with "Now do you know what that means?"

"Do you yourself know what that means!" shot back the Teacher. "I'd like to hear you explain it. You know what the scribe in your synagogue taught you what it means, that's all you know and if you learned enough Greek here to shout in my face, you're the better for it. What do any of you know, you hardheaded Galilean Jews? Coming to Egypt for refuge, and leaving as hardheaded as you came."

My mother was anxious.

The Teacher looked at me.

"And to take this child, this brilliant child—."

"And what would you have us do?" asked Alphaeus.

"Oh, no, don't ask such a thing!" my mother whispered. It was so unusual for her to speak up.

Joseph glanced at her, and then looked at the Teacher. The Teacher went on.

"It's always the same," said the Teacher with a great drawn-out sigh. "In times of trouble, you come down to Egypt, yes, always to Egypt, she receives the dregs of Palestine. . . ."

"The dregs!" Cleopas said. "You call our forefathers the dregs?"

"They didn't speak Greek either," said Alphaeus.

Cleopas laughed. "And the Lord on Sinai didn't speak Greek," he said.

Uncle Simon said quietly, "And the High Priest now in Jerusalem, when he lays his hands on the goat, he probably forgets to tell all our sins in Greek."

They were all laughing. The older boys laughed. Aunt Mary laughed. But my mother was still crying. I had to stay by her side.

Even Joseph smiled.

The Teacher was angry. He went on:

". . . if there's a famine, come down to Egypt, if there's no work, come down to Egypt, if there's a murderous rampage on the part of Herod, come down to Egypt, as if King Herod took the slightest care as to the fate of a handful of Galilean Jews such as you! A murderous rampage! As if—."

"Stop," Joseph said.

The Teacher stopped.

All the men stared at the Teacher. No one said a word. No one moved.

What had happened? What had the Teacher said? *Murderous rampage.* What were these words?

Even James had the same look on his face as the men.

"Oh, you think people don't talk about these things?" asked the Teacher. "As if I believe travelers' tales."

They said nothing.

Then in a soft voice Joseph spoke.

"The Lord made patience for this!" he said. "But I don't have it. We go home because it is our home," he went on, staring at the Teacher, "and it is the Lord's land. And because Herod is dead."

The Teacher was taken aback. Everyone else was surprised. Even my mother was surprised, and I could see the women looking at each other.

Now, we little ones all knew Herod was the King of the Holy Land, and we knew he was a bad man. Only lately had he done a terrible thing, a desecrating of the Temple, or so we'd heard as all the men talked about it but we didn't know much more than that.

The Teacher was frowning at Joseph.

"Joseph, it's not wise to say such a thing," the Teacher said. "You can't speak of the King in this way."

"He is dead," said Joseph. "The news will come by the Roman post in two days."

The Teacher was cold. All the others were quiet, eyes on Joseph.

"How do you know?" asked the Teacher.

No answer.

"It will take a little while to prepare for our journey," Joseph said. "Our boys will have to work with us until then. No more school for them now, I fear."

"And what will Philo think?" asked the Teacher, "when he hears that you're taking Jesus?"

"What has Philo to do with my son," said my mother. Her voice shocked everyone.

Another silence followed.

I knew this was not an easy moment.

A while back, the Teacher had taken me to Philo, a rich man and a scholar, to show me to him as a fine pupil, and Philo had taken a great liking to me, and even taken me to the Great Synagogue which was as large and beautiful as the pagan temples of the city, where the rich Jews gathered on the Sabbath, a place to which my family never went. We went to the little House of Prayer in our own street.

It was after those visits that Philo had given work to us from his house, to make wooden doors and benches and book stands for his new library, and soon his friends had given our family similar jobs which meant good wages as well.

Philo had treated me as a guest when I was brought to him.

And even today when we had put in the doors on their pivots, and picked up the painted benches from the men who did the painting and taken them to Philo, I had seen him and he had taken time with us to tell Joseph kind things about me.

But to talk of this now, that Philo had taken a liking to me? It was not right, and I felt the men were uneasy as they looked at the Teacher. They had worked hard for Philo and for Philo's friends.

The Teacher did not answer my mother.

Finally Joseph said: "Philo should be surprised that my son goes home with me to Nazareth?"

"Nazareth?" said the Teacher coldly. "What is Nazareth? I've never heard of such a place. You came here from Bethlehem. Your terrible stories, why you——. Philo thinks Jesus is the most promising scholar he's ever seen. Philo would educate your son if you would allow. That's what Philo has to do with your son, that's what Philo's said. Philo would see to it—."

"Philo has nothing to do with our son," said my mother, again shocking all that she spoke up, her hands clasping my shoulders tightly.

No more the rich house with its marble floors. No more the library of parchment scrolls. Smell of ink. Greek is the language of the Empire. See this? This is a map of the Empire. Hold the edge for me there. Look. All this Rome rules. There is Rome, here is Alexandria, here is Jerusalem. See, there Antioch, Damascus, Corinth, Ephesus, all great cities, and in all these cities the Jews live and speak Greek and have Torah in Greek. But there is no city outside of Rome as great as Alexandria where we are now.

I shook off the memory. James was staring at me. The Teacher was talking to me.

". . . but you liked Philo, didn't you? You liked answering his questions. You liked his library."

"He stays with us," said Joseph calmly. "He will not go to Philo."

The Teacher continued to stare at me. This was not right.

"Jesus, speak up!" he said. "You want to be educated by Philo, don't you?"

"My lord, I do as my father and mother want," I said. I shrugged. What was I to do?

The Teacher turned and threw up his hands.

"When will you go?" he asked.

"As soon as we can," said Joseph. "We have work to finish."

"I want to send word to Philo that Jesus is leaving," said the Teacher, and with that he turned to go. But Joseph stopped him.

"We've done well in Egypt," he said. He took money out

of his purse. He pressed it into the hand of the Teacher. "I thank you for teaching our children."

"Yes, yes, and you take them back to—where was it? Joseph, there are more Jews living in Alexandria than there are in Jerusalem."

"There may be, Teacher," said Cleopas, "but the Lord dwells in the Temple in Jerusalem, and his land is the Holy Land."

All the men laughed to approve and the women too and so did I and Little Salome and Judas, Joses and Symeon.

The Teacher couldn't say anything to this, but only nodded.

"And if we finish our work quickly," Joseph said with a sigh, "we can reach Jerusalem in time for Passover."

We all gave cries of delight when we heard it. Jerusalem. Passover. We were all excited. Salome clapped her hands. Even Uncle Cleopas was smiling.

The Teacher bowed his head. He put two fingers to his lips. Then he gave us a blessing:

"May the Lord go with you on your journey. May you reach your home in peace."

The Teacher left.

At once all the family was speaking our native tongue for the first time in the whole afternoon.

My mother looked at me, ready to nurse my cuts and bruises. "Why, they're gone," she whispered. "You're healed."

"It wasn't much," I said. I was so happy we were going home.

2

THAT NIGHT, AFTER SUPPER, while the men were dozing on their mats in the courtyard, Philo came.

He sat down to a cup of wine with Joseph, just as if he wasn't wearing white linen and wouldn't be soiled, and crossed his legs like the other men. I sat beside Joseph, hoping to hear all that was said, but then my mother took me inside.

She listened behind the curtain and she let me listen. Aunt Salome and Aunt Esther were there too.

Philo wanted to keep me and instruct me and send me back to Joseph an educated young man. Joseph listened to all this in silence but said no. Joseph was my father and Joseph must take me back to Nazareth. He knew that this was what he had to do. He thanked Philo, and offered him wine again, and said that he would see to it that I was educated as a Jew.

"You forget, my lord," he said in his gentle manner, "that on Sabbath all Jews are philosophers and scholars the world wide. It's no different in the town of Nazareth, believe me."

Philo was pleased at that and nodded and smiled.

"He'll go to school in the mornings, as all the boys do," Joseph went on. "And we will have our disputes over the Law and the Prophets. And we'll go up to Jerusalem and there at the Feasts, maybe he'll listen to the teachers in the Temple. I have many a time."

When Philo offered a gift for my education, a little purse that he wanted to put into Joseph's hand, Joseph said no.

Philo took his ease awhile, and he talked of many things with Joseph, of the city and of the jobs our men had done, and of the Empire, and then he asked Joseph how Joseph was so certain that King Herod was dead.

"The news will reach here soon with the Roman post," Joseph said. "As for me, I knew it in a dream, my lord. And it means for us we will go home."

My uncles who had sat quietly all this time in the dark came in with their agreement, and how much they had despised the King.

The strange words of the Teacher, his talk of murderous rampages, were in my mind, but the men never spoke of that, and finally it came time for Philo to go.

He didn't even dust off his fine linen as he stood up, and he thanked Joseph over and over for the good wine, and wished us well.

I ran out. I walked a way with Philo up the street. He had two slaves with him who carried torches and I'd never seen the Street of the Carpenters so brightly lighted at this hour, and I knew people were watching from the courtyards where they took their ease in the breeze from the sea that came with the dark.

Philo told me to always remember Egypt and the map of the Empire which he had shown me.

"But why don't all the Jews go back to Israel?" I asked him. "If we are Jews, shouldn't we live in the land the Lord gave to us? I don't understand."

He thought for a moment. Then he said, "A Jew can live anywhere and be a Jew. We have the Torah, the Prophets, the Tradition. We live as Jews wherever we are. And don't we take the Word of the One True Lord wherever we go? Don't we establish his Word among the pagans wherever we live? I live here because my father lived here and his father before him. You go home because your father wants you to go home."

My father.

A chill passed over me. *Joseph was not my father.* I had always known this, but it wasn't something to be said to anyone, ever. And I didn't say anything about it now.

I nodded.

"Remember me," Philo said.

I kissed his hands, and he bent down and kissed me on both cheeks.

He was going home to a fine supper perhaps, in his house of marble floors and lamps everywhere, and rich curtains, and the upper rooms open to the sea.

He turned back once to wave to me and then he and his servants with their torches were gone.

I felt sad for a moment, just a moment, enough never to forget it, this stabbing sadness. But I was too excited to be returning to the Holy Land.

And I hurried back home.

In the darkness, I came up quietly on the courtyard, and I heard my mother crying. She sat next to Joseph.

"But I don't know why we can't settle in Bethlehem," she was saying. "It seems we were meant to return there."

Bethlehem, where I was born.

"Never," said Joseph. "We can't even consider such a thing." He was kind as always with her. "How could you think this, that we could ever go back to Bethlehem?"

"But I've been hoping all this time," my mother pressed. "It's been seven years, and people forget, if they ever understood. . . ."

My uncle Cleopas who lay flat on his back with his knees crooked was laughing softly, the way he laughed at so many things. My uncle Alphaeus said nothing. He appeared to be looking up at the stars. I could see James in the doorway watching, and listening too perhaps.

"Think of all the signs," said my mother. "Think of the night when the men from the East came. Why, that alone—."

"That's just it," said Joseph who sat beside her. "Do you think anybody there has forgotten that? Do you think they've forgotten anything? We can never go there."

Cleopas laughed again.

Joseph paid no mind to Cleopas and neither did my mother. Joseph put his arm around my mother.

"They'll remember the star," said Joseph, "the shepherds coming in from the hills. They'll remember the men from the East. Above all, they'll remember the night that—."

"Don't say it, please," said my mother. She put her hands to her ears. "Please don't say those words."

"Don't you see, we must take him and go to Nazareth. We have no choice. Besides . . ."

"What star? What men from the East?" I asked. I couldn't hold back anymore. "What happened?"

Again, my uncle Cleopas laughed under his breath.

My mother looked up at me. She hadn't known I was there. "You mustn't worry about it," she said.

"But what happened in Bethlehem?" I asked.

Joseph was looking at me.

"Our house is in Nazareth," said my mother to me. Her voice was stronger. It was a voice for me. "You have more cousins than you can count in Nazareth. Old Sarah's waiting for us, and Old Justus. These are our kindred in common. We're returning to our house." She stood up and beckoned for me to come.

"Yes," said Joseph. "We'll leave as soon as we can. It will take us a few days, but we'll be in time for Passover in Jerusalem and then go on home."

My mother took me by the hand and started to lead me inside.

"But who were the men from the East, Mamma?" I asked. "Can't you tell me?"

My uncle would not stop his soft laughing.

Even in the dark, I could see the strange expression on Joseph's face.

"Some night, I'll tell you all of it," said my mother. Her tears were gone. She was strong for me as always, not the child she was with Joseph. "You mustn't ask me these things now. Not now. I'll tell when the time comes."

"This is true," said Joseph. "I don't want you to ask, do you understand?"

They were gentle, but these were clear and strange words. All the words they'd spoken were strange.

I should have let them go on talking. I would have learned more. And I knew it was a great secret, this that they talked about. How could it not be? And as for me hearing it, they knew they'd made a mistake.

I didn't want to sleep. I lay on my blanket trying to sleep, but sleep didn't come and I didn't want it. I never wanted it. But now my thoughts were racing. We were going home, and I had so much to think about because so much had happened, and now they were saying these strange things.

And what had happened today? What had happened

with Eleazer and what had happened with him, that, and the memory of the sparrows insofar as I could remember it— these were like bright shapes in my mind for which I didn't have words. I'd never felt anything before like the power that had come out of me just before Eleazer fell dead in the dust, or the power that had come out of me just before he'd risen from the mat. *Son of David, Son of David, Son of David . . .*

Little by little everyone came in to sleep. The women were in their corner, and I had Little Justus snuggled up to me, Simon's youngest son. Little Salome was singing softly to Baby Esther who was, by some miracle, quiet.

Cleopas was coughing, talking to himself but saying nothing, then sleeping again.

I felt a hand on mine. I opened my eyes. It was James next to me, James, my elder brother.

"What you did," he whispered.

"Yes?"

"Killing Eleazer, bringing him back?"

"Yes?"

"Never, never do that again," he said.

"I know," I answered.

"Nazareth is a small place," he said.

"I know," I said.

He turned away.

I rolled over, my head on my arm. I closed my eyes. I stroked the head of Little Justus. Without waking he snuggled closer.

What did I know?

"Jerusalem," I whispered. "Where the Lord dwells in the Temple." No one heard me. Philo had told me, It is the biggest Temple in all the world. I saw the clay sparrows that I had made. I saw them spring into life, heard the flap of wings, heard my mother's breath, Joseph's cry: "No!" and they were gone, tiny dots against the sky. "Jerusalem." I saw Eleazer rise from the mat.

Philo had said on that day when he received me in his house that the Temple was so beautiful that thousands came to see it, thousands, pagans and Jews from all the cities of the Empire, men and women journeying there to offer sacrifice to the Lord of All.

My eyes snapped open. All around me the others slept.

What did I think had happened in all this? A *great stumbling*.

Where had that power come from? Was it still there?

Joseph hadn't spoken one word to me about it. My mother hadn't asked me what had happened. Had we ever talked of the sparrows made on the Sabbath?

No. No one would talk of these things. And I couldn't ask anyone, now, could I? To talk of such things outside the family, that could never happen. Any more than I could stay in the great city of Alexandria and study with Philo in his house of marble floors.

I must be very very watchful from now on, that even in the smallest things I might misuse what was inside me, this power that could make Eleazer die and come back to life.

Oh, it had been all very well to make everyone smile at my quickness at learning, Philo and the Teacher and the other boys, and I knew so much of the Scripture in Greek, and in Hebrew thanks to Joseph and Uncle Cleopas and Uncle Alphaeus, but this was different.

I knew something now that was beyond what I could put into words.

I wanted to go to Joseph, to wake him up, to ask him for help in understanding this. But I knew he'd tell me not to ask about this any more than I should ask about the other things, the things I'd heard them saying. Because this power, this power was somehow linked to the things they'd been saying, and to the strange talk of the Teacher which had made them all go silent and look at him. It had to be linked.

It made me sad, so sad I wanted to cry. It was my fault we had to leave here. It was my fault, and even though everyone was happy, I felt sad and to blame.

All this was mine to keep inside. But I'd find out what had happened in Bethlehem. I'd find out some way, even though I had to do as Joseph said.

But for now, what was the very deep secret of all this? What was the inside of it? I must not misuse who *I am*.

A coldness came over me. I felt still and I felt very small. I pulled the blanket up around me. Sleepiness. It came as if an angel had touched me.

Better to sleep as all of them were sleeping. Better to drift as they drifted. Better to trust as they trusted. I stopped trying to stay awake and think on these things. I felt drowsy, so drowsy that I couldn't think anymore.

Cleopas was coughing again. Cleopas was going to be sick as he so often was. And that night I knew it would be bad. I heard the rattle down in his chest.

3

WITHIN DAYS THE NEWS ARRIVED in the port that Herod was dead. It was the talk of the Galileans and Judeans everywhere. How had Joseph known? The Teacher came storming back, demanding to know, but Joseph said nothing.

We were busy long hours completing the tasks we'd taken on, finishing doors, benches, lintels, and such that had to be leveled and smoothed, and finished, and then delivered to the painters. After that came the picking up of the items already painted and the putting of them into place in the houses of those who had hired us, which I liked because I saw many rooms, and different people, though we always worked with our heads down and our eyes down out of respect, but still I saw things. I learned things. And all this meant coming home after dark, tired and hungry.

It was more work than Joseph had thought but he didn't want to leave any promise unfulfilled, and meantime my mother wrote home to Old Sarah and her cousins that we were coming, James penning the letters for her and both of us taking them to the post, and all life was excited with preparations.

The spirit in the street was with us again now that everyone knew we were soon going. Other families gave us presents to take with us—small pottery lamps, and one a stoneware cup, and another a fine bit of linen.

It was almost resolved to go by land, with the purchase of donkeys planned, when Uncle Cleopas rose from his bed one night coughing badly and said:

"I don't want to die in the desert." He had become very pale, and thin, and had not been working much with us anymore, and this was all he had to say. No one answered him.

And so it was resolved, we would go by ship. It would cost us, everybody knew, but Joseph said we would do it. We would go to the old harbor of Jamnia. And we would reach Jerusalem in time for the Feast, and after that Cleopas slept better.

Then came time to leave. We were dressed in our finest woolen robes and sandals, everyone loaded with packs of goods. And it seemed the whole street turned out to see us off.

Tears were shed, and even Eleazer came to nod at me, and I at him, and then we were pressing our way through the thickest crowd I'd ever seen in the port, with my mother herding us together, and I clutching Salome's hand tight, and James telling us over and over to stay together. Over and over the heralds blew their trumpets for ships. And at last came the call for a ship to Jamnia, and then another, and another. Everywhere people were shouting and waving.

"Pilgrims," said Uncle Cleopas, laughing again the way he used to before he got sick. "The whole world's headed for Jerusalem."

"The whole world!" Little Salome shrieked. "Did you hear that?" she said to me.

I laughed with her.

We went pushing and shoving and clinging to our bundles with the men hollering and gesturing over our heads, the women cleaving together, and reaching out ,to snatch our arms and pull us in, and suddenly we were on the gangplank, very nearly falling into the murky water.

In all my life, I had never known such a thing as hitting the deck boards of this ship and as soon as the bundles had all been set down all together, and the women had climbed on top of them and faced each other with veils drawn, and James had given us his more serious and warning face, Salome and I dashed off and made for the rail of the ship, slipping under everyone to reach the point where we could see the port and all the other hurrying people who were still waving and disputing and carrying on, even though we were all but crushed by the bellies and backs against us.

We saw the plank drawn up, the ropes tossed aboard, the last sailor jumping onto the boat, and the water widen between us and the harbor, and suddenly there came that lurch as the boat moved out, and all aboard gave a loud shout, and we slipped away onto the belly of the sea and I squeezed Little Salome to myself, and we laughed for joy to feel the boat borne along beneath us.

We waved and hollered to people we didn't even know, and they waved back and I could feel the high spirits of everyone around me.

For moments, I thought Alexandria would disappear behind all her ships and their masts, but the farther out we moved, the more I could see the city, really see it as I'd never seen it, and a shadow passed over me, and if it hadn't been for Little Salome's happiness, I might not have been so happy too. But I was.

The wind picked up; the smell of the sea was suddenly clean and wonderful, and it caught at our hair and was cool on our faces. We were really leaving Egypt behind, and I wanted to break down and cry like a baby.

Then everyone was shouting for us to look at the Great Lighthouse, as if we could not see it looming over us to the left.

Now many times, I'd looked out to sea at the Great Lighthouse.

But what was that to passing before it now?

Heads were turned, and people were pointing, and finally Salome and I had a good view of it. It stood on its own little island—a great torch reaching the sky. And we passed it as if it was a holy thing, wondering and murmuring.

The ship moved on, and what had seemed slow now seemed very fast, and the sea was tossing up and down, and there were cries from some of the women.

People began to sing hymns. The land grew ever more distant. The lighthouse became small and then disappeared.

The crowd of those looking broke up, and for the first time I turned and saw the sight of the giant square sail filled with the wind and the sailors working the ropes, and the whole scene of the men at the tillers and all the families now huddled around their bundles, and I knew we had better get back to our own who were no doubt missing us.

People were singing louder and louder, and soon one hymn gripped the whole crowd, and Little Salome and I joined in, but the wind came scurrying to take the words away.

We had to pick our way through the families to find our own, but at last we did, and there were my mother and my aunts trying to sew as if their veils weren't being almost torn from their heads, and my aunt Mary saying that Uncle Cleopas was feverish and he himself curled up and sleeping beneath a blanket tucked tight and missing everything.

Joseph was just a little apart, seated on one of the few trunks we had with us, quiet as he always was, staring at the blue sky, and the mast above the sail where there was a top-sail, but my uncle Alphaeus was deep into arguing with other passengers on board about trouble ahead in Jerusalem.

Now James was all ears for this, and I was soon listening to it too, though I didn't dare move too close for fear they'd leave off if they noticed me. They were shouting against the growing wind, standing together, in a little space, fighting to keep their mantles from being blown off, shifting this way and that as the boat moved uneasily over the water.

At last, I had to hear what they were saying, and moved away towards them. Little Salome wanted to come, but her mother snatched her back, and I made a motion for her to wait, trying to tell her I'd come back to her.

"I tell you it's dangerous," one of the men said in Greek. He was a tall man with very dark skin and richly dressed. "I wouldn't be going to Jerusalem if I were you. For me it's home, and my wife and children are there. I have to get there. But I tell you, it's no time for all these pilgrim ships to be sailing."

"I want to be there," said the other, his Greek just as easy, though he was a rougher man. "I want to see what happens. I was there when Herod burnt alive both Matthias and Judas, two of the finest scholars of the Law we ever had." He nodded to both my uncles. "I want justice from Herod Archelaus. I want the men who served his father in this to be punished. How Archelaus handles this will argue for everything else."

I was amazed. I'd heard many bad things about King Herod. I didn't know a thing about the new Herod, his son, who was Archelaus.

"Well, what does he tell the people?" asked my uncle Alphaeus. "He must tell them something."

My uncle Cleopas, having roused himself from the company of the women, suddenly joined in. "He probably tells whatever lies he has to," he said as if he knew all about it. "He has to wait for Caesar to say whether he'll be King. He can't rule without Caesar confirming his crown. Nothing he says means anything anyway." My uncle gave one of his mocking laughs.

I wondered what they thought of him.

"He tells everyone to be patient, naturally," said the first man in his good Greek. It flowed easily like Greek did from our Teacher, or from Philo. "And he waits for Caesar's confirmation, yes, and he tells the people to wait. But the crowds don't even listen to his messengers. The crowds don't want patience right now. They want action. They want vengeance. And they just might get it."

This puzzled me.

"You have to realize," said the rough man, the more angry man, "that Caesar didn't know all the evil that old Herod did. How can Caesar know everything that goes on in the Empire? I tell you there has to be a reckoning for the things he did."

"Yes," said the tall one, "but not in Jerusalem at Passover, not when pilgrims have come from all over the Empire."

"Why not?" said the other, "why not when the whole world is there? Why not when the news will carry to Caesar that Herod Archelaus is not master of those who insist upon justice for the blood of those who were murdered?"

"But why did Herod burn alive the two teachers of the Law?" I asked. I did it suddenly, surprising myself.

At once Joseph turned from his thinking, though he was far away, and he looked over at me and then at the men.

But the taller one, the calm one, was already answering me.

"Because they pulled down the golden eagle Herod had

put above the great Temple gate, that's why," he said calmly. "The Law says plainly there shall be no image of a living thing in our Temple. You are old enough to know that, child. Don't you know it? Just because Herod built the Temple did not mean he could put an image of a living thing in it. What was the point to labor rebuilding a magnificent temple so that he could transgress the law and put on its walls an image that was a desecration?"

I understood him though his words were not so simple to understand. I shivered.

"These men were Pharisees, teachers of the Law," the tall man went on, fixing me with his eye. "They led their pupils with them to take down the eagle. And Herod took their lives for this!"

Joseph was at my side.

The angry man said, "Don't take him away, let him learn. He would know the names of Matthias and Judas. Both these boys should know." He nodded to me and James. "It was the right and just thing to do. And they knew what a monster Herod was. Everyone knew. You in Alexandria, what did it have to do with you?" He looked at my uncles. "But for us, we lived with him and his monstrosities. They were visited on great and small, I tell you. Once on a whim, a mad whim, fearing a new King had been born, a Son of David, he sent his soldiers two miles' walk from Jerusalem to the town of Bethlehem and . . ."

"No more!" Joseph said, though he smiled and nodded as he put up his hand.

He drew me away. Quickly and firmly, he brought me towards the women. James he allowed to stay there.

The wind swallowed up all their words.

"But what happened in Bethlehem?" I asked him.

"You'll hear stories about Herod's deeds all your life," Joseph said under his breath. "Remember, I told you that there were some questions that I didn't want for you to ask."

"Will we still go to Jerusalem?"

Joseph didn't answer. "Go there, and sit with your mother and the children," he said.

I did what he said.

The wind was blowing hard now and the boat was heaving. I felt a little sick. I was getting a little cold.

Little Salome was waiting to question me. I snuggled in between her and my mother. It was warm here and I felt better.

Joses and Symeon were already asleep in their lumpy bed among the bundles. Silas and Levi were huddled together with Eli, who was the nephew of Aunt Mary of Uncle Cleopas, who had come to live with us. They were pointing to the sail and to the rig.

"What were they saying?" Salome wanted to know.

"Trouble in Jerusalem," I said. "I hope we go," I said. "I want to see it." I thought of all the words I'd heard. I said excitedly, "Salome, just think of it, people from all over the Empire are going to Jerusalem."

"Yes, I know," she said. "It's the best thing we've ever done."

"Yes," I said with a big sigh. "I hope Nazareth is a fine place as well."

My mother sighed and threw back her head.

"Yes, you must see Jerusalem first," she said sadly. "As for Nazareth, it is the will of God it seems."

"Is it a big town?" asked Little Salome.

"Not a town at all," my mother said.

"No?" I asked.

"A village," she said. "But it was once visited by an angel."

"People say that?" Little Salome asked. "That an angel came to Nazareth? It really happened?"

"No, people don't say it," said my mother, "but I know it."

She went quiet. It was her way. To say small things, and nothing more. After that, she wouldn't say anything even though we asked her over and over again.

My uncle Cleopas came back, sick and coughing, and lay down and my aunt covered him and patted him.

He heard us talking about angels in Nazareth—saying that we hoped we would see them—and he began his not so secret laughing.

"My mother says Nazareth was once visited by an angel," I told him. I knew that he just might tell us something. "My mother says she knows this." And his laughter only ran on as he curled up to sleep.

"What would you do, Father?" Little Salome asked him. "If you saw an angel of the Lord with your own eyes in Nazareth?"

"Just what my beloved sister did," he answered me. "Obey the angel in everything he told me to do." And again came his low private laughing.

A terrible anger came over my mother. She looked over at her brother. My aunt shook her head as if to say let it all go. This was her way with her husband.

And usually it was my mother's way too, to let things go with her brother, but not this time.

Little Salome saw all of this, this look of anger on my mother's face, something so surprising I didn't know what to make of it, and I looked up and saw that James too was there, watching, and I knew that he had heard it. I was very sorry to see this. I didn't know what to do. But Joseph sat quietly away from all of this just thinking to himself.

I had a sense of something then, and why I'd never sensed it before I don't know. It was that Joseph put up with Cleopas but never really answered him. For him, he'd made this voyage over sea rather than land. And for him, he'd go to Jerusalem, even if there were trouble. But he never answered him. He never said anything to all Cleopas' laughing.

And Cleopas laughed at everything. In the House of Prayer, he would laugh when he thought the stories of the prophets were funny. He would start to laugh very low and then the little children, such as myself, would start to laugh with him. He had laughed in that way at the story of Elijah. And when the Teacher had become angry, Cleopas had insisted that the story had parts that were funny. He had said that the Teacher ought to see that. And then all the men had begun to argue with the Teacher about the story of Elijah.

My mother turned back to her mending. Her face became smooth. She had a piece of fine Egyptian cotton that she was mending. It was as if nothing had happened.

The Shipmaster was hollering at the sailors, and it seemed they had no rest.

I knew not to say another word.

All around us was the sparkling sea, so blessed, and the boat rising and falling beneath us, sweetly carrying us along, and other families were singing, and we knew the hymns and we too picked it up, singing with all our hearts. . . .

Never mind about the secrets.

We were going to Jerusalem.

4

EVEN LITTLE SALOME AND I were weary of the tossing ship when we finally reached the small harbor of Jamnia. It was a port that only the pilgrims and the slow cargo ships used now, and we had to anchor far out on account of the shallows and the rocks.

Little boats carried us in, the men dividing themselves to care for the women in one boat and the little ones in another. The waves were so rough I thought we would be pitched into the sea. But I loved it all the same.

At last we were able to jump out and make our way through the foaming tide to the land.

We all fell to our knees and kissed the ground that we'd reached the Holy Land safely, and we hurried inland, wet and shivering, to the town of Jamnia, which was quite a way from the coast, where we rested at the inn.

It was crowded after the boat, a little upstairs room full of hay, but we were so happy to be there that it didn't matter at all to us. And I went to sleep listening to the men disputing with the other men, and voices hollering and laughing below and more and more pilgrims came in.

The next day there were donkeys aplenty for sale for all of

us pilgrims and we began our journey across the beautiful plain with its distant groves of trees, saying goodbye to the misty sea, and heading slowly towards the hills of Judea.

Cleopas had to ride on the donkey, though he protested at first, and we made our way slowly, many of the other families in the great crowd passing us as we went, but we were all of us so happy to be in Israel that we didn't care to hurry, and Joseph said we had plenty of time to be in Jerusalem for the purification.

When we put up at the next roadside inn, we made our beds in a large tent beside the building, and there were warnings from those traveling down to the sea that we shouldn't go on, that we should just go north right to Galilee. But Cleopas was by this time out of his head, and singing "If I forget thee, O Jerusalem" and every other song of the city he could remember.

"Take me to the gates of the Temple and leave me there, a beggar, if you will!" he said to Joseph, "if you mean to go on to Galilee!"

Joseph nodded and said we would go on to Jerusalem and to the Temple.

But the women were growing afraid. They were afraid of what we would find in Jerusalem and afraid for Cleopas.

His cough came and went but he was hot all the time, and thirsty and restless. And laughing, always laughing under his breath. He laughed at the little children, and the things other people said, and he looked at me and he laughed. And sometimes he was laughing just to himself, maybe remembering things.

The next morning we began the hard slow climb into the hills. Our ship companions had long ago gone ahead, and we were with those who had come from many different places. I still heard Greek spoken around us as much as Aramaic. And even some Latin.

But our family had stopped speaking Greek to others, and was using only the Aramaic.

It wasn't until the third day that we finally saw our first view of the Holy City from the slope above it. We children jumped up and down with excitement. We were shouting. Joseph stood smiling. Ahead of us lay twists and turns in the road, but we could see it all before us—this sacred place which had been in our prayers and in our hearts and in our songs since we were born.

There were camps about the high walls with tents of all sizes, and cooking fires, and as we drew closer and closer, the crowds were so big that we hardly moved for hours at a time. People everywhere were speaking Aramaic now, though I still heard some Greek, and all of the men were on the lookout for those they knew, and here and there clasping hands and waving and calling out to friends.

For a long time, I couldn't see anything. I was in a crowd of the children, mingled with the men, my hand in Joseph's hand. I only knew we were moving little by little, and we were close to the walls.

Finally we passed through the open city gates.

Joseph reached down and caught me up under his arms, and put me on his shoulders and I saw the Temple clearly above the small city streets.

I felt sad that Little Salome couldn't see this, but then Cleopas said loudly he had to have her up with him on the donkey, and so Aunt Mary lifted her and she could now see too.

And look! We were in the Holy City of Jerusalem, and the Temple was right in front of us.

Now in Alexandria, I had, like any good Jewish boy, never let my eyes stray to the pagan temples. I had not looked up at the pagan statues. What were idols to a Jewish boy who was forbidden to make such things and held them to have no meaning? But I'd passed the temples and the processions with their music, looking only to the houses to which Joseph and I had to go, which seldom took us out of the Jewish quarter of the city anyway, and I suppose that the Great Synagogue was the grandest building that I had ever entered. And besides pagan temples were not for entering anyway. Even I knew that they were supposed to be the house of the pagan gods for whom they were named and put together.

But I knew of these temples, and somehow from the corner of my eye, I had taken their measure. I had taken a measure as well of the palaces of the rich, and had some idea of what any carpenter's son would call the scale of things.

And for the Temple of Jerusalem I had no measure at all. No words from Cleopas or Alphaeus or Joseph, or even Philo had made me ready for what I saw.

It was a building so big and so grand and so solid, a building so shining with gold and whiteness, a building stretching to the right and to the left so far that it swept out of my mind anything I'd ever seen in the rich city of Alexandria, and the wonders of Egypt passed away from me, and my breath was taken out of me. I was struck dumb.

Cleopas now had Little Symeon in his arms so he could see, and Little Salome was holding Baby Esther who was bellowing for no reason, and Aunt Mary was holding up Joses, and Alphaeus had my cousin Little James.

As for Big James, my brother, James who knew so much, James had seen it before, when he was very small and had come here with Joseph before I was ever born, even he

seemed amazed by it, and Joseph was quiet as if he had forgotten us and everyone around us.

My mother reached up and put her hand on my hip and
I looked down at her and smiled. She was pretty to me as
always, and shy with her veil drawn over most of her face,
and clearly so happy that we were here at last and she looked
up as I did to the Temple.

All through the crowd, and it was a great crowd of those
shifting and moving and coming and going, there was this
feeling of people falling quiet and still just to look at this
Temple, trying to know its size, trying to take it in, trying
perhaps to remember this moment because many of them
were here from far away and long ago or for the first time.

I wanted to go on, to enter the Temple—I thought that's
what we would do—but that was not to be.

We were pushing towards it but losing our sight of it, and
dipping down into crooked and tight streets, the buildings
seeming to close over our heads, people pressing against one
another, and our men asking for the synagogue of the
Galileans, where we were to lodge.

I knew Joseph was tired. After all, I was seven years old,
and he'd been carrying me a long while. I asked him to put
me down.

Cleopas was now very feverish, and yes, laughing with
happiness. He asked for water. He said he wanted to bathe
now, and Aunt Mary said he couldn't. The women said we
had to get him to bed right away.

My aunt was almost in tears over him and Little Symeon
started to cry so I picked him up but he was too heavy and
James took him in his arms.

And so it was through the crooked and narrow streets we
went, streets that might have been in Alexandria, though

they were much more crowded, Little Salome and I laughing that "the whole world *was* here," and everywhere there was fast talk, raised voices, people speaking Greek, even Hebrew, people *speaking* Hebrew, and some speaking Latin but not very many, and most Aramaic like us.

When we reached the synagogue, a big building of three stories, the lodgings were full as everyone expected, but as we were turning away to look for the synagogue of the Alexandrians, my mother cried out to her cousins, Zebedee and his wife, and their children who were just coming in, and they all flocked to her with much embracing and kissing, and they wanted us very much to come up with them and share the space already made for them on the roof. Other cousins were already there waiting. Zebedee would see to it.

Now the wife of Zebedee was Mary Alexandra, my mother's cousin, who was always called Mary same as my mother, and same as my aunt Mary who was married to my mother's brother, Cleopas. And when these three women hugged and kissed they cried out: "The Three Marys!" and this made them very happy, as if nothing else was going on.

Joseph was busy paying the price, and we pushed our way with Zebedee and his clan, and Zebedee had brothers with wives and children, through the crowded courtyard where the donkeys were given over for care and feeding, and then we climbed the stairs, and then went up a ladder, the men carrying Cleopas who was laughing all the way in his low manner because he was ashamed.

On the roof, a swarm of kindred greeted us.

Standing out from all the rest was an old woman who reached out for my mother as my mother called her name.

"Elizabeth." And this name I knew well. And that of her son John.

My mother fell into this woman's arms. There was much

crying and hugging as I was brought to her, and to her son, a boy of my age who never spoke a word.

Now as I said, I knew of Cousin Elizabeth, and I knew of many of the others because my mother had written many letters home from Egypt and received many from Judea and from Galilee too. I'd often been with her when she'd gone to the scribe of our district to dictate these letters. And when she had received letters, they had been much read and reread, and so the names had stories to them which I also knew.

I was much taken by Elizabeth as she had a very slow and pretty manner to her, and I thought her face pleasing in a way I couldn't put into words to myself. I often felt this way about old people, that the lines in their faces were very worth study, and that their eyes were bright in the folds of their skin.

But as I am trying to tell you this story from the point of view of the child that I was, I will leave it at that.

My cousin John, too, had about him this same manner as his mother, though he made me think of my own brother James. In fact, the two of them marked each other, just as I might have expected. John had the look of a boy of James' age, though he wasn't, and John's hair was very long.

John and Elizabeth were clothed in white garments that were very clean.

I knew from my mother and her talk of her cousin that John had been dedicated from his birth to the Lord. He would never cut his hair, and he would never share in the wine of supper.

All this I saw in a matter of moments, because there were greetings and tears and hugs, and commotion all around.

The roof couldn't hold any more people. Joseph was finding cousins, and as Joseph and Mary were cousins themselves of each other, that meant happiness for both of them, and at the same time, Cleopas was fussing that he wouldn't drink the water his wife had brought, and Little Symeon was crying, and then Baby Esther began to cry and Simon her father picked her up.

Zebedee and his wife were making room for our blanket to be put down, and then Little Salome tried to hold Little Esther. And Little Zoker got loose and tried to run. Little Mary was also wailing—and all in all so much happening around me—that it was hard to pay much attention to any one thing.

Before anyone knew it, I had grabbed Little Salome's hand and tugged her away, slipping under this person and that, and stepping over this person and that, and we were at the edge of the roof.

There was a little wall there, just high enough so we couldn't fall—.

I could see the Temple again! The crowded roofs of the city lay all in front of it, rising and dipping on the hills and coming up to the Temple's mighty walls.

There was music coming from the streets below, and I could hear people singing, and the smoke of cooking fires smelled good, and everywhere people chattered, below and on the roofs and it became like a holy chant.

"Our Temple," said Little Salome proudly to me, and I nodded. "The Lord who made Heaven and Earth dwells in the Temple," she said.

"The Lord is everywhere," I answered.

She looked at me.

"But He's in the Temple!" she said. "I know that the Lord is everywhere. But for now we should talk of his being in the Temple. We are here to go to the Temple."

"Yes," I said. I looked at the Temple.

"To dwell with his people, He's in the Temple," she said.

"Yes," I said. "And . . . everywhere." I looked only at the Temple.

"Why do you say that?" she asked.

I shrugged my shoulders. "You know that it's true. The Lord is with us, you and me, right now. The Lord is always with us."

She laughed and so did I.

The cooking fires made a mist in front of us, and all the noise was like a mist of another kind. It made my thoughts clearer. *God is everywhere and God is in the Temple.*

Tomorrow we would go to it. Tomorrow we would stand in the court inside its walls. Tomorrow, and then the men would go for the first sprinkling of the purification of the blood of the red heifer in preparation for the Feast of Passover which we would all eat together in Jerusalem to celebrate our coming out of Egypt long, long ago. I would be with the children and the women. But James would be with the men. We would watch from our place, but we would all be within the walls of the Temple. Nearer to the altar where the lambs of Passover would be sacrificed. Closer to the Sanctuary into which only the High Priest would go.

We had known about the Temple ever since we had known about anything. We had known about the Law ever since we had known anything. We had been taught at home by Joseph, and Alphaeus and Cleopas and then in school by the Teacher. We knew the Law by heart.

I felt a quiet inside myself in all the noise of Jerusalem. Little Salome seemed to feel that way too. We stood close to each other without talking or moving, and all the talking and laughter and crying babies, and even the music didn't touch us for a little while.

Joseph came up to us, and guided us back to the family.

The women were just coming back with food they'd

bought. It was time for everyone to gather and time for prayer.

For the first time I saw worry in Joseph's face as he watched Cleopas.

Cleopas still fought with his wife over the water, not wanting to take it.

I turned and looked at him, and I knew right away he didn't know what he was doing. He wasn't right in the head.

"You come sit by me!" he said to me.

I did it, sitting at his right hand, crossing my legs. We were all very close together. Little Salome sat on his left, watching everything he did.

He was angry but not at anybody there. Suddenly he asked when we would get to Jerusalem? Did anybody remember we were going to Jerusalem? It frightened everyone.

My aunt suddenly was very tired of it and threw up her hands. Little Salome went quiet also, just looking at her father.

Cleopas looked around himself and he knew he had said something wrong. Then he seemed himself again, just like that. He picked up the cup of clean water and he drank it. He took a deep breath and looked at his wife. My aunt came nearer again. My mother moved beside her, and put her arm around her. My aunt needed to sleep, I could see it, but she couldn't do that now.

The sauce was hot from the brazier. I was very hungry. The bread was warm too.

It was time for the blessing. The first prayer we all said together in Jerusalem. I bowed my head. Zebedee, being the eldest, led us in the prayer in our family tongue, and the words were a little different to me. But it was still very good.

Afterwards, my cousin John bar Zechariah stared at me

as though he had something very important on his mind but he didn't say anything.

At last we began dipping our bread. It was so good—not just a sauce but a thick pottage of lentils and soft cooked beans and pepper and spices. And there were plenty of dried figs to chew after the hot flavor of the pottage, and I loved it. I didn't think about anything except the food. And Cleopas was eating a little which made everyone happy.

It was the first really good supper since we'd left Alexandria. And there was plenty of it. I ate until I almost couldn't eat anymore.

Afterwards, Cleopas wanted to talk to me and made everyone leave us alone. Aunt Mary just made a quitting gesture again and moved away to rest for a moment, and then went to other chores with the clearing away, and Aunt Salome was tending to Little James and the other children. Little Salome was helping with Baby Esther and Little Zoker whom she loved so much.

My mother came near to Cleopas.

"Why, what are you going to say?" my mother asked him. She sat down on his left, not very close but close enough. "Why should we go away?" She said this in a kind way but she had something on her mind.

"You go away," he told her. He sounded like he had drunk himself drunk but he hadn't. He had drunk less wine than anybody else. "Jesus, come in so you can hear me if I whisper in your ear."

My mother refused to leave. "Don't you tempt him," my mother said.

"And what do you mean by that?" Cleopas asked. "You think I've come to the Holy City of Jerusalem to tempt him?"

Then he clutched at my arm. His fingers were burning.

"I'm going to tell you something," he said to me. "You remember it. This goes in your heart with the Law, you hear me? When she told me the angel had come, I believed her. The angel had come to her! I believed."

The angel—the angel who'd come in Nazareth. He'd come to her. That was what he'd said on the boat, wasn't it? But what did this mean?

My mother stared at him. His face was wet and his eyes very big. I could feel the fever in him. I could see it.

He went on.

"I believed her," he said. "I am her brother, am I not? She was thirteen, betrothed to Joseph, and I tell you, she was never out of the sight of us outside of our house, never could there have been any chance of anyone being with her, you know what I'm saying to you, I mean a man. There was no chance, and I am her brother. Remember, I told you. I believed her." He lay back a little on the clothes bundled behind him. "A virgin child, a child in the service of the Temple of Jerusalem, to weave the great veil, with the other chosen ones, and then home under our eyes."

He shivered. He looked at her. His eyes stayed on her. She turned away, and then moved away. But not very far. She stayed there with her back to us, close to our cousin Elizabeth.

Elizabeth was watching Cleopas, and watching me. I didn't know whether she heard him or not.

I didn't move. I looked down at Cleopas. His chest rose and fell with each rattling breath and again he shivered.

My mind was working, collecting every bit of knowledge I had ever learned that could help me make sense of what he had said. It was the mind of a child who had grown up sleeping in a room with men and women in that same room and in other rooms open to it, and sleeping in the open courtyard with the men and women in the heat of summer, and living always close with them, and hearing and seeing many things. My mind was working and working. But I couldn't make sense of all he'd said.

"You remember, what I said to you, that I believed!" he said.

"But you're not really sure, are you?" I whispered.

His eyes opened wide and a new expression came over him, as if he was waking from his fever.

"And Joseph isn't either, is he?" I asked in the same whisper. "And that is why he never lies beside her."

My words had come ahead of my thoughts. I was as surprised as he was by what I'd said. I felt chilled all over. Prickly all over. But I didn't try to change what I'd said.

He rose up on his elbow, and his face was close to mine.

"Turn it around," he said. He struggled for breath. "He never touches her because he does believe. Don't you see? How could he touch her after such a thing?" He smiled, and then he laughed in that low laugh of his, but no one else heard it. "And you?" he went on. "Must you grow up before you fulfill the prophesies? Yes, you must. And must you be a child first before you are a man? Yes. How else?" His eyes changed as if he stopped seeing things in front of him. Again he struggled for breath. "So it was with King David. Anointed, and then sent back to the flocks, a shepherd boy, wasn't it? Until such time as Saul sent for him. Until such time as the Lord God sent for him! Don't you see, that's what confounds them all! That you must grow up like any other child! And half the time they don't know what to do with you! And yes, I am sure! And have always been sure!"

He fell back again, tired, unable to go on, but his eyes never left me. He smiled and I heard his laughter.

"Why do you laugh?" I asked.

He shrugged. "I am still amused," he answered. "Yes, amused. Did *I* see an angel? No, I did not. Maybe if I had, I wouldn't laugh, but then maybe again I would laugh all the more. My laughter is the way I speak, don't you think? Remember that. Ah, listen to them down in the streets. Over there, over here. They want justice. Vengeance. Did you hear all that? Herod did this. Herod did that. They've stoned Archelaus's soldiers! What does it matter to me now? I would like to breathe without it hurting me for one quarter of an hour!"

His hand came up, groping for me. He touched the back of my head, and I bent down and kissed his wet cheek.

Make this pain go away.

He drew in his breath, and then he appeared to drift and to sleep, and his chest began to rise and fall slowly and easily. I placed my hand on his chest and felt his heart. *Strength for this little while. What harm is there in it?*

When I moved away, I wanted to go to the edge of the roof. I wanted to cry. What had I done? Maybe nothing. But I didn't think it was nothing. And the things he'd said to me—what did they mean? How was I to understand these things?

I wanted the answers to questions, yes, but these words only made more questions, and my head hurt. I was afraid.

I sat down and leaned against the low wall. I could barely see over it now. With all the families huddled so near, and so many backs to me and so much chatter and soft singing to children, I thought I was hidden.

It was dark now and there was torchlight all over the city, and loud happy cries, and plenty of music. Cooking fires still, or maybe fires for warmth as it was a little colder. I was a little colder. I wanted to see what was going on below. Then I didn't. I didn't care.

An angel had come to my mother, an angel. I was not Joseph's son.

My aunt Mary caught me by surprise. She pulled me hard around to look at her. She was crouching over me. Her face was full of glittering tears, and her voice was thick:

"Can you cure him!" she asked.

I was so surprised I didn't know what to say to her.

My mother came down upon us and tried to pull her away. They stood over me, their robes brushing my face. Words were whispered. Angry words.

"You can't ask this of him!" my mother whispered. "He's a little child and you know it!"

Aunt Mary sobbed.

What could I say to my aunt Mary? "I don't know!" I said. "I don't know!" I said again.

Now I did cry. I drew my knees up and I crouched even closer to the wall. I wiped at my tears.

They went away.

The families close to us were settled down, the women having gotten the little ones to sleep. Down below a man played the pipe and another man sang. The sound was clear for a moment, and then gone in the hush.

I couldn't see the stars for the mist. But the sight of all the torches of the city, tumbling uphill and downhill, and above all, the Temple rising like a mountain with its great fluttering torches drove every other thought from my mind.

A good feeling came over me, that in the Temple I would pray to understand all these words—not only what my uncle had said to me, but all the other things I had heard.

My mother came back.

There was just room near the wall by me for my mother to kneel down and then to sink back on her heels.

The torchlight hit her face as she looked towards the Temple.

"Listen to me," she said.

"I am," I answered. I answered in Greek without thinking.

"What I have to say to you should have waited," she said. She spoke Greek as well.

With the noise in the streets, with the low nighttime talk on the roof, I could still hear her.

"But it can't wait now," she said. "My brother has seen to that. Would that he could suffer in silence. But it's never been his way to do anything in silence. So I say it. And you listen. Don't ask questions of me. Do as Joseph told you in that regard. But listen to what I say."

"I am," I said again.

"You're not the child of an angel," she said.

I nodded.

She turned towards me. The torchlight was in her eyes.

I said nothing.

"The angel said to me—that the power of the Lord would come over me," she said. "And so the shadow of the Lord came over me—I felt it—and then in time came the stirring of life inside me, and it was you."

I said nothing.

She looked down.

The noise of the city was gone. The torchlight made her look beautiful to me. Beautiful perhaps as Sarah looked to Pharaoh, beautiful as Rachel to Jacob. My mother was beautiful. Modest, but beautiful, no matter how many veils she wore to hide it, no matter how she bowed her head or blushed.

I wanted to be in her lap, in her arms, but I didn't move. It wasn't right to move or say a word.

"And so it happened," she said, looking up again. "I have never been with a man, not then, not now, nor will I ever. I am consecrated to the Lord."

I nodded.

"You can't understand this . . . can you?" she asked. "You can't follow what I'm trying to tell you."

"I do follow," I said. "I do see." Joseph wasn't my father, yes, I knew. I had never called Joseph Father. Yes, he was my father according to the Law, and married to my mother, but he wasn't my father. And she was so like a girl always, and the other women like her older sisters, I knew, yes, I knew. "Anything is possible with the Lord," I said. "The Lord made Adam from the dust. Adam didn't even have a mother. The Lord can make a child with no father." I shrugged.

She shook her head. She wasn't like a girl now, but not like a woman either. She was soft and almost sad. When she spoke again, she didn't sound like herself.

"No matter what anyone ever says to you in Nazareth," she said, "remember what's been said tonight."

"People will say things . . . ?"

She closed her eyes.

"This is why you didn't want to go back there . . . to Nazareth?" I asked.

She gave a deep breath. She put her hand over her mouth. She was amazed. She took a deep breath, and she was gentle:

"You haven't understood what I've said to you!" she whispered. She was hurt. I thought she might cry.

"No, Mamma, I do see, I understand," I said at once. I didn't want her to be hurt. "The Lord can do anything."

She was disappointed, but then she looked at me and for my sake, she smiled.

"Mamma," I said. I reached out for her.

My head was pounding with thoughts. The sparrows, Eleazer dead in the street and rising living from the mat, too many other things, things slipping away in my mind, and my mind too full. And all Cleopas' words and what were they? *You must grow up like any other child or was it Little David back to the flock until they called him? Don't let her be sad.*

"I see. I know," I said to her. I smiled a little smile I never gave to anyone but to her if it was giving. More a little sign than a giving. She had her smile for me. A little thing.

And now, she shook off everything that had gone before, and she reached out for me.

I went up on my knees, and she did too, and she held me tight to her.

"It's enough for now," she said. "It's enough for you to have my word," she whispered in my ear.

After a while, I got up with her and we went back to the family.

I lay down on my bed of bundles, and she covered me, and under the stars, with the city singing, and Cleopas singing, I went sound asleep.

After all, it was the farthest place to which I could go.

5

IN THE MORNING, we found the streets almost too crowded for us to move, but move we did, all of us, even the babies in the arms of the mothers, to the Temple.

Cleopas was rested, and a little better, though very weak still and needing to be helped along the way.

I rode on Joseph's shoulders, and Little Salome on Uncle Alphaeus, and we managed to hold hands, and to see wonderfully as the whole people carried us round the crooked lanes and under archways, until we came to the great open space before the huge stairs and the rising golden walls of the Temple.

There we parted, the women and babies away from the men, moving slowly into the ritual baths, to bathe thoroughly before we would enter the Temple walls.

Now this was not the sprinkling and cleansing for Passover. That had to be done in three stages, starting with the first sprinkling of the men within the Temple today.

This was an overall cleansing that we would do because of our long journey from Egypt, and one that would prepare us to enter into the precincts of the Temple itself. And it was one which our families wanted, and the baths were there, and so we did it though it was not required in the Law.

It took us a long time. The water was cold, and we were glad when we had our clothes on again and we could go back out into the light and rejoin the women, and Little Salome and I could see each other and link hands again.

It seemed the crowds were growing, though how even more people could fit into this space I didn't know. People were chanting the Psalms in Hebrew. And some were praying with their eyes half closed. And others were merely talking to each other. And children were crying naturally as they always will do.

Once more Joseph put me on his shoulders. And, nearly blinded by the light flashing off the Temple walls, we started the climb up the stairs.

Now as we went up step by step everyone was as over-come by the size of the Temple as I was, and the whole crowd seemed to be praying out loud even if the words they were saying were not prayers.

It seemed impossible that men could have built walls of this height, let alone decorated them with marble of such pure whiteness, and the voices were echoing off the walls, but as we reached the top and pressed slowly to get through the gates, I could see there were soldiers in the square below and some of them were on horseback.

They weren't Roman soldiers; I didn't know what they were. But the crowd didn't like them. I could see even at this great distance that people were raising fists to them, and the horses were dancing as horses do and I thought I saw stones flying through the air.

I could hardly bear the slow pace of waiting. I think I wanted Joseph to push harder for us to get through the gate. He gave way so easily. And we did all have to keep together, and that included now Zebedee and his people, and also Elizabeth and Little John, and cousins whose names I didn't remember.

At last we entered the gates, and to my surprise found ourselves in a huge tunnel. I could barely see the beautiful decorations all around us. The prayers of the people echoed off the roof and the walls. I joined in the prayers, but mostly I just looked around myself, and felt the breath taken out of me again, just as surely as when Eleazer had kicked me hard and I couldn't breathe.

Finally, we came out into the great open space inside the first court of the Temple and it seemed that everyone shouted at once.

Far, far away on either side of us were the columns of the roofed porches and in between people went on forever, and before us, there rose up high the wall of the Sanctuary. And the people on top of the roofs were so tiny that I couldn't even make out their faces so big was this holy place.

I could hear and smell the animals that were gathered at the far porches, the animals offered for sale for sacrifice, and the noise of everybody rose in my ears.

But the whole feeling of the crowd changed. Everyone was happy to be here. All the children were laughing with happiness.

The sunshine was bright as it had never been in the tight streets of the city. The air was sweet and fresh.

I heard the sound of horses, too, not the hooves, but the whinnying of horses being pulled up short, and I heard shouting.

But for the moment, I was lost in looking ahead at the shining walls in front of me that enclosed the courts of the men and the women. I was too little to be taken to the court of the men. I would be staying with the women today, I knew. But I'd be able to see the men as they were sprinkled with the first purification for Passover.

All of it was such a wonder to me, and the wonder of being inside it was beyond any words in me to describe it. I knew full well there were people around me from all over the Empire who had come to be here today and it was as wonderful as we had hoped it would be. Cleopas had lived to be here. Cleopas had lived to be purified and to eat the Passover meal with us. Maybe Cleopas would live to go home.

It was our Temple and it was God's Temple and it seemed so splendid that we could enter it and come so close to God's presence.

There were many many men running on top of the faraway porches. And men on other roofs, but they were tiny as I said, and I couldn't hear them though I knew they were shouting by the way their arms moved in the air.

Suddenly, we were pushed this way and that. I thought Joseph would fall but he didn't.

A huge cry went up from the crowd.

People broke into shouting and women screamed. I think the children were thrilled. I was still on Joseph's shoulders, and we were packed in so tight that he couldn't move.

For the first time I saw at the far left many armed soldiers on horseback coming right towards us through the crowd. We were all swept backwards as if the crowd were water and then forwards, and my mother and my aunt Mary were screaming and Little Salome was screaming and reaching out to me but we were too far apart for me to catch her hand.

Most everyone around us was shouting in Aramaic, but many were shouting in Greek.

"Get out, get out," men shouted. But there was no way to move. I could hear the bleating of the sheep suddenly, as if someone had made all the animals run. Then came the bellow of the cows or the oxen—a dreadful sound.

The soldiers were coming closer and closer to us, and they had their spears raised. There was no way to move.

Then out of nowhere stones began to fly.

Everyone was screaming. I saw one soldier struck by many stones before he fell from his horse. Hands pulled at him and he went down into the crowd. A man in a robe and mantle scrambled up on the horse and began to fight with another soldier, and the soldier stabbed the man twice in the belly with his sword. The blood just gushed out of him.

I thought my breath had stopped. It was like the kick in the belly from Eleazer. I opened my mouth but the air wouldn't come. Joseph tried to drag me down from his shoulder but the crowd was too tight for him to do it, and I didn't want to come down. Terrible as it was, I wanted to see.

Prayers rose from everywhere, but they weren't the joyful Psalms. They were cries for help, cries for deliverance. Some people were falling to the ground.

But things like this were happening on all sides. All of us went back again like a wave in the sea.

Joseph reached up, and with other hands helping him, he lifted me over his head and down, his arms around me as he dragged me through the tight squeeze of people struggling and screaming.

When my feet hit the marble, I couldn't move. Even my tunic was caught up against those in front and behind me.

"Little Salome!" I cried. "Little Salome, where are you?"

"Yeshua," she called in the Aramaic. "Reach for me."

I saw her head before me as she struggled, as if she was swimming towards me, through the bodies that closed in on her.

I pulled her right beside me and in front of Joseph, and above me I could hear Cleopas laughing. He stood in front of me and he was laughing his old laugh.

The crowd moved to the side and then forward, so that we fell. Everyone fell. Hands pulled me down, and I pulled Little Salome under me, my right hand on top of her head.

"Get on your knees and stay there!" Joseph commanded. What could we do? We were on our knees and pitched forward.

My mother's voice came up in my ear.

"My son, my son."

Joseph and Cleopas threw up their hands and prayed to the Lord. I held Salome and threw up my left hand.

"Oh Lord, you are my refuge!" Joseph cried. Cleopas said another prayer. "I stretch forth my hands to you, Oh Lord," my mother cried. Little Salome cried: "Oh Lord, deliver me!"

All around us people called on the Lord. "Let the wicked fall in their own snares," cried James right near me.

"Deliver me, Lord, deliver me, from the evil around me," I prayed, but I couldn't hear my own voice. The prayers grew louder and became like a rumbling rising so high it almost rose above the screams and cries of those who fought.

The bellowing of the oxen was terrible, and the high thin screams of the women hurt me.

I looked up, lifting my head as much as I dared, and I saw that everyone all around us was kneeling and bowing. Zebedee rose up to implore the Lord and then bowed, but he was only one of so many I couldn't count.

But people came rushing through this big sea of those who prayed, scrambling over us, pushing down on shoulders and backs as they tried to get out.

For a moment, I was crushed right to the marble tiles of the floor, slipping beside Little Salome, my hand not leaving her head.

A wild will came over me and I struggled to get up and free. I pushed and jerked to the side until I wasn't under Joseph, and I climbed to my feet as if I was running.

I saw the great big square. Far ahead of us, people ran in all directions, the sheep were running wild with quick jerky steps, and soldiers rode down on the people, and the people, even the people who knelt and bowed, rose up all over and threw stones at the soldiers.

Some groups of people were like mounds of the dead.

The psalms rose to Heaven. " 'I flee unto you, O Lord, to hide me. . . . I cried to you, O Lord—.' "

Soldiers on horseback came racing after the people, both men and women who ran right towards us.

"Joseph, look," cried my mother. "Get him, pull him down."

I pulled free of the hands that tried to tug at me.

The people ran on top of those kneeling, right over them as if they were rocks by the sea. The prayerful groaned and cried out, and as a single horseman drove his way towards us, the bodies fell back to either side.

Down I went with a hand on the back of my head and another on my back. I could hear the snorting of the horse and the clatter of his hooves.

My head was pressed right to the stones.

Yet out of the corner of my eye I saw the legs of the horse right beside us, and as the horse shied backwards, I saw a man rise from the mounds of huddled figures. He drew a stone from under his robe and thew it at the soldier.

He cried out in Greek:

"There is no one but the Lord Himself who has a right to rule over us! Take those words to Herod. Take them to Caesar!"

Then came another stone from under his mantle and another.

The soldier's spear came down right into the man's chest. It went deep into him and through him.

The man dropped the stone he held, and fell back with his eyes wide.

My mother sobbed. Little Salome screamed, "Don't look, don't look."

But was I to look away from this man in his last moments? Was I to turn away from his very death?

The soldier pulled up his spear and the man rose with it. Blood poured out of the man's mouth.

The body was cast this way and that, and then the spear pulled free and let the body drop.

The man rolled onto his left side, and he stared right at us, right at me.

I couldn't see the horse anymore. I could only hear it, and the terrible noise of its running wild. I saw the soldier in the grip of men all around him, those who had pulled him from the horse which was now gone.

His body was lost in the crowd that covered him, as elbows rose and fell over him.

Our men bowed and prayed.

The dying man if he heard it, if he knew it, didn't care.

He didn't see us. He didn't know about the soldier. Blood came out of his mouth onto the stones.

Terrible cries came out of my mother.

The people who'd taken hold of the soldier got up and were running away. More people got up and ran. Beyond them more stayed on their knees and prayed.

The body of the soldier was covered with blood.

The man who stared at us reached out his hand, but his arm flopped down, and he died.

People ran between us and the man. I heard the sheep again.

I felt my mother slip over on her side on the ground, and I tried to catch her, but she sank down on the ground with her eyes closed.

Again the stones flew from everywhere over our heads.

Who had come into this Temple that did not carry stones for this war?

The stones rained down on us, and hit us on our heads and shoulders.

When Joseph raised his arms in the chanting, I managed to get out from under him, and I got up on my knees.

The crowd was loose and broken. Bodies lay everywhere like heaps of bloody wool for the wash.

Everywhere I looked men fought and men died.

On top of the beautiful porches, men who looked tiny and black against the sky were fighting, soldiers with their swords drawn stabbing those who tried to beat them with clubs.

I saw way out on the stones where there was no crowd anymore another man attack a soldier, rushing right against the spear that went through him. Women ran right to the dead to cry over them. They did not care where they were, these women. They cried and screamed. They howled like dogs. The soldiers didn't hurt them.

But no one came to our dead man, the man who lay on his side with the blood all over his mouth, staring and not seeing. He lay alone.

At last the soldiers were everywhere, so many soldiers I could never count them. They came on foot into the crowd.

They moved through the families of those kneeling and came closer and closer on the left and on the right.

All the fighters were gone.

"Pray!" said Joseph to me, breaking his chant for only a moment.

I obeyed him. I raised my arms and prayed.

"But the souls of the righteous are in the hands of the Lord, and no torment can harm them."

New soldiers came riding out. They raised their voices, and they spoke in Greek. At first I couldn't hear them, but then one of them came nearer to us, walking his horse.

"Leave, go to your homes!" he said. "Get out of Jerusalem, by the King's order."

6

THE QUIET WAS NOT QUIET. It was full of crying and
sobbing and the clatter and noise of the horses, and the soldiers shouting at us to go.

Some bodies were dead all alone on the tops of the
porches. I could see them. And our dead man was all alone.
The sheep wandered everywhere, the sheep without blemish
that would have been the Passover sacrifice. Men ran after
them. They ran after the oxen that were still bellowing and
that bellowing was the loudest noise of all.

At last we rose to our feet, because Joseph rose, and we
followed, all of us together, Cleopas very shaky, and laughing
still under his breath, but not so any soldier could hear him.

Aunt Salome and Aunt Esther had my mother by her
arms. She started to sink again and she groaned. Joseph
struggled to get close to her, but the little ones were underfoot. I had hold of Little Salome.

"Mamma, we have to go now," I said to my mother, staying close to her. "Mamma, wake up. We're going now."

She was trying to be strong. But they turned her and they
pushed her along. Uncle Alphaeus had a time with Silas and
Levi who were whispering questions to him, but I couldn't

hear them. Now they were each past their fourteenth year, and they took all of this perhaps not the same as we little ones did.

All the people moved to the gateway.

Cleopas was the only one of us like Lot's wife, who turned back and back.

"Look," he said to anyone who could hear him. "See the priests there?" He pointed to the top of the faraway wall of the Inner Court. "They had sense enough to run for cover, didn't they? Did they know the soldiers were going to attack us?"

We saw them for the first time, the gathering of men up there above the gates, who could have watched the whole thing from there. I could barely make them out. I think they were in their fine robes and headdresses, but maybe not.

What did they think as they looked on this? And who would come for our dead man? How would this blood be cleaned away? The whole Temple was defiled with it. The whole Temple would have to be cleansed.

But there wasn't much time to look. And I only wanted to get out now. I was not afraid yet. I was wide eyed. The fear would come later.

The soldiers came behind us, crying out their orders. They spoke in Greek, then they spoke in Aramaic.

These were the same now who had killed others. We moved as fast as we could.

There would be no celebration of Passover this year, the soldier called out. "The Festival is over, no Passover! No Passover! You go to your homes."

"No Passover!" Cleopas said under his breath, laughing. "As if they can say there is no Passover! As long as there is one Jew alive in the world there is Passover when there is Passover!"

"Quiet," said Joseph. "Keep your eyes off them. What would you have them do? Mingle the blood of more Jews and Galileans with their sacrifices? Don't taunt them!"

"It's an abomination," said Alphaeus. "We should get out of the city as quickly as we can."

"But is it right to leave now of all times?" asked my cousin Silas. My uncle Alphaeus told him firmly to be quiet with a gesture and a sound.

My uncle Simon, the quiet one, said nothing.

As we entered the tunnel, people hurried past us. Joseph picked me up, and Little Salome with me. The other men were picking up the little ones. Cleopas tried to pick up Little Symeon, his youngest, who was crying to be picked up, but then Cleopas started coughing again, and so the women took him. My mother took him.

This was a good sign. She had the child in her arms, and she would be all right.

I couldn't see very well in the dark. But it didn't matter now. Little Salome was sobbing and sobbing, and nothing Aunt Mary said to her could comfort her. I couldn't reach her as she was too far behind me.

"No Passover!" Cleopas said, then he coughed more before he could go on. "So this King who doesn't wait on Caesar to confirm him on his throne has just done away with the Passover! This King who is as full of blood now as his father, who takes his stand with his father—."

"Don't say any more," said Alphaeus. "If they hear one word, they'll turn on the lot of us."

"Yes, and how many innocents did they slay in there just now?" Cleopas said.

Joseph spoke up as he had in Alexandria.

"You will not say another word on this until we are out of Jerusalem!"

Cleopas didn't answer. But he didn't say any more. No one did.

We reached the bright light, only to see soldiers everywhere who spoke the orders as if they were cursing us.

People lay dead in the streets. They looked like they were sleeping. All the women started crying at the sight of the dead because we had to walk around them or step over them, and the mourners on their knees cried, and some begged for alms.

The men began to give out coins where they could, as others did. Some people were too miserable to want such a thing or they didn't need it.

But everywhere people cried even as they hurried. All of our women were crying, and Aunt Mary sobbed that this was her very first pilgrimage, that all her life in Egypt she had longed for this, and what had been done before our very eyes?

At the synagogue, we found everyone very afraid. Joseph gathered us inside the courtyard only to wait while the women rushed up to the roof for our bundles. He and Alphaeus went to get the donkeys. James told us to stand still and be quiet, to hold on to the babies. I had Little Symeon by the hand. Cleopas leaned against the wall and smiled and said things no one could hear.

The wailing over the dead still filled my ears. I couldn't stop thinking of our dead man, the dead man who had died so close to us. Did anyone come to bury him? What happened if nobody did?

I hadn't looked at the face of the soldier who killed him. I hadn't looked at the face of any soldier. All I saw of them was their strung-up boots and their armor, dark and tarnished, and their spears. How could I ever forget their spears?

"Leave Jerusalem," someone shouted even now in Hebrew here in the synagogue courtyard. "Leave Jerusalem and go to your homes. There is no Passover."

And our dead man. He must have known the soldier would kill him when he threw the stone he had hidden under his robe. He'd brought his stones to the Temple so that he might throw them.

Yet he had looked just like the rest of us. Same simple mantle, tunic, same dark curly hair, a beard like the beards of Joseph and my uncles. A Jew like us, though he shouted in Greek, why Greek, and why had he done it? Why had he almost flung himself at the soldier, when he knew the soldier had the spear?

I saw in my mind the spear go into our dead man. I saw it over and over, and the look on his face. I saw the dead all over the court of the Temple and the wandering sheep. I put my hands over my eyes. I couldn't stop seeing these things.

I felt cold. I huddled near to my mother, who at once opened her arms. I stood against her, against her soft robe.

We stood beside Cleopas, letting Little Symeon twist and turn and play. I said to my uncle,

"Why did that man throw those stones when he knew the soldier would kill him?"

Cleopas had seen it. We had all seen it, hadn't we?

Cleopas appeared to think, looking up into the bit of light that came in over the high walls. "It was a good moment to die," he said. "It was the finest moment perhaps that he'd ever seen."

"Did you think it was good?" I asked.

He laughed his soft slow laugh.

He looked down at me. "Did you?" he asked. "Did you think it was good?"

He didn't wait for my answer.

He said in my ear:

"Archelaus is a fool," Cleopas said. He spoke Greek. "Caesar should laugh him to scorn. King of Jews!" He shook his head. "We're in exile in our own land. That's the truth of it. That's why they were fighting! They want to get rid of this miserable family of Kings who build pagan temples and live like pagan tyrants!"

Joseph took Cleopas by the arm and pulled him away.

"Don't talk," said Joseph, staring at Cleopas. "No more of this here, you understand me? I don't care what you think, you say nothing more."

Cleopas said nothing. He began coughing again. And he made sounds under his breath as if he was talking but he wasn't talking.

Joseph went to the task of tying the bundles on the donkey. In a softer voice he said, "Nothing now, you understand me, brother?"

Cleopas didn't answer. My aunt Mary came to Cleopas and wiped some of the sweat from his forehead.

So I was wrong that Joseph never answered him.

But Cleopas gave no sign that he had heard. He was lost in his laughing and staring away, as if Joseph hadn't told him these things. And there was sweat all over his face now, and the day wasn't hot.

At last the clans were all together, and Joseph and Zebedee led us out of the courtyard.

"My brother," Joseph said to Cleopas. "When we get outside the gates, I want you to ride on this animal."

Cleopas nodded.

We were packed tighter than a herd of sheep as we tried to move up the street.

The sound of the women crying was loud under the archways and in the narrow high-walled places through which we had to go. I saw that windows and doors were shut tight. The wooden gates of courtyards had been closed. People stepped over the beggars and those huddled here and there. The men gave out coins. Joseph put a coin in my hand and said to give it to a beggar and I did, and the man kissed my fingers. He was an old man, thin and white haired with bright blue eyes.

My legs ached and my feet hurt me on the rough paving, but this was no time to complain.

As soon as we came out of the city, we saw all around us a sight that was even worse than what we'd seen in the Temple Court.

The tents of the pilgrims were torn apart. Bodies lay everywhere. Goods were scattered and people had no thought to pick them up.

And the soldiers rode wildly back and forth through the helpless people, crying out their orders, with no thought to the dead. We were to move on, everyone was to move on. They held up their spears. Some had drawn swords. They were all around us.

We could not stop to help anyone here any more than we could have stopped in the city. The soldiers even pushed at people with their spears, and the people hurried so as not to be touched in this shameful way.

But more than anything else, it was the number of the dead that caught our eyes. The dead were beyond number.

"This was a massacre," said my uncle Alphaeus. He drew his sons, Silas and Levi, to him and Eli, and said so all of us could hear: "Look on the doings of this man. See it and never forget it."

"I see it, Father, but shouldn't we stay! Shouldn't we fight!" Silas said. He said it in a whisper but we all heard it and at once the women cried out low and secretly to him that he must not say such a thing, and Joseph told him firmly there would be no talk of staying.

I started to cry. I started to cry and I didn't know why I was crying. I felt I couldn't breathe, and I couldn't stop it.

My mother said, "We'll be out in the hills soon, away from all this. You're with us. And we're going to a peaceful place. There is no war where we're going."

I tried to swallow the crying, and I became afraid. I don't know that I'd ever been afraid before in my life. I started to see in my mind our dead man again.

James was looking at me. And so was my cousin John, the son of Elizabeth. Elizabeth rode on a donkey. And when I saw these two looking at me, James and my cousin John, I stopped crying. It was very hard.

The walk was getting hard. And that was a thing to think about, climbing the road as we went up and up until we could look down on the city. The harder we climbed, the less afraid I was. And soon Little Salome was up with me. We couldn't see the city over the big people even if we wanted to, but I didn't want to see it now, and no one stopped to say how beautiful the Temple was.

The men had made Cleopas get onto one donkey, and Aunt Mary was told to ride on the other. Both of them held babies in their arms. Cleopas was talking under his breath.

And on went the caravan.

Yet it seemed a wrong thing to me to leave Jerusalem in this way. I thought of Silas, and what he'd said. It did feel wrong to be going. It felt wrong to be hurrying away from the Temple in the hour when the Temple was in need of care. But then there were hundreds of priests, priests who knew how to cleanse the Temple, and many of them lived in Jerusalem, and so they couldn't go away. And they would stay—they and the High Priest—and they would cleanse the Temple the way it ought to be cleansed.

And they would know what to do with our dead man. They would see to it that he was washed and wrapped and buried as he ought to be. But I tried not to think of him because I knew I'd start crying again.

The hills closed us up. Our voices were echoing off the sides of the mountains. People began to sing, but this time they sang mournful Psalms of pain and affliction.

When riders came through, we pressed ourselves to the side. The women screamed. Little Salome was asleep on the donkey with Cleopas, who slept and talked and laughed to himself and they were slippery bundles.

I started to cry. I couldn't help it. So many riders passing us, and so quickly and no more Jerusalem.

"We'll be there again next year," Joseph said to me. "And the year after. We're home now."

"And maybe there will be no Archelaus by next year," Cleopas said under his breath without opening his eyes, but James and I heard it. "The King of the Jews!" he scoffed. "The King of the Jews."

7

A DREAM. Wake up. I was sobbing. The man went down, the spear through his chest. He went down again, the spear through his chest. Wake up, they said, more voices. Something wet was against my face. Sobbing. I opened my eyes. Where were we? "Wake up," said my mother. I was in the middle of the women, and the fire was the only light, except that something out there was lighting up the sky.

"You're dreaming," said my mother. She held me.

James ran past us. Little Salome was calling to me.

"Jesus, wake up!" said my cousin John, who'd never spoken a word until now.

What was this place, a cave? No. This was the home of my kinfolk here—this was the house in which John and his mother lived. Joseph had been carrying me by the time we got here.

All the women were wiping my face. "You're dreaming." I was coughing from so much crying. I was so afraid, afraid and never never would I ever be not afraid as I was now. I clung to my mother. I pushed my face against her.

"It's the royal palace," someone shouted. "They've set it on fire!"

There was a loud noise, the sound of horses. A darkness fell. Then the red light flickered on the ceilings.

My cousin Elizabeth prayed in a low voice, and one of the men said for the children to get back from the door.

"Put out the lamps!" said Joseph.

Again came the noise, the noise of horses rushing past, and screams outside.

I didn't want to see what they were talking about, all the children screaming and shouting, and the prayers of Elizabeth running underneath. The fear swallowed me.

Even with my eyes closed, I could see the red flashes of light. My mother kissed the top of my head.

James said: "Jericho is burning. The palace of Herod is in flames. All of it's burning."

"They'll rebuild it," Joseph said. "They've burned it before. Caesar Augustus will see to it that it's rebuilt." His voice was steady. I felt his hand against my shoulder. "Don't you worry, little one. Don't you worry at all."

For a moment I slipped back into sleep—the Temple, the man rushing towards the spear. I gritted my teeth and cried, and my mother held me as tightly as she could.

"We're safe, little one," said Joseph. "We're in the house here, we're all together, and we're safe."

The women who'd been right beside me got up. They went to see the fire. Little Salome was shrieking with excitement the way she shrieked when we played. They were all rushing back and forth, and fussing to get into the doorway to see it.

Little Symeon shouted, "The fire, the fire!"

I looked up. I could see out of the open door past them, and the very sight of the red flashing sky made me shiver. Never had I seen a sky like that. I turned and saw my uncle Cleopas stretched out against the wall, his eyes shining. He smiled at me.

"But why?" I asked. "Why are they burning Jericho?"

"And why shouldn't they?" asked Cleopas. "Let Caesar Augustus see how we despise the man who sent his soldiers to mingle our blood with our sacrifices! This word will reach Rome before Archelaus does. The flames reach farther than words."

"As if flames had the purpose of words," said my mother under her breath, but I don't think they heard her.

My cousin Silas came running into the house, crying, "It's Simon, one of Herod's own slaves. He's crowned himself King and gathered a huge force. He's lit fire to the palace!"

"You stay in this house, here!" said my uncle Alphaeus. "Where is your brother?"

But Levi was there, and when I saw his face, his expression was terrible. He was afraid, and it made me more afraid.

All the men got up and were headed out of doors to see the fire. I looked at all those black shapes against the sky, so many moving back and forth, as if everyone was dancing.

Joseph rose to his feet.

"Yeshua, you come and see this," he said.

"Oh, but why?" asked my mother. "Must he go out?"

"Come, you can look at what a band of robbers and murderers have done," said Joseph. "You can see how they run rampant to celebrate the death of Old Herod. You can see what lies beneath the surface when a King rules by cruelty and terror. Come."

"And why should they let tyrants live in luxury?" Cleopas said. "Tyrants who murder their own people? Tyrants who build theaters and circuses in Jerusalem, the Holy City itself, places no good Jew would go. And the High Priests he appoints—men he wants to advance, as if the High Priest were not the man who enters the very Holy of Holies, as if the High Priest were nothing but a paid servant."

"My brother," said my mother, "I'm going mad!"

I was shaking so hard I feared to get up, but I did get up and I took Joseph's hand.

He led me out of the house. The whole family stood on the prow of the hill, even the women except for my mother, and gathered all around were others in the night who'd spilled out of the village.

The clouds over the plain below were boiling with fire. The air was hot and cold, and people were talking loudly as they might at Festival, and the children were running in circles and dancing and rushing to look again at the fire. I huddled close to Joseph.

"He's very little still," said my mother. She stood behind me.

"He should see," said Joseph.

It was a great growing, licking blaze, and suddenly a wall of flame rose up, so fierce, and it seemed to reach for the stars of Heaven. I turned my head. I couldn't look at it. I went into wild crying. The cries came out of me like knots in a rope being pulled out one after another. Against my eyes I saw the flickering. I couldn't get away from it. The smell of the smoke filled me. My mother was trying to lift me and I didn't mean to fight her, but I was fighting her, and then Joseph had hold of me, and said my name over and over.

"We're far away from it!" he said. "We're safe from it. Listen to me!"

I couldn't stop until he crushed me against his chest, and I couldn't twist or turn there.

He walked fast with me back into the house.

I couldn't stop my cries. They hurt my chest. They hurt my heart.

We sank down on the floor, and my cousin Elizabeth took my face and held it. I saw her eyes just in front of me.

"Listen to what I say to you, my child," she said. "Stop crying. Do you think the angel of the Lord would have come to your father, Joseph, and told him to bring you home if you weren't safe? Who is to say what are the purposes of the Lord? Now, stop your cries and trust in the Lord. Lie against your mother's breast, here, and stop your crying. Let your mother hold you. You are in the hands of God."

"Angel of the Lord," I whispered. "Angel of the Lord."

"Yes," said Joseph, "and the angel of the Lord will be with us until we reach Nazareth."

My mother took me.

"We are passing through this," she said. Her voice was low and sweet in my ear. "We are passing through this, and we'll be home soon, in our own house. We will eat the figs of our own tree, and the grapes of our own garden. In our own oven we'll bake our daily bread," she said to me as we settled down beside Cleopas once again. I sobbed against her neck. She stroked my back.

"That's right," said Cleopas very near to me.

I wrapped my fingers around my mother's neck. I took deeper and deeper breaths.

"We'll be in Nazareth," said Cleopas, "and no one, I promise you, my little one, no one will ever look for you there."

I was drowsy, so very drowsy all at once. But what did he mean, Cleopas, that no one would look for me? Who was looking for me? I didn't want to sleep. I wanted to ask him what he meant by those words, look for me, who was looking for me? What did all the strange stories mean? What did it mean what my mother had said about the angel coming to her? In all this misery and woe, I had forgotten about what she'd said on the rooftop in Jerusalem, the strange words she'd spoken. And Elizabeth had just said that an angel came to Joseph. Joseph hadn't said an angel came to him.

It seemed for a moment as I was sliding deeper and deeper into sweet rest that it was all connected. I ought to make something of it. Yes! Angels. An angel had come before and an angel had come again, and an angel was here. I knew that, didn't I? No. But then I felt purely drowsy, and I felt so safe.

My mother was singing to me in Hebrew, and Cleopas was singing with her. He was better now, much better, though he still coughed. But my aunt Mary did not feel well, though no one was worried about her.

And tomorrow we would leave this terrible place. We would leave my cousins here, the strange solemn boy John, who said so little and looked at me so much, and our beloved Elizabeth, his mother, and we'd go on to the refuge of Nazareth.

8

RIGHT AFTER THE COMING OF THE LIGHT, men on horseback came on a "rampage" through the village.

We left our little circle in which all had only just begun to listen to our cousin Elizabeth, and crowded into the back room of the house together.

Cleopas had never moved from there, as he had coughed very badly in the night and was feverish again. He lay smiling in his usual way, his eyes wet as he stared up at the low roof over our heads.

We could hear screams and the braying of the lambs and the screech of the birds. "They're stealing everything," said my cousin Mary Alexandra. The other women told her to be quiet, and her husband Zebedee patted her arm.

Once Silas tried to get up to go to the curtain, but his father ordered him to go to the far corner with a firm gesture.

Even the little ones who were always excited by everything were quiet.

Aunt Esther, Simon's wife, had Baby Esther in her arms, and every time the baby started to cry, she gave her the breast.

I wasn't afraid now, and I didn't know why. I stood

among the women with the other children, except for James who stood beside his father. James was really not a child anymore, I thought to myself, looking at him. Had we stayed in Jerusalem, had there been no rebellion, James would have gone into the Sanctuary of the Sons of Israel with Silas and Levi and with all the men.

But I was interrupted in this thought by the sudden fear that gripped everyone, and the feel of my mother's fingers closing around my upper arm.

Strangers were in the front room. Little Salome crushed up against me and I hugged her tight as my mother hugged me.

Then the curtain was ripped off the door. I was blinded and blinked, struggling to see. My mother gripped me very tight. No one spoke a word, and no one moved. I knew we were to be quiet and to do nothing. Everyone knew it, even the very littlest ones knew it. The babies cried but it was soft and it had nothing to do with these men who had torn the curtain away.

There were three or four of them, black against the daylight, big rough figures, with rags tied around their legs under the lashings of their sandals. One wore animal skins and another a gleaming helmet. The light hit their swords and their daggers. They had rags around their wrists.

"Well, look here," said the man with the helmet. He spoke in Greek. "What do we have here? Half the village."

"Come on, everything!" said another forcing his way towards us. He too spoke Greek. His voice was ugly. "I mean it, every denarius you have, all of you, now. Your gold or your silver. You women, your bracelets, take them off. We'll cut you open for what you swallowed if you don't give up what you've got!"

No one moved. The women did nothing.

Little Salome began to cry. I held her so tight I must have hurt her. But no one answered the men.

"We're fighting for freedom for our land," said one of the men. More Greek. "You stupid fools, don't you know what's happening in Israel?"

He stepped towards us and flashed his dagger at us, glaring into the face of Alphaeus, then Simon, then Joseph. But the men said nothing.

No one moved. No one spoke.

"Did you hear me? I'll cut your throats one by one, starting with the children!" said the man, stepping back.

One of the others kicked at our well-bound bundles, another lifting a blanket and letting it fall.

Very softly in Hebrew, Joseph spoke.

"I can't understand you. What do you want us to do? We are people of peace. I can't understand you."

Very softly in Hebrew, Alphaeus said: "Please do not harm our innocent children and our women. Do not let it be said of you that you shed innocent blood."

Now it was the turn of the men to be still as stone, and finally one of them turned away.

"Oh, you stupid worthless peasants," he said in Greek. "You miserable ignorant filth."

"They've never seen any money in their lives," said the other. "There's nothing in this place but old clothes and stinking babies. You pitiful wretches. Eat your dirt in peace."

"Yes, grovel while we fight for your freedom," said another.

They turned and went out with heavy steps, kicking baskets and bedrolls out of their way.

We waited. I felt my mother's hands on my shoulders. I

could see James, and he looked so much like Joseph, it was a wonder I never saw it before.

Finally the cries and the noise were over.

Joseph spoke. "Remember this," he said. He looked from James to me and to Little Joses, and to my cousins who stared up at him, and to John who stood beside his mother. "Remember. Never lift your hand to defend yourself or to strike. Be patient. If you must speak, be simple."

We nodded. We knew what had happened. All of us knew. Little Salome was sniffling. And all at once, my aunt Mary, who had been feeling so sick, broke into crying, and turned and sat down beside Cleopas, who was still staring up as he had been before. He looked like he was already dead. But he wasn't dead.

All at once we children rushed to the doors of the little house. People were pouring out into the street. They were in a fury against the robbers. Women were chasing after fluttering birds and I saw the body of a man lying in the very middle of all that was going on, and he was staring up at the sky the same way that Cleopas had stared, but with blood streaming from his mouth. He was like our dead man in the Temple.

No soul in him.

People were going around him, and nobody wept for him, and nobody knelt beside him.

Finally two men with a rope came and they looped it over him and under his arms and they dragged him away.

"He was one of them," said James. "Don't look at him."

"But who killed him?" I asked. "And what will they do with him?" In the light of the day it was not so frightening as it had been in the night. But I knew, even at this moment, that the darkness of the night would come. And it would be very frightening again. I knew the fear was waiting. The fear was something new. The fear was terrible. I didn't feel it but I remembered it, and I knew it would come back. It would never go away.

"They'll bury him," said James. "His dead body can't be left unburied. It's an offense to the Lord in Heaven. They'll put him in a cave or in the earth. It doesn't matter."

We were told to go inside.

The room had been cleared, the floor swept and beautiful rugs had been put down, rugs covered with flowers woven in the wool. We were told to sit down and be still and listen because Elizabeth wanted to talk to us before we left to go on.

I remembered now that we had been gathered for this purpose before, but the rugs had not been unbound yet when the first horsemen had come.

Now as if nothing had happened, as if no one had died in the street we went on.

We made a big thick, crowded circle. The babies were quiet enough for Elizabeth to be heard. I sat before Joseph, my legs crossed, as were his, and Little Salome was right by me, leaning back against her mother. Cleopas was still in the other room.

"I'll make my words quick," Elizabeth said. When I'd awakened this morning, she'd been talking of grandfathers and grandmothers, and who had married who and gone to what village. I couldn't remember all those names. Both the women and the men had been repeating what she'd been telling, in order to remember it.

Now, she shook her head before she began and she lifted her hands. I saw her gray hairs under the edge of her veil, running through her darker hair.

"This is what I must tell you, what I never put in a letter to you. When I die, which will be soon—and no, don't say that it won't. I know that it will. I know the signs. When I die, John will go to live with our kindred among the Essenes."

All at once there was fussing and crying out. Even Cleopas appeared in the door, huddled over, with his hand around his chest.

"No, why in the world have you made such a decision!" he said. "To send that child to people who don't even worship in the Temple! And John, the son of a priest! And you married all your life to a priest, and Zechariah, the son of a priest, and before him?"

Cleopas limped, holding his stomach, until he reached the circle and then dropped to his knees, my mother right there to help him and pull his robe free, and straighten it around him. On he went. "And you would send John, whose mother is of the House of David, and whose father is of the House of Aaron, to live with the Essenes? The Essenes? These people who think they know better than all the rest of us what is good and what is bad, and who is righteous and what the Lord demands?"

"And who do you think the Essenes are!" said Elizabeth in a low voice. She was patient but wanted to be understood. "Are they not from the Children of Abraham? Are they not of the House of David and the House of Aaron, and from all the Tribes of Israel? Are they not pious? Are they not zealous for the Law? I'm telling you, they will take him out in the wilderness and there they'll educate him and care for him. And he, the child himself, wants this and he has reason."

My cousin John was looking at me. Why? Why not at his mother as everyone else was, when they were not looking at him? His face didn't show much. He stared at me and I could see only a calmness in him. He didn't look like a little boy. He looked like a little man. He sat opposite his mother, and he wore a plain white tunic of far better wool than mine, or any of ours, and over that a robe of the same fine weave. And these things I'd seen before but not thought of, and now as I took them in, I felt a great wondering about him, but Cleopas was talking and I had to follow his words.

"The Essenes," Cleopas said. "Will none of you speak up for this boy before he becomes the son of men who don't stand before the Lord at the appointed times? Am I the only man here with a voice? Elizabeth, on the heads of our grandparents, I swear this must not—."

"Brother, calm yourself," said Elizabeth. "Save your passion for your own sons! This son is mine, entrusted to me by the Lord in my old age against all probability! You don't speak to a woman when you speak to me. You speak to Sarah of old, to Hannah of old. You speak to one chosen for a reason. Am I not to provide for this child what I think the Lord will have?"

"Joseph, don't let this pass," said Cleopas.

"You stand closest to the boy," said Joseph. "If you must speak against his mother, then speak."

"I don't speak against you," said Cleopas. Then the cough came up in his chest, and he was in pain. My aunt Mary was worried and so was my mother. Cleopas raised his hand, begging for patience. But he couldn't stop the cough. Finally he said, "You speak of Sarah, the wife of Abraham," he said, "and you speak of Hannah, the mother of Samuel, but did either of these men fail to do what the Lord commanded, and you talk of sending your boy to live with those who turn their backs on the Temple of the Lord?"

"Brother, you have a poor memory," said Elizabeth. "To whom did your sister, Mary, come when she learned that she was chosen to bear this child Yeshua? She came to me and why? Now, before some other calamity befalls this village, I beg you to listen to my decision, and I have asked you to listen to it, not to dispute with me. I don't put it before you for judgement, you understand. I tell you, the boy goes to the Essenes."

Never had I heard a woman speak with this kind of authority. True, there had been venerable women in the Street of the Carpenters in Alexandria, women who could bring the children to silence with the clap of their hands, and women who asked questions in the synagogue to make the Teacher go to his scrolls. But this was stronger, and more clear than anything I'd ever heard.

Cleopas fell silent.

Elizabeth lowered her voice and spoke on.

"We have brethren with them, grandsons of Mattathias and Naomi, who went out long ago to the desert to live with them, and I've spoken with them, and they will take him, even now. It's their way to take children and bring them up strictly, abiding by their rules of purity and fasting, and strict community, and all these are natural things to my son. And he will study with them. He will learn the prophets. He will learn the word of the Lord. The desert is where he wants to be, and when I'm gathered to my ancestors there he will go until such time as he is a man and decides for himself what he will do. I have already provided for John with the Essenes and they wait only for my word, or for him to come to those that live on the other side of the Jordan and they will take him far out away from here to where he's to be brought up removed from the affairs of men."

"Why can't you come with us to Nazareth?" asked Joseph. "You are welcome. Your brother surely will say so, as it's the house of his parents that we go to, all of us—."

"No," said Elizabeth. "I will stay here. I'll be buried with my husband, Zechariah. And I will tell you the reason why this child is to go."

"Well, say the reason," said Cleopas. "And you know I want you to come to Nazareth. Surely it is right for John and Yeshua to be brought up together." Then he started coughing again, trying to hide it. But I knew if he hadn't been coughing he would have said a lot more.

"This is what I couldn't write to you in a letter," said Elizabeth. "Please listen because I only want to tell it one time."

The mothers said hush to the babies. Cleopas cleared his throat. "Come out with it," he said, "or I may die without hearing it."

"You know that after you left for Egypt, you, Mary and Joseph and the little one, Herod was of restless and cruel mind."

"Yes," said Cleopas. "Out with it." He began to cough again.

"And you know that John was born to me and to Zechariah when both of us were in our extreme old age, as were Sarah and Abraham when Isaac was born." She stopped and looked to each and every one of us little ones who were in the inner circle and we nodded that we understood. "You know of Hannah's prayer for a child, do you not, children, when she stood before the Lord at Shiloh praying, and who was it that thought she was drunken, can you tell me, any of you?"

"Eli the priest," said Silas quickly. "And she told him that she was praying and why she was praying, and he prayed for her as well."

"Yes," said Elizabeth, "and so I too often prayed, but

what you may not know, all you young ones, is that the birth of my child was foretold."

I had not known it. And I could see that the others had not known it. As for John, he sat quietly, watching his mother, but it seemed nothing was disturbing him and he was deep in his thoughts.

"Well, how that is explained to you, I leave it up to your fathers, because there are reasons not to speak of it, but I will say only that it was known that the child came to us late in life by the will of Heaven, and when he was born I consecrated him to the Lord. You will see that no razor has ever touched his head, and he takes nothing of the grape. He belongs to the Lord."

"The Lord of the Essenes?" asked Cleopas.

"Let her speak," said my mother. "Do you forget everything you know?"

He was quiet.

Elizabeth went on.

Again she looked at each and all. And no one spoke, all of us waiting to see what all this could mean.

"We are of the House of David," Elizabeth said. "And you know that Herod so hated all of us, and any of us with the faintest claim to royal blood, that he burned all the records in the Temple by which everyone suffered the loss of the archives in which the names of all their ancestors had been written for all time.

"And you know what happened before you went to Egypt, you know what sent my beloved cousin Mary and her newborn into Egypt with Joseph and with you, Cleopas. You know perfectly well."

I didn't dare to ask the question that was on my lips. I didn't know what had sent us into Egypt! But she went on.

"King Herod had his watchers everywhere," she said, her voice getting rougher and deeper.

"We know this," said my mother softly. She lifted her hand just a little, and her cousin Elizabeth took her hand and held it and they nodded at one another, their veils almost touching, as if telling each other without words a secret.

Then Elizabeth said,

"Now, Herod's men, his soldiers, rough as those thieves who just came into our village, into this very house thinking to rob us for their petty wars, soldiers like that came into the very Temple and sought out my Zechariah to ask him about the son born to him, the son of the House of David. They would see this son for themselves."

"We knew nothing of this," Joseph said in a whisper.

"I told you I would not write this in a letter," said Elizabeth. "I had to wait until you came. What was done could not be undone. Now they accosted him in the Temple, these soldiers, as he came out of the Sanctuary where he had fulfilled his duty as it was his time as a priest. And do you think he would tell them where to find his son? He had already hidden me away with the baby. We had gone into the caves near the Essenes and they had brought food to us. And he wouldn't tell these soldiers where we were.

"They pushed him and knocked him to his knees, and this right outside the Sanctuary, and the other priests could not stop them. And do you think they even tried? Do you think the scribes came to his defense? Do you think the chief priests came to protest?"

Now my cousin Elizabeth's eyes were fixed on me. Slowly she looked at Joseph and Mary, and then again at each and every one listening. "They beat Zechariah. They beat him because he would say nothing, and with one fine blow to his head, they killed him. Right before the Lord."

We waited in silence as she went on.

"Many saw what happened. But they didn't know the reason for it. Some of the priests knew. And they sent word to me. Our kinsmen were told, and they told other kinsmen and some came to the Essenes and told. And I was told."

All were dazed by this terrible news. My mother leaned forward and put her head on the shoulder of Elizabeth, and Elizabeth held her. But then Elizabeth drew herself up, and so did my mother, and Elizabeth spoke on.

"The kinsmen of Zechariah, all of them priests, saw to his burial with his ancestors," she said. "And do you think I have gone into the Temple since? Not till you came to Jerusalem. Not till the tyrant was dead, and gone to eternal fire. Not till the stories of Yeshua and John were forgotten, and what do we find when we go before the Lord?"

No one dared to answer her.

"He goes to the Essenes and soon. There he will be hidden. Now you take your leave of me and go on to Nazareth before more bandits come through here. I have nothing for them to take. I'm old and John is little, and they'll leave us in peace. But I won't see you again. No. And surely John is meant to hear the voice of the Lord. He is consecrated to the Lord, and the Essenes know that he is under the vow. And they will take care of him and he'll study until the time comes for him. Now you, you go."

9

HEROD'S SOLDIERS, the bandits, the man killed in the Temple, my cousin killed in the Temple, a priest killed searching for the whereabouts of a child, and my cousin was the child.

Yeshua and John. Why was he foretold, and why were we linked, and behind it all was the great question: What had happened in Bethlehem? What had happened, and was it the thing that had made my family go to Egypt where I'd lived all my life?

But I couldn't think now except in bursts of curiosity and fear. The fear became part of my thinking. The fear became part of the story. My cousin Zechariah, a priest with gray hairs, being kicked by the soldiers of Herod. And here we were in the village that was filled with the angry voices of those who'd been robbed by the bandits, and expected more of the same.

We found our beasts still tethered on the outskirts. An old woman without teeth stood there laughing.

"They tried to steal them!" she cried. "But the animals wouldn't move." She bowed her head and slapped her knees as she laughed. "They couldn't make them move." And an old man who was sitting in the dirt beside a small house was laughing too.

"They stole my shawl," he cried out. "I said to them, 'Go on, brother, take it!' " He waved his hand and he laughed and laughed.

We loaded our bundles quickly, put Cleopas firmly in place, and Aunt Mary in place, and then my mother took Elizabeth in her arms and they cried.

Little John stood there staring at me.

"We'll go around Jericho and on through the valley home," Joseph said to all of us.

When my mother finally came, we set off.

Little Salome and I went ahead with James, and some of the other cousins followed.

Cleopas began to sing.

"But who are the Essenes?" Little Salome asked me.

"I don't know," I said. "I heard what you heard. How could I know?"

James said: "They don't hold with the priesthood in the Temple. They believe they have the true priesthood. They are the descendants of Zadok. They wait until they can purify the Temple. They dress in white; they pray together. They live apart."

"Are they good or are they bad?" Little Salome asked.

"They're good enough for our kindred," said James. "How can we know? There are Pharisees, there are the priests, there are the Essenes. We all say the prayer, 'Hear O Israel, the Lord our God is One.' "

We murmured the prayer after him in Hebrew as he'd said it. We said it every day always in the morning when we rose and in the evening. I hardly thought about it. When we said it everything stopped, and we said it with a true heart.

I didn't want to say anything about the things that troubled me. A bad feeling came over me that James knew all about it, and I didn't want to say anything with Little Salome there. My feelings grew darker and darker and the fear was there, very near.

We were moving fast it seemed to me, down and down through the mountains, and the plain was spread out and beautiful in the sunlight with palm trees everywhere, even though smoke was still pouring up from the burnt places, and there were many houses on all sides. It wasn't hard to see that people everywhere were going on with what they had to do as if the bandits had never come.

Bands of pilgrims passed us, some singing, and some were on horseback, and they had cheerful greetings for us.

We drew near villages where children were playing, and we could smell the cooking food.

"You see," said my mother, as if she knew my thoughts, "it will be this way all the way to Nazareth. These robbers, they come and they go, but we are who we are." She smiled at me and it seemed I'd never be afraid again.

"Do they really fight for the freedom of the Holy Land?" Little Salome asked. She was looking to the men now for an answer, as we were somewhat drawn together.

Cleopas laughed at the question. He rubbed her head.

"Little daughter, if men want to fight, they find a reason," he said. "Men have been fighting for the freedom of the Holy Land by raiding the villages whenever they want to for hundreds of years."

Joseph merely shook his head.

Alphaeus reached out to gather Little Salome up to him.

"You don't worry," he said. "Once it was Cyrus the King who watched over us, now it's Augustus Caesar. We don't care, because the Lord in Heaven is the only King we know in our hearts, and what man thinks he is King here on Earth, we don't care."

"But David was King of Israel," I said. "David was King, and Solomon after him. And King Josiah, he was a great King of Israel. We've known this for as long as we've known anything. And we're the House of David, and the Lord said to David, 'I will make you reign over Israel forever.' Isn't that so?"

"Forever . . ." Alphaeus said. "But who is to judge the ways of the Lord? The Lord will keep his promise to David in the Lord's way."

He looked away as he spoke. We were in the valley now. The crowd of those coming out of the mountains was large. We pressed together. "Forever . . . what is forever in the mind of the Lord?" he said. "A thousand years is nothing but a moment to the Lord."

"A King will come?" I asked.

Joseph turned and looked at me.

"The Lord keeps his promises to Israel," said Alphaeus, "but how and when and in what way we don't know."

"Do angels come only in Israel?" Little Salome asked.

"No," said Joseph. "They come anywhere and everywhere and whenever they want."

"Why did we have to go to Egypt?" asked Little Salome. "Why did King Herod's men——."

"This is no time to tell you," said Joseph.

My mother spoke up. "There will come a time, a time to tell you everything slowly so that you understand. But now is not that time."

I knew they would say this, or words like it. But there had been a chance, and I was glad that Little Salome had spoken up. I didn't know where my older cousins, Silas and Jus-

tus, had gone, or any of the others, or what they thought of
what Elizabeth had said. Maybe those older boys knew
things, surely they knew things. Maybe Silas knew.

I dropped back slowly in the press of the family, until I
was walking close to my uncle Cleopas on the donkey.

Cleopas had heard us talking, I was sure of it. Had anyone made me promise not to ask him questions? I didn't
think so.

"I pray I live to tell you things," said Cleopas.

But no sooner had he spoken these words, than Joseph
stepped back beside him, and began to walk with us and he
said quickly:

"I pray you live to let me tell my child what I will." He
was gentle but he meant it. "Enough questions. Enough talk
of the bad things of long ago. We're out of Jerusalem. We're
away from the troubles. We have good daylight and we can
go far before making our camps."

"I wanted to go into Jericho!" cried Little Salome.
"Couldn't we go into Jericho for a little while? I want to see
the palace of Herod where they burned it."

"We want to see Jericho!" cried Little Symeon.

Suddenly all the children around us took up the cry, even
children of new pilgrims who were with us, and I started to
laugh at the way in which Joseph smiled.

"You listen to me," Joseph said. "We will bathe tonight in
the River Jordan! The River Jordan! We'll wash our bodies
and our clothes in it for the first time! And then we'll sleep
out in the valley under the stars!"

"The River Jordan!" Everyone was shouting it with great
excitement.

Joseph was telling the tale of the leper who'd come to the
Prophet Elisha and been told to bathe in the River Jordan

and how he would be cleansed. And Cleopas began a story of how Joshua had crossed the Jordan, and then Alphaeus was telling James another story, and I went from story to story as we moved on.

Zebedee and his people caught up with us, whom we hadn't seen since we'd left Elizabeth, and he too had a tale of the Jordan River, and Zebedee's wife, Mary, who was my mother's cousin, Mary Alexandra, but always called Mary, soon began to sing, "Blessed be all those who fear the Lord; that walk in his ways!"

She had a sweet high voice. We sang with her.

"For you will eat the labor of your hands; and you will be happy and all will be well!"

We were such a large clan that we moved slowly, with many stops for the women to take their ease, and for Little Esther to be wrapped in fresh swaddling clothes. My aunt Mary was sick, for certain, but my mother said it was good news, a baby coming, and I stopped worrying about it. And Cleopas had to come down off the donkey many times to cover his feet, as they say, which meant to find a private place to relieve himself away from the road.

He was weak and my mother went with him, holding his arm, which made him angry, but he needed the help, and she wouldn't let the men do it. She said, "This is my brother," and she went with him alone.

He did it so many times that he told us the funny story from Scripture of the time King Saul was warring with young David, fearing young David because he knew that David was to be King. King Saul went into a cave to cover his feet, and his enemy David was in there, and might have killed him. But did David do it? God forbid. David crept up to Saul in the darkness of the cave as Saul relieved himself, a man off guard, and David cut a tassel from Saul's kingly robe, a tassel like no other man wore.

And hours later, in hope of making peace with King Saul, David sent this tassel to him, to let him know that he, David, might have slain King Saul, but would David have slain an anointed King? God forbid.

We all loved the stories of David and Saul. Even Silas and Levi who were usually bored with stories came up to listen as Cleopas told these tales. Cleopas was speaking in Greek all the while, and we were all very used to it, and liked it, though nobody said so.

Cleopas told us the marvelous story of how Saul, when the Lord ceased to speak to him, went to the Soothsayer of Endor, to beg her to summon from Sheol the spirit of the dead Prophet Samuel, to tell Saul his fate. There was to be a great battle on the next morning, and Saul, who no longer found favor with the Lord, was desperate, and sought out a woman who could talk to the dead. Now this was forbidden by Saul's own orders, along with all soothsaying. But such a woman was found.

And out of the Earth by her power came the spirit of the Prophet asking, "Why have you disturbed my rest?" Then he foretold that Saul's enemies would defeat Israel, and that Saul and his sons would all die.

"And what happened then?" asked Cleopas, looking around at all of us.

"She made him sit down and eat a meal for his strength," said Silas.

"And that's what we'd like to do right now." Everyone laughed.

"I tell you, we will not eat or drink until we reach the river," cried Cleopas.

And so we pushed on.

And to the river we finally came.

Beyond the tall grass, it was red with the light of the sun that was almost gone away.

Many people were bathing in the river. People streamed down to the banks from all directions, and others had made camps nearby. We could hear the singing coming from everywhere, and songs blended into songs.

We ran into the water and the water came up to our knees. We washed our bodies and our clothes. We were singing and shouting. The cool air did not bother us, and we were soon warm and the water felt warm.

Cleopas came down from the back of the beast and walked into the river. He threw up his hands. He sang aloud so all could hear him.

"Praise to the Lord, Praise to the Lord, my soul, sing! While I live I will praise the Lord; I'll sing praises unto my God while I have any life in me; Put no trust in princes, nor in others, in whom there's no help; the breath of your men goes out of them; they return to the earth; in that very day their thoughts are gone, gone!"

All began to sing with him:

"Happy is the one that has the Lord of Jacob for his help!"

The whole river was full of singing, and those on the banks began to sing.

I'd never seen my uncle as he was now, looking up at the red sky, and with his arms up, and his face so full of his prayers. All the cleverness was gone from him. All the anger was gone. He didn't care about the people. He didn't sing for the people. He sang and sang without looking at anyone. He looked up at the sky, and I looked at it, at the sky darkening with ribbons of red from the dying sun, and the first of the bright stars.

I moved through the water as I sang, and when I reached him, I put my arm up around his back, and felt him shivering under his robe that was trailing in the water.

He didn't even know I was there.

Stay with me. Lord, Father in Heaven, let him stay with us. Father in Heaven, I ask this! Is this too much? If I cannot have answers to my questions, let me have this man for a little while, for as long as you will.

I was weak. I needed to hold on to him or I would have fallen. Something happened. It happened quickly and then slowly. There was no more river, no more dark sky and no more of the singing, but all around me there were others and there were so many others that no one could count them; they were beyond the grains of sand in the desert or in the sea. *Please, please, with me, please, but if he has to die, so be it——.* I reached out with both arms. I reached up. I knew, just for a moment, a tiny moment, the answer to everything, and I worried about nothing, but that moment vanished, and all these countless others went upward away from me, away from where I could see them and feel them.

Darkness. Stillness. People laughing and talking as they do late at night.

I opened my eyes. Something fled away from me, like the water washing away on a beach, just being pulled back, so big and strong you can't stop it. Gone, whatever it was. Gone.

I was afraid. But I was dry and wrapped up and it was soft here, soft and close and dark. The stars were sprinkled all over the sky. People still sang and there were lights moving everywhere, lights of lanterns and candles and fires by the tents. I was covered up and warm and my mother had her arm over me.

"What did I do?" I asked.

"You fell down in the river, you were tired, you were praying and you were tired. There were so many people, and you were praying and you cried out to the Lord. You're here now, and you go to sleep. I put you to bed. You close your eyes now, and when you wake in the morning, you'll eat and you'll be strong. It's all too much, and you're little but not little enough, and you're a big boy, but not big enough."

"But we're here and we're home," I said. "And something happened."

"No," she said. She meant it. She didn't understand. She smiled. I could see that in the firelight, and I could feel the heat of the fire. She told the truth as she always did. I looked over and saw James fast asleep, and beside him Zebedee's little brothers, and so many others, I didn't know all their names. Little Symeon was asleep bundled up against Little Judas. Little Joseph was snoring.

Mary, the wife of Zebedee, was talking to Mary, the wife of Cleopas, in a fast, worried manner but I couldn't hear her words. They were friends, now, I could see that, and Mary, the Egyptian, the wife of Cleopas, was gesturing and making pictures with her hands. Mary of Zebedee was nodding.

I closed my eyes. *The others, the great crowd of others, so sweet, like the blanket, like the wind with the smell of the river.* Were they here? Something stirred in me, knowledge as clear as if a voice was speaking: this is not the most difficult part.

It was only a moment. Then I was myself.

New voices sang from here and from there, and people who passed us were singing. I was happy with my eyes closed.

"The Lord shall reign forever," they sang, "even your Lord, O Zion, unto all generations. Praise to the Lord."

I heard the voice of my aunt Mary of Cleopas. "I don't

know where he is. He's out there over by the river singing with them, talking. They're shouting at each other one minute and the next singing."

"Look to him!" whispered my mother.

"But he's stronger now, I tell you. His fever's gone. He'll come back when he needs to lie down. If I go to him with the men he'll be angry. I'm not going. What's the use of going? What's the use of trying to tell him anything? When he needs to come, he'll come."

"But we should see to him," said my mother.

"Don't you know," said my aunt Salome to her, "that this is what he wants? If he's to die, let him die quarreling over kings and taxes, and over the Temple, and by the River Jordan, shouting to the Lord. Let him have his last strength."

They were quiet.

Their voices went low. Talk of common things. And then the worries, but I didn't want to hear it. Bandits everywhere, villages burning. Archelaus had gone to the sea to sail to Rome. If the Romans weren't on the march yet from Syria they soon would be. Weren't the signal fires telling them what happened? The whole city of Jerusalem was in a state of riot. I snuggled close to my mother. And my whole body was like a fist.

"Enough," said my mother. "Nothing ever changes."

Sleep. I went away in my half sleep.

"Angels!" I said out loud. I opened my eyes. "But I didn't really see them."

"You lie quiet," said my mother.

I laughed to myself. She had seen an angel before I was born. An angel had told Joseph to bring us back, I had heard it said. And I had seen them. I had seen them but only for a moment. Less than a moment. They came in great numbers, numberless like the stars in their numbers, and I'd seen them for a moment. Hadn't I? What had they looked like? Let it go. *This is not the most difficult part.*

I turned over, my head against the soft bedroll. Why hadn't I paid more attention to what they looked like? Why hadn't I held on to the sight of them, and not let them go? Because the truth of it was they were always there! You just had to be able to see them. It was like opening a wooden door, or pulling back a curtain. But the curtain was thick, and heavy. Maybe that's how it was with the curtain of the Holy of Holies—it was thick and heavy. And the curtain could fall down, closed, just like that.

My mother had seen an angel who spoke to her, who must have stepped out of the numberless ones, who came towards her, said words to her, but what was the meaning of the words?

I wanted to cry again, but I didn't. I was happy and sad. I was filled with feeling, as a cup can be of water. I was so full of it my body curled up under the covers, and I held tight to my mother's hand.

She slipped her fingers out of mine.

She lay down beside me. I almost dreamed.

That's how to do it, I thought. Thoughts began to slide. That's how to do it, so that no one knows. And don't tell anyone ever. Don't ever tell, not even Little Salome or my mother. No. But Father in Heaven, I did do it, didn't I? And I will find out what happened in Bethlehem. I'll find out everything.

They came again, so many of them but this time I only smiled and I didn't open my eyes. *You can come, you aren't going to make me jump and wake up.* No, you can come, even if there are so many of you there are no numbers for you. You come from the place where there are no numbers. You come from where there are no robbers, no fires, no man dying on a spear. You come, but you don't know what I know, do you? No, you don't know.

And how do I know that?

10

WHAT WAS THE PEACE OF THAT NIGHT? How soon was it shattered?

The next morning, the river valley was flooded with those fleeing the uprisings. We woke up to shouts and crying. The nearby villages were in flames. We packed up the donkeys and made our way north.

First we went straight along the river, but soon the sight of flames and the sound of cries drove us far to the west, only to find fighting there and people running, their bundles and children under their arms.

When we crossed the river, the other way, we found the same terrors. The road was crowded with the miserable and the weeping who told stories of bands of robbers, and would-be kings, swooping down upon them for livestock and gold, and even burning their villages for no good reason. My fear rose in me and became a thing always with me so that all happiness seemed finally to be a dream, even in the brightest sunlight.

I lost count of the days, and the names of the towns and places we passed did not drop a hook into my mind. Again and again we were stopped by the bandits themselves. They forced their way into the crowds, shouting and cursing, and seeking to rob everyone.

We huddled together and said nothing, and before dark, pitched our camp away from the settlements which were more often than not empty or burnt out.

In one town we hid from them while they set fire to the houses around us. Little Salome started to cry and it was I who comforted her, I who had been crying so hard outside Jericho and now held her and told her we'd be home soon. Silas and Levi were in a passion that they couldn't fight the men who accosted us, and James repeated the stern warnings of his father to be silent, to do nothing in the face of their huge numbers.

After all, these "rogues," the men said, carried swords and daggers. They killed at whim. They were "thirsty for blood." We were to give them no "provocation."

Sometimes we walked late into the night, even as other pilgrims pitched camp, and the men quarreled, with Cleopas always in the middle of it. Aunt Mary said he was having a high time of it with so many new men to listen to his speeches.

He didn't have any more fever.

People didn't talk about it now.

I stayed close to him to learn what he had to say. And he would not stop speaking his mind about King Herod Archelaus, no matter what Joseph said to him, and Alphaeus gave up too. Archelaus had sailed to Rome. The word was out. But so had others of Herod's children, "those who had been lucky enough to survive," said Cleopas. For it seemed the King had murdered five of his own sons as well as countless other helpless men over the thirty and more years of his reign.

Joseph's brother Simon was quiet too, and so were his boys and girl, as they'd always been. They had no interest in these things. And neither had my mother.

When we parted from Zebedee and my mother's dearest cousin, Mary Alexandra, there was much crying because "the three Marys" wouldn't be together again until the next Festival in Jerusalem and with things as they were, who knew when it would be safe to go?

And Elizabeth, what about Elizabeth, they sobbed, alone in the world and Little John going to the Essenes, and though they had left her a long time ago back beyond Jericho, they cried about her all over again. They cried about people I didn't know, and then off they went on their beasts, Zebedee and his kindred, towards the Sea of Galilee, to Capernaum. I wanted to go to the Sea of Galilee too. I wanted to see it with all my heart.

I missed the sea. That is, if I had a single thought of not being afraid, I missed the sea. Alexandria was a narrow piece of land between the Great Sea and the lake. You could always smell the water in Alexandria. You could always feel the cooling breeze. But we were inland, and the land was rocky and the paths hard. And there were sudden rains.

These were the last of the lesser rains, said the men, who knew the seasons, and it was late for them, and in any ordinary time, they would have been good. But now there was no one thinking about the harvest or the crops, only of getting away from the rebellions and the troubles. And the rains made us huddle together under our cloaks, and they made us cold.

The rains put the women in a terrible fear for Cleopas, but Cleopas didn't take sick. He no longer coughed at all.

Those who passed us on the road brought stories of more

riots in Jerusalem. It was said the Roman soldiers were on the march from Syria, there was no question of it. Our men threw up their hands.

As we went on, there were still many with us—pilgrims returning to towns in Galilee, and we began to climb into higher, green country and I liked this very much.

Everywhere I turned there were forests of trees, and the sheep grazing on the slopes, and here at last we did see the farmers at work, just as if there were no wars at all.

I would forget about bandits and trouble. Then out of nowhere, over the rise of the hill would come a pack of the riders, sending us all screaming. Sometimes the great number of homeless pilgrims was too much for them, and they rode off into the fields and around us and left us in peace. Other times they tormented the men who gave them nothing but humble answers as if the men were stupid when the men were not.

Night after night, new men were at our dinner circle, some of them Galileans headed north to other villages, some of them our kindred but distant whom we really didn't know, and some of them refugees from the raids and the fire. The men sat around the fire and passed the wineskin and they argued and disputed and shouted at one another, and Little Salome and I both loved to listen to what they had to say.

Rebel leaders had risen everywhere, said the men. There was Athronges, with his brothers, gathering forces, and on the rampage, and many going to him. And also in the north, Judas bar Ezekias, the Galilean.

And not only were the Romans on the march, but they had been joined by the men of Arabia Petrea, and the Arabians were burning villages because they hated Herod and there was no Herod here to fight back and make order. And the Romans were doing what they could.

All this encouraged us, and all who were around us, to move quickly towards Galilee even though we never knew where we might meet with these terrible forces.

The men disputed wildly.

"Yes, everybody talked about the evils of King Herod, what a tyrant and what a monster he was," said one of the men, "but look what happens to this nation in the blink of an eye! Must we have a tyrant to rule us?"

"We could do well and good with the Roman governor of Syria," said Cleopas. "We don't need a Jewish King who isn't a Jew."

"But who would be here, here in Judea and Samaria and Peraea and Galilee with the authority!" asked Alphaeus. "Would it be Roman officials?"

"Better than the Herods," said Cleopas. And many others said the same thing.

"And what if a Roman prefect comes marching into Judea with a statue of Caesar Augustus as the Son of God?"

"But they wouldn't do that, they would never do that," said Cleopas. "In every city of the Empire, we're respected. We keep the Sabbath, we're not required to join in the army. They respect our ancestral Laws. I say better them than this family of madmen who plot against each other and slaughter their own blood!"

The talk went on and on. I liked to fall asleep listening to it. It made me feel safe.

"I'll tell you this much because this much I've seen," said my uncle Alphaeus. "When the Romans put down a riot, they kill the innocent with the bad."

"But why do the innocent suffer?" James asked, James, my brother, who was now one of them, as if he had ever been anything else.

"How are soldiers to tell who is innocent or guilty when

they come down on a mob in a city, or on a village?" said a stranger, a Jew from Galilee. "You can be swept up like that by them. I'm telling you when they come, you get out of the way. They don't have time to listen to you tell them you've done nothing. It's one swarm of locusts after another, the thieves first and the soldiers second."

"And these men, these great warriors of old," Cleopas said, "these new kings of Israel rising up out of slavery all around us, these sudden anointed leaders, where will they take this land except into more and more misery?"

My aunt Mary, the Egyptian, cried out.

I opened my eyes and sat up.

My aunt Mary rose up suddenly from among the women and came over to them, her hands shaking, her eyes streaming with tears. I could see her tears in the firelight.

"Stop it, don't say any more," she shouted. "We came out of Egypt to listen to this? We came from Alexandria to make our way through the Jordan Valley in fear and terror of these fools, and when it's quiet and we're almost home, you frighten the children with all your shouting, all, all your prophesies, you don't know the will of the Lord, you don't know anything! We could get home tomorrow and find Nazareth's been burnt to the ground."

Tomorrow. Nazareth. In this beautiful land?

Two of the other women caught hold of her and took her away from the men. Cleopas shrugged his shoulders. The other men went on talking but in quieter voices.

Cleopas shook his head, and drank his wine.

I got up and went close to James, who was looking into the fire as he often did.

"We're going to be in Nazareth that soon?" I asked.

"Perhaps," he said. "We're close."

"But what if it is all burned?" I asked.

"Don't be frightened," said Joseph in a low voice. "It won't be burnt up. I know it won't. You go back to sleep."

Alphaeus and Cleopas looked at him. Some of the men were whispering their night prayers, heading for their beds under the sky.

"How are we to know the will of the Lord?" Cleopas said in a mutter, looking away. "The Lord wanted us to leave beautiful Alexandria for this, the Lord wanted us—." He stopped because Joseph had turned away.

"What's happened to us so far?" Alphaeus asked.

Cleopas was angry and spoke low. Joseph looked at him the whole time.

Cleopas couldn't find his words.

"What's happened?" Alphaeus asked. "Now, tell me, Cleopas. What's happened?"

They were all watching Cleopas.

"Nothing has happened to us," Cleopas whispered. "We have been through it."

Everyone was satisfied. That was the answer they had wanted.

When I lay down, Joseph brought the blanket up over me. The ground under me was cool, and I could smell the grass. I could smell the sweet smell of the trees not far off. We were all scattered over the slope of the hill, some under the trees, and some in the open as I was.

Little Judas and Symeon snuggled up next to me, without even waking up.

I looked up at the stars. I'd never seen the stars like this in Alexandria, so clear, so many like dust, like sand, like all the words I'd learned and sung.

All the men had left the fire. The fire had gone out. All the better could I see the stars, and I didn't really want to go to sleep. I never wanted to sleep.

Far off people shouted. I heard screams. It was down the hill. I could barely hear the voices crying out down there, and then turning, I saw flames way off from us down there, and I hated the way they shivered, the flames, but the men didn't get up. No one moved. We were in darkness. Nothing changed in our camp, and it was the same for all those camped near us. I heard horses down there in the little valley.

Cleopas lay down beside me.

"Nothing changes," he said.

"How can you say that?" I asked. "Everywhere we go it's changing."

I wanted badly for the screams to die away. And they almost did. More flames. I was afraid of the flames.

There was a song of screams coming closer and closer. It was one woman screaming. I thought it would stop, but it didn't stop. And with it I could hear feet running, faint and then loud, stomping feet.

A man's voice rose in the dark, crying out terrible words, words I knew were hateful and mean as he flung them out, over the woman's screams.

In Greek he called the woman a harlot, he said he would kill her when he caught her, and terrible oaths came from him, terrible words I'd never heard spoken before.

Our men rose up. I rose up.

All at once the woman's steps were right near us, pounding up the slope. She was breathing hard and couldn't scream anymore. The distant fire showed nothing yet.

Cleopas rushed forward, and so did Joseph, and the other men, and I saw through the dark that they reached out for the woman as soon as she appeared, arms waving, against the fiery sky. They brought her down to the ground, and pushed her behind them into the blankets. They stood still. I heard her breathing, and her coughing and sobbing, and the women hushing her as if she was a little child, and pulling her away.

I was on my feet, and James was right behind me.

Against the faraway flames, I saw the man rise up and stop. He was a big black shape like the rocks around us. He was drunk. I could smell the wine on him. I could see him wag his head.

In an evil voice, he called out to the woman, in vile names, names I knew only from now and then in the market-place, and names I knew were never to be said.

Then he went quiet.

The whole night was quiet, except for his breathing, and the crunch under his feet as he tried to get his footing.

The woman let out a cry, more like a choke, as if she couldn't help it.

At that the man laughed and he headed right towards my father and my uncles, and they took hold of him. It was one big shape of darkness taking over another great lump of dark-ness. The night was full of soft, but loud sounds.

Off they went up the hill, all of them, and it did seem now that there were a lot of them, maybe Alphaeus' two sons, too, because it was so quick and there were so many of those sounds. I knew what the sounds were. They were beat-ing him.

And he had stopped his cursing and raging. And from everyone else nothing except the women shushing the hurt one.

They were gone!

I don't know why I didn't move.

I started to run after them.

I heard my brother James say:

"No."

The woman sobbed softly:

"A widow alone, I tell you, alone with my servant girl, and my husband not dead two weeks, and they come down on me like locusts, I tell you. What am I to do? Where am I to go? They burnt my house. They took everything. They broke what little I had. This is the dregs, I tell you. And my son believes they fight for our freedom. I tell you, all the filth is rising, and Archelaus is in Rome, and slaves killing their masters and all the world in flames." She went on and on.

I couldn't see anything. I listened for the sounds of the men. I heard nothing. I felt my skin all over.

"What are they doing with him?" I asked James. I could barely see him. A little bit of light in his eye.

Down below, in the valley, the fire burned but its great flames were finished.

"Say nothing," he said. "Go back to your bed."

"My house," said the woman, her voice full of hurt, "my farm, my poor girl, Riba—if they caught her, she's dead. There were too many of them. She's dead, she's dead, she's dead."

The women comforted her the way they comforted us when we were sad. They made sounds, more than they spoke.

"Go back to your bed," said James again to me.

He was my older brother. I had to do what he said. And Little Salome was crying a little, half asleep.

I went to her and hushed her and kissed her. She curled her fingers around mine, and I knew she was sleeping again.

I lay awake until the men returned.

Cleopas lay beside me as before. Little Symeon and Judas were sleeping all this time as if nothing had happened. Little children like that, once they fall into deep sleep, nothing wakes them up. All was quiet. Even the women weren't making much noise.

Cleopas began to whisper in Hebrew. I could not make it out, what he said. The other men were whispering too.

The women were all talking in such low voices they might have been praying.

I prayed too.

I couldn't think of the poor girl, down there where the house was burnt. I prayed for her without thinking about her. And somehow I went to sleep.

I I

WHEN I WOKE UP, I saw the blue sky and the trees before
I said anything.

Nazareth in this land—of trees and fields.

I stood up, said the morning prayers with my arms
outstretched.

"Hear, O Israel, the Lord our God is One,

"And you shall love the Lord your God with all your
heart, and with all your soul, and with all your might."

I was happy.

Then I remembered the night.

They were just coming back from the woman's house, or
so the women told me. The woman was with us, and here
also came the maidservant, not dead, and with her proper
veil and tunic and robe, who was crying and in the arms of
Cleopas who brought her up the slope.

The woman cried out and ran to her.

The men had bundles of belongings from the house
below. And a heifer also they brought up, a big slow-walking
heifer with frightened eyes which they led with a rope.

They spoke Greek together, the maid and the woman,
and hugged each other. When the woman talked to the other

women, she spoke our tongue. The women crowded around these two newcomers and hugged them and comforted them and kissed them.

Bruria was the name of this woman, and the servant, Riba, was like a daughter to Bruria. And Bruria was offering prayers of thanks that Riba had been spared.

Finally we joined the crowd of people on the road and headed towards Nazareth.

I learned from the talk that the bandits had taken everything that Bruria had—fine silks and plate, grain, wineskins, and whatever they could carry, and burnt out the whole place. Not even the olive groves were left unburnt. But they hadn't found what was hidden in the tunnel under the house. So Bruria had her gold now with her, all that had been left to her by her husband. And Riba had hidden in the tunnel, which the bandits didn't find.

As we walked on towards Nazareth, I learned they would now be with us, these two.

There was more news on the road, too.

Not only Jericho had been burnt but another palace of Herod, the palace at Amathace. And the Romans could not stop the Arabians from their rampaging. They were burning village after village.

But the men of last night's attack had been common drunkards, said Bruria, and so did Riba, who had barely made it to the tunnel alive, and both women were crying as we walked on.

A tunnel under a house. I had never seen a tunnel under a house.

"There is no King, there is no peace," said Bruria, who was the daughter of Hezekiah, son of Caleb, and she told off all the names of her family going back, and the names of her husband's family.

Even the men listened to her. There were nods and mur-
murs at this name and that name. The men didn't look at her,
or at the maidservant, but they walked close to the women,
and they were quiet, and they listened.

"Judas bar Ezekias—he's the rebel," the woman said.
"Old Herod had him in prison. But he didn't execute him,
which he should have done. Now he's stirring up the young
men. He's set up court in Sepphoris. He's raided the armory
there. He rules from there, but the Romans are already on the
march from Syria. I weep for Sepphoris. All those who don't
want to die should flee from Sepphoris."

Now I knew the name of the city, Sepphoris. I knew that
was where my mother had been born, that her father Joachim
had been a scribe, and his wife, Anna, my grandmother, had
been born there, too. They had come to Nazareth only when
my mother had been betrothed to Joseph, who with his
brothers lived in the house of Old Sarah and Old Justus, who
were kindred of my mother and Joachim and Anna, as well as
Joseph, too. Part of the house had been given over to Joachim
and Anna and my mother, as it was a big house which had in
it many rooms for families to live on one large courtyard, and
it was there that they lived until they went to Bethlehem
where I was born.

When I thought about it, it came clear to me that I
didn't know parts of the story. I did know that Joseph and my
mother had been married in Bethany, in the house of Elizabeth and Zechariah, and that house was near to Jerusalem.
But Elizabeth and her son John didn't live there now.

No, they had gone into hiding, as my cousin Elizabeth
had told us.

And when I thought of this, all the questions came back
to me.

But I was too eager to see Nazareth to think of all this just now. It hurt too much to think of all this. And the land around me was so beautiful. I knew that word from the Psalms and when I looked at this land I knew what the word meant.

Old Sarah and Old Justus were waiting in Nazareth. We'd written to them. We'd told them we were coming home. Old Sarah was the aunt of my grandmother Anna. And the aunt of one of Joseph's people, but I couldn't trace it all back.

The land was greener and greener as we moved on. And when there came a light rain we didn't even stop.

We'd listened to her letters many times, and she thought to name all of the children when she wrote to us, and she knew by now we were coming home.

The men were not talking much, but Bruria and Riba talked on and on, and the men listened, or so I thought. Finally Bruria said she would confess her worst sorrow. She couldn't keep it inside. Bruria's son had run off to join the rebels in Sepphoris! His name was Caleb, and Caleb might as well be dead, said Bruria. She had no hope of seeing him again.

The men said nothing. They only nodded.

"Who would bother with Nazareth?" Cleopas said under his breath.

"It will be good," said Joseph. "I know it."

And the sun moved high in the sky. And the clouds were clean and like the sails of ships, and there were women in the fields.

We'd been walking up and up into the hills for a long time when we came to a small village that was broken down and empty. The grass was high. The roofs had fallen in. People had gone from here a long time ago. Nothing was burnt. Most of the people on the road walked on.

But all our kindred stopped here.

Cleopas and Joseph led us past the broken buildings.

We found a small spring coming out of the rock, and water filling a big basin surrounded by heavy, leafy trees. It was a beautiful thing to behold.

We made a camp, and my mother said we'd stay the night and go on to Nazareth in the morning.

The men went alone to the spring to bathe, and the women brought fresh robes for them. We waited. Then the women took all of us little ones, and we bathed and dressed the same. The women had a tunic and robe, each, for Bruria and Riba.

The water had been cold, but everyone had laughed and had fun, and the clean clothes smelled good. They even smelled like Egypt.

"Why can't we go on to Nazareth?" I asked. "It's early in the day."

"The men want to rest," said my mother. "And it looks like rain again. If it rains we'll go into the old buildings. If not, we stay here."

The men were not themselves. I hadn't thought much about it until now. But they had been quiet all day.

With all the troubles, we changed every day. And we had to make do with what we found. But this time the men were different. Even Cleopas was quiet. He sat with his back to the bark of a tree, looking out over the hills, and he didn't seem to see the people passing down on the road, going on to Galilee. But when I looked to Joseph as I always did at such times, he was steady. He had taken out a little book to read, a bound book with cut pages, and he was whispering to himself. The letters in the book were Greek.

"What is it?" I asked him.

"Samuel," he answered. "About David," he said.

I listened as he read. David had been fighting, and he

wanted a drink of water from the well of his enemies, and when the water was brought to him, David couldn't drink it, because men had put themselves in great danger to get the water. Men might have died in the getting of it for David.

Joseph got up after he was finished, and told Cleopas to come with him.

The women and the children were all gathered around Bruria and Riba, and they talked on and on of the many things that had happened in the country.

Joseph and Cleopas, and Alphaeus, and his two sons, and James—they all asked for Bruria to come and talk to them.

They went off towards a grove of trees that were moving in the wind in a way I liked to watch.

Their voices were small but I could hear some of it.

"No, but you lost your farm. No, but you . . . And everything that you owned . . ."

"I tell you, you have a right . . ."

"It's ransom."

Ransom.

And the woman with her hands up, shaking her head, left them. "I will not!" she called out.

They all came back and lay down, and became quiet again. Joseph was thinking. He was worried. Then he became steady.

People passed on the road without even seeing us. Horsemen passed.

And after the meal, when everyone slept, I thought about the man in the darkness, the drunken man.

I knew they'd killed him. But I didn't say so to myself. I just knew it. And I knew why they'd killed him. I knew what he meant to do to the woman. And I knew that the men had washed and put on new garments according to the Law, and they wouldn't be clean until sundown. That's why they didn't go on to Nazareth on this day. They wanted to be clean to go home.

But could they ever be clean of such a thing? How to wash away the blood of a man, and what do you do with the money he had, the money he stole, the money soaked in blood?

12

AT LAST WE'D REACHED THE TOP of the hill.

Only a great valley spread out in front of us, and what a sight of olive trees and blowing fields it was. It seemed a glad land.

But the great devil, the fire, was burning again, big and far away, and the smoke went up to Heaven, to the white clouds. My teeth chattered. The fear came up in me, and I pushed it back down.

"It's Sepphoris," my mother cried, and so did the other women. The men cried out the same. And our prayers went up, as we looked but didn't move.

"But where is Nazareth?" Little Salome cried. "Is it burning too?"

"No," said my mother. My mother bent down and she pointed.

"There is Nazareth," she said, and I followed her pointing to see a village laid out on a hill. White houses, some on top of others, and the trees very thick and to the right and the left other soft slopes and gentle valleys, and far beyond other villages scarcely visible under the brightness of the sky. Beyond was the great fire.

"Well, what do we do?" asked Cleopas. "We hide in the hills because Sepphoris is gone up, or we go home? I say we go home!"

"Don't be so hasty," said Joseph. "Perhaps we should remain here. I don't know."

"What, from you?" asked his brother Alphaeus. "I thought you knew the Lord would take care of us, and now we're less than an hour from home. If those thieves come riding this way, I'd rather be hiding under the house in Nazareth than up in these hills."

"We have tunnels?" I asked quickly, not meaning to interrupt the men.

"Yes, we have tunnels. Everyone in Nazareth has tunnels. We all have them. They're old and need to be repaired but they are there. And these murdering bandits are everywhere we go."

"It's Judas bar Ezekias," said Uncle Alphaeus. "He's probably finished with Sepphoris and on the move."

Bruria began to cry for her son, and Riba with her. And my mother to say hopeful things.

Joseph thought this over and then he said:

"Yes, the Lord will take care of us, you're right. And we'll go. I don't see anything bad happening in Nazareth, and nothing between here and there."

We followed the road down into the soft valley, soon passing between groves of fruit trees and even bigger stands of olive trees, and past the best fields I'd ever seen. We walked slowly as ever and we children were not allowed to run ahead.

I was so eager to see Nazareth and so filled with happiness at the land around us that I wanted to sing, but no one was singing. I sang in my heart. "Praise the Lord, who covered the Heavens with clouds, who prepared the rain for the Earth, who made the grass to grow upon the mountains."

The road was rocky and uneven, but the wind was gentle. I saw trees full of flowers, and little towers way back away on the small rises, but there was no one in the fields.

There was no one anywhere.

And there were no sheep grazing, and no cattle.

Joseph said for us to walk faster, and we did our best to hurry, but it wasn't easy with my aunt Mary, who was now sick, as though the woes had passed from Cleopas to her. We pulled at the donkeys, and took turns carrying Little Symeon, who fussed and cried for his mother, no matter what we did.

Finally we were climbing the slope to Nazareth! I begged to run ahead, and so did James in the same voice, but Joseph said no.

In Nazareth, we found an empty town.

One great lane leading uphill with little lanes that went off one side and the other, and white houses, some with two and three stories, and many with open courtyards, and all lying quiet and empty as if no one lived there at all.

"Let's hurry," said Joseph, and his face was dark.

"But what's happening up there to make everyone hide like this!" Cleopas said in a low voice.

"Don't talk. Come," said Alphaeus.

"Where are they hiding?" Little Salome asked.

"In the tunnels, they have to be in the tunnels," said my cousin Silas. His father told him to be quiet.

"Let me go up on the highest roof," said James. "Let me look."

"Go on," said Joseph, "but keep low, don't let anyone see you, and come right back to us."

"May I go with him?" I begged. But the answer was no.

Silas and Levi were sticking out their lips that they couldn't go with James.

Joseph led us faster and faster up the hill.

He brought us to a stop in the main lane maybe halfway up the rise. And I knew we were home.

It was a big house, far bigger than I had ever dreamed it could be, and very old and tired. It needed plaster everywhere, and even sweeping, and the wood I could see that held the vines was rotting away. But it was a house for many families, as we'd been told, with an open stable in its great courtyard, and three stories. And its rooms came out on either side of the big courtyard with a large roof hanging over all around for shade, and with many dusty old wooden doors. In the courtyard was the biggest fig tree I'd ever seen.

It was a bent fig tree, a fig tree with twisted branches, and its branches reached all over the worn old stones of the courtyard to make a living roof of new spring leaves, very green.

There were benches under the tree. And the vines grew on the rotted wood frames above the low wall at the street making a gateway.

And it was the most beautiful house I had ever beheld.

After the crowded Street of the Carpenters, after the rooms in which women and men slept on either side bundled up with babies crying, it was a palace to me, this house.

Yes, it had a mud roof, and I could see the old branches that had been laid over it, and I could see the water stains on the walls, and holes in which the pigeons were nesting and cooing—the only living things in this town—and the stones of the courtyard were worn. Inside, we would probably find mud floors. We had had mud floors in Alexandria. I didn't even think about it.

I thought about the whole family in this house. I thought about the fig tree, and the glory of the vines with their peeping white flowers. I sang a secret song of thanksgiving to the Lord.

Where was the room in which the angel came to my
mother? Where? I had to know.

Now all these happy thoughts were crowded in an instant
in me.

Then a sound came, a sound so frightening to me that it
wiped out everything else. Horses. Horses coming up the
lanes of the village. Rattling and scratching and the sound of
men calling in Greek words I couldn't make out.

Joseph stared one way and then the other.

Cleopas whispered a prayer, and told Mary to get everyone inside.

But before she could move, the voice came again, and
now we could all hear it, and it was saying in Greek for everyone to come out of their houses now. My aunt stood still as if
she'd turned to stone. Even the little ones were quiet.

From up the hill and down came the riders. We went into
the courtyard. We had to go, to get out of their way. But
that's as far as we went.

They were Roman soldiers in full armor, the riders, their
brows covered by their helmets, and they carried spears.

Now, I'd seen Roman soldiers in Alexandria everywhere
all my life, coming in and going out, and in processions, and
with their wives in the Jewish quarter. Why, even my aunt
Mary, the Egyptian, wife of Cleopas, who was standing here
with us, was the daughter of a Jewish Roman soldier, and her
uncles were Roman soldiers.

But these men were not like any I'd ever seen. These men
were in a sweat and covered in dust, and looking from their
right and to their left with hard eyes.

There were four of them, two waiting for the other two
who were coming down the slope and all four met before our
courtyard, and one of them shouted for us to stand where we
were.

They pulled up their horses, but the horses were dancing and wet and foaming, and they wouldn't stop going back and forth, and kicking up the dust. They were too big for the street.

"Well, look at this," said one of the men in Greek, "it seems you're the only people that live in Nazareth. You have this whole town for yourselves. And we have the entire population gathered in one courtyard. Isn't that good for us!"

No one said a word. Joseph's grip on my shoulder almost hurt. No one moved.

Then another soldier who waved for the other to be quiet moved forward as best he could on his restless horse.

"What do you have to say for yourselves?" he asked.

The other soldier called out, "Is there some reason we shouldn't crucify you with all the rest of the rabble down the road?"

Still no one spoke. Then in a soft voice, Joseph began.

"My lord," he said in Greek, "we've only just come from Alexandria, to find our home here. We know nothing of what goes on here. We've just arrived, and found the village empty as you see." He pointed to the donkeys with their baskets and blankets and bundles. "We're covered with the dust of the road, my lord. We're at your service."

This long answer surprised the soldiers, and the leader, the one who was doing all the talking, made his dancing horse come close to us, the horse moving into the courtyard, making our donkeys shy back. He looked at all of us, and our bundles, and the woman huddled together and the little ones.

But before he could speak, the other soldier said:

"Why don't we take two and leave the rest? We don't have time to raid every house in the village. Pick out two of them and let's go."

My aunt screamed and so did my mother, though they

tried to cover their screams. At once Little Salome started crying. Little Symeon began to howl, but I'm not sure he knew why. I could hear my aunt Esther murmuring in Greek, but I couldn't make out the words.

I was so scared I couldn't breathe. They had said "crucify," and I knew what crucifixion was. I'd seen crucifixion outside Alexandria, though only with quick looks because we wanted never, never to stare at a crucified man. Nailed to a cross, stripped of all clothes and miserably naked as he died, a crucified man was a terrible shameful sight.

I was also in terror because I knew the men were in complete dread.

The leader didn't answer.

The other said, "That'll teach the village a lesson, two, and let the others go."

"My lord," said Joseph very slowly, "is there anything that we might do to show you we're not guilty here, that we've only just returned from Egypt? We're simple, my lord. We keep to our law and your law. We always have." He showed no fear at all, and none of the men showed fear. But I knew they were in dread. I could feel it as I could feel the air around me. My teeth began to chatter. I knew if I cried I would sob. I couldn't cry. Not now.

The women were shaking and crying so softly it could almost not be heard.

"No, these men have nothing to do with this," said the leader. "Let's get on."

"No, wait, we have to come back with somebody from this town," said the other. "You can't tell me this town didn't support the rebels. We haven't even searched these houses."

"How can we search all these houses?" asked the leader. He looked us over. "You just said yourself we can't search all these houses, now let's go."

"We take one, at least one, to set an example. I say, one." This soldier moved up before the leader and began to look over the men.

The leader said nothing.

"I'll go then," said Cleopas. "Take me."

The women in one voice cried out, my aunt Mary collapsing against my mother, and Bruria sinking to the ground in sobs. "It was for this moment that I was spared. I will die for the family."

"No, take me if someone is to go," said Joseph. "I will go with you. If one is to go, I will go. I don't know what I'm accused of, but I'll go."

"No, I'll go," said Alphaeus. "If someone must go, let me be the ransom. Only tell me why I should die?"

"You will not," said Cleopas. "Don't you see, this is why I didn't die in Jerusalem. This is the perfect moment. I'm to offer my life for the family now."

"I will be the one," said Simon, and he stepped forward. "The Lord doesn't spare a man to die on the cross. Take me. I've always been the slow one, the late one. You know it, all of you know. I'm never good at anything. I'll be good for something now. Let me have this moment to offer for my brothers and all my kindred now."

"No, I tell you, I will be the one!" Cleopas said. "I'm going. I will be the one."

At that, all the brothers began to shout at each other, even pushing gently at each other, and trying to get ahead of one another, each saying why he should die instead of the others, but I couldn't make out all the words. Cleopas because he was sickly anyway, and Joseph because he was the head of the family, and Alphaeus because he left behind two strong sons, and on and on.

The soldiers, who said nothing in their amazement, suddenly broke into laughter.

And James came down from the roof, my brother James, twelve years old, remember, he dropped into the courtyard, and ran up and said that he wanted to be the one to go.

"I'll go with you," he said to the leader. "I've come home to the house of my father, and of his father, of his father, and his father, to die for this house."

The soldiers laughed even more at that.

Joseph pulled James back and they all started fighting again, until the soldiers looked towards the house. One of them pointed. We all turned around.

Out of the house, our house, there came an old woman, a woman so old her skin looked like weathered wood, and in her hands she had a tray piled with cakes, and over her shoulder she carried a skin of wine. This had to be Old Sarah, we knew.

We children looked at her because the soldiers looked past the men at her. But the men were still fighting over who was to be crucified, and when she spoke we couldn't hear her words.

"Stop it, all of you now," shouted the leader. "Can't you see the old woman wants to speak!"

Quiet.

Old Sarah came forward with quick steps almost to the gate.

"I would bow, my lords," she said in Greek, "but I'm far too old for that. And you are young men. I've sweet cakes to offer you and the best wine from the vineyards of our kindred in the north. I know you're weary and in a strange land." Her Greek was as good as Joseph's Greek. And she spoke like one who is used to telling tales.

"You'd feed an army that's crucifying your own people?" asked the leader.

"My lord, I'd prepare for you the ambrosia of the gods on Mount Olympus," she said, "and call up dancing girls and flute girls and fill golden goblets with nectar, if you would only spare these children of my father's house."

The soldiers all broke into such laughter now it was as if they'd never laughed before. It wasn't mean laughter, it never had been mean, and their faces were soft now and they did seem tired.

She went towards them and offered up her cakes, and they took the cakes, all four of the men, and the mean soldier, the soldier who wanted to take one of us, he took the skin of wine and drank.

"Better than nectar and ambrosia," said the leader. "And you're a kind woman. You make me think of my grandmother at home. If you tell me that none of these men are bandits, if you tell me they have nothing to do with the rebellion in Sepphoris, I'll believe you, and tell me why there's nobody else in this town."

"These men are as they told you," said the old woman. James took the empty tray from her, as the men ate their cakes. "They've been in Alexandria for seven years. They're craftsmen who work in silver, wood, and stone. I have a letter from them telling me they were coming home. And this child, my niece, Mary, is the daughter of a Jewish Roman soldier stationed in Alexandria, and his father was in the campaigns in the north."

My aunt Mary, who couldn't stand up by herself any longer, and was being held up by the other women, nodded at this.

"Here, I carry the letter from these children, which came to me from Egypt only a month ago, and it by the Roman post. I'll show it to you. You read it. It's in Greek, written by the scribe of the Street of the Carpenters. You can see for yourself."

She drew out a little packet of parchment, the very parchment my mother had sent her from Alexandria when I was with my mother.

"No, that's all right," said the soldier. "You know, we had to put this down, this rebellion, you do know that. And a good part of the city has gone up in flames. It's no good for anyone when it's like this. You don't want it like this. Look at this village. Look at the farmland here. This is rich land, good land. Why this stupid rebellion? And now half the city burnt and the slave traders dragging away the women and children."

One of the other soldiers was quietly scoffing, and the mean soldier held his peace. But the first soldier went on.

"These leaders have no chance to unite this country. Yet they're putting on crowns and declaring themselves Kings. And the signals from Jerusalem tell us things are worse there. You know the better part of the army's marching south to Jerusalem, don't you?"

"Pray when death comes to any of us," said the old woman, "that our souls be together in the bundle of life in the light of our Lord."

The soldiers looked at her.

"And not in the bundle flung out, like the souls of those who do evil, as if from a sling," she said.

"A good prayer," said the leader.

"And wait till you taste the wine," said the soldier who now gave him the wineskin.

The leader drank.

"Ah, that's good," he said, "that's very good wine."

"For the life of my family," asked the old woman, "would I give you bad wine?"

They laughed again. They liked her.

The leader tried to give the skin back to the old woman, but she refused it.

"You take it with you," she said. "What you have to do is a hard thing to do."

"It is a hard thing to do," said the soldier. "Battle's one thing. Execution is another."

A quiet came over everyone. The leader looked at us and at the old woman as if he was speaking but he wasn't. Then he said: "I thank you, old woman, for your kindness. As for this village, let it be as it is." He reined in his horse and turned to make his way out into the street.

All of us bowed.

The old woman spoke and the leader stopped to listen: " 'The Lord bless you, and keep you; the Lord make his face shine upon you; and be gracious to you; the Lord lift up his countenance upon you, and give you peace.' "

The leader looked at the old woman for a long time, as the horses danced and pawed at the dust, and then he nodded and smiled.

And they rode away.

As they had come, they went—with a lot of noise and clatter, and rattling. And then Nazareth was as empty and as quiet as before.

Nothing moved but all the little flowers and leaves on the green vines that grew around us. And the new leaves of the fig, so brightly green.

I could hear but the cooing of doves, and the soft song of other birds.

Joseph spoke in a low voice to James,

"What did you see from the rooftops?"

James said,

"Crosses and crosses, on both sides of the road out of Sepphoris. I couldn't see the men, but I could see the crosses. I don't know how many. Maybe fifty men crucified."

"It's over," Joseph said, and everyone began to move and to talk at once.

The women crowded around the old woman and took her hands and showered her with kisses, and gestured for us to come and to kiss her hands.

"This is Old Sarah," said my mother. "This is the sister of my mother's mother. All of you come here to Old Sarah," she said to us children. "Come and let me present you to Old Sarah."

Her robes were dusty but soft, and her hands small and wrinkled like her face. Her eyes were under hoods of wrinkles. But they were bright.

"Jesus bar Joseph," she said. "And my James, and here, let me take my place under the tree, you come, you children, come here, all of you, I want to see everyone, and here, you put that baby in my arms."

All my life I'd heard of Old Sarah. All my life we'd read letters from Old Sarah. Old Sarah was the place where my father's family and my mother's family were joined. I couldn't remember all those links, no matter how often they were told to me. But I knew the truth of it, nonetheless.

And so we gathered under the fig tree, and I sat at Old Sarah's feet. The place was a place of shade and of sunlight. The air was fresh and almost warm.

The old stones were so worn that they showed hardly any of the marks of the mason's tools anymore, and they were big stones. I loved the vines with their white flowers fluttering in the breeze. There was space here and a softness to things, or so it seemed to me, that there hadn't been in Alexandria.

The men went to tend to the beasts. The older boys were taking the bundles into the house. I wanted to be with the men and help them, but I wanted to hear Old Sarah too.

My mother held Little Judas in her lap, as she told Old Sarah the story of Bruria and her slave woman, Riba, and they, Bruria and Riba, said they would be our servants forever and this very day they would prepare the meal for us, with their hands, and they would wait on everyone, if only we told them what they could use and where it was. There was talk all around me.

As for the rest of Nazareth, people were hiding in the tunnels under their houses, said Old Sarah, and some had fled to caves in the hills.

"I'm too old to be crawling in a tunnel," said Old Sarah, "and they never kill old people. And let us pray they don't come back."

"There are thousands of them," said James, the one who had seen them from the rooftops.

"May I go up on the roof and see them?" I asked my mother.

"You go in to see Old Justus," said Old Sarah. "Old Justus is in bed, and can't move."

At once, we went into the house, Little Salome, James and I, and my two cousins of Alphaeus. We went through four rooms in a row before we found him. His bed was up off the floor, and there was a lamp burning there that gave off a perfume. Joseph was already with him, seated on a wooden stool by the bed.

Old Justus raised his hand, and tried to sit up on his bed but he couldn't. Joseph said our names to the old man but he only looked at me. Then he lay back on his bed, and I saw that he couldn't speak. He closed his eyes.

Old Justus we'd spoken of, yes, but he himself never wrote. He was older even than Old Sarah. He was her uncle. And kin to Joseph and to my mother, just as Old Sarah was. But again, how, I couldn't have told out as my mother could, as if it were a psalm.

Now there was the smell of food in the house—fresh baked bread and a meat pottage on the brazier. These things Old Sarah had prepared.

Even though it was bright sunlight, the men made us all go into the house. They closed up the doors, even the doors to the stable where the animals were—our beasts were the only ones—and the lamps were lighted, and we sat in the shadows. It was warm. I didn't mind it. The rugs were thick and soft, and the supper was my whole thought.

Oh, I wanted with all my heart to see the fields around, and the trees, and to run up and down the street, and see the people of the town, but all that would wait until the terrible troubles were gone.

Here we were safe together, and the women were busy, and the men were playing with the little ones, and the fire in the brazier had a pretty glow.

The women brought out dried figs, raisins in honey, and sweet dates, and spiced olives, and other fine things, which we'd brought all the way from Egypt in our bundles, and that with the thick meat pottage, full of lentils and lamb, true lamb, and the fresh bread, was a feast.

Joseph blessed the cups of wine as we drank, and we repeated the blessings:

"Oh Lord of the Universe, maker of vine from which we drink, maker of wheat for the bread we eat, we give you thanks that we are home safe at last, and keep us from evil, Amen."

If there was anyone else in the town, we didn't know it. Old Sarah said for us to have patience, and have faith in the Lord.

After the supper, Cleopas came to Aunt Sarah and took her in his arms, and kissed her hands, and she kissed his forehead.

"And what do you know," he asked, "about gods and goddesses who drink nectar and eat ambrosia?" he asked her. There was a little laughter from the other men.

"Look in the boxes of scrolls when you have the time for it, curious one," she said. "You think my father had no room there for Homer? Or for Plato? You think he never read to his children in the evening? Don't think you know what I know."

The other men came to Old Sarah one by one and kissed her hands and she received them.

It struck me that it was very late, their coming to her, and that none of them said a word of thanks to her for what she had done.

When my mother put me to bed in the room with the men, I asked her about this, how it was they didn't offer their thanks. She frowned and shook her head and said in a whisper that I mustn't speak of it. A woman had saved the lives of the men.

"But she has many gray hairs," I said.

"She's still a woman," my mother said, "and they are men."

In the night, I woke up crying.

For a time I didn't know where we were. I couldn't see anything. My mother was near me and so was my aunt Mary, and Bruria was talking to me. I came to know we were home. My teeth were chattering, but I wasn't cold. James came up close to me and told me that the Romans had moved on. They'd left soldiers to keep guard on the crucified, and put down any last bit of rebellion, but most of them had moved on.

He sounded very sure and strong. He lay beside me with his arm over me.

I wished it was daylight. I felt my fear would go away if it was daylight. I began to cry again.

My mother softly sang to me: "It is the Lord who gives salvation even unto Kings, it is the Lord who delivered even David from the hateful sword; Let our sons grow as plants grow, and let our daughters be cornerstones, polished as if they were the cornerstones of the palace . . . happy is that people, whose God is the Lord."

I drifted in dreams.

When daylight came I saw it under the door to the courtyard. The women were already up. I went out before anyone could stop me. The air was sweet and almost warm.

James came fast after me, and I ran up the ladder to the roof, and up the next ladder to the roof above that. We crawled to the edge and looked towards Sepphoris.

It was so far away that all I could see were the crosses, and it was as James had said. I couldn't count them. People were moving around the crosses. Others were coming and going on the road as people do and I saw wagons, and donkeys. The fire was out, though there was still smoke streaming up to the sky, and there was plenty of the city that wasn't burnt. But again it was hard to see.

To my right the houses of Nazareth went up the hill one against another, and to the left they went down. No one was on all the roofs we saw, but we could see mats and blankets here and there and all around the village the green fields and the forests of thick trees. So many trees.

When I came down, Joseph was waiting, and he took us both sternly by the shoulders and said, "Who told you that you could do this? Don't you go up there again."

We nodded. James blushed, and there passed between them a quick look, James ashamed, and Joseph forgiving him.

"It was my doing," I said. "I ran up."

"And you won't do it again," said Joseph, "because what if they come back?"

I nodded.

"What did you see?" Joseph asked.

"It's quiet," said James. "They're finished. People are taking away the bodies of the dead. There are villages that were burnt."

"I didn't see the villages," I said.

"They were out there, little places, near the city."

Joseph shook his head, and took James with him to work.

Old Sarah sat, bundled up against the open air, under the old bones of the fig tree. The leaves were big and green. She was at her sewing, but mostly pulling out threads.

An old man came to the gate, nodded and moved on. Women passed with their baskets, and I heard children.

I stood listening, and I heard the cooing of the pigeons again, and I thought I could hear the leaves moving, and a woman singing.

"What are you dreaming?" asked Old Sarah.

In Alexandria there had been people—people everywhere, and always we were with each other, crowded and eating and working and playing and sleeping crowded together, and there had never been this . . . this quiet.

I wanted to sing. I thought of my uncle Cleopas and the way that he would sing all of a sudden. And I wanted to sing.

A little boy came to the entrance to the courtyard, and then another behind him, and I said to them,

"Come in."

"Yes, you come in now, Toda, and you too, Mattai," said Old Sarah. "This is my nephew, Jesus bar Joseph."

At once Little Symeon came out from behind the curtain of the doorway, and so did Little Judas.

"I can run to the top of the hill faster than anyone," said the boy Mattai.

Toda told him they had to get back to work.

"The market's open again. Have you seen the market?" Toda asked.

"No, where is it?"

"You go," said Old Sarah.

The town was coming back to life.

13

THE MARKETPLACE was only a gathering at the foot of the hill. People threw up canopies and laid their goods out on blankets, and women sold the vegetables from their gardens that they didn't need. A peddler was there with some goods, including some silver plate. And another peddler had linen to sell, and lots of dyed yarn, as well as trinkets of all kinds, and some cups of limestone and even one or two small bound books.

I met more friends, but the mothers were keeping the children close. And James came to look for me quick enough.

The town grew busier and busier. Women passed on their way to market, and old men and women were out in the court-yards, and some men were coming and going from the fields.

But people were worried, and they spoke of the woes of Sepphoris in hushed voices, and no one was at ease except perhaps those of us who were little and could forget about it for a little while.

When I got back home, I saw new children in the court-yard come to play with Little Salome and the others, but most of the family was hard at work.

It was our job to take stock of the repairs that had to be

done, and we climbed up first to see the roof of mud and branches, and where the holes had to be fixed, and then to pass through each room to be sure of its mud plaster, and how the floors on the upper stories were holding up. There was much white painting to be done where the plaster had gone gray or black. And on the walls of the lower rooms in the flood of light from the open doorways, I could see the traces of fine painted borders in different colors and designs that had once been very beautiful, no doubt.

Joseph and Cleopas talked about repainting all of this, and I'd seen them do this work in Alexandria with great speed. I wasn't old enough to do it, to keep a long strip of green border perfectly straight.

But there was much I could do with them now.

The cribs in the stable needed repairing, and the frames of the lattices for the vines on the front of the courtyard had to be rebuilt as I'd seen when I first came.

But what most surprised me was to discover the huge cisterns which the house had, both of them holding much rainwater even though they needed to be patched.

And then the final discovery was the big mikvah that had been cut into the stone beneath the house many many years ago.

Now the mikvah was a pool for purification, which I hadn't seen in Egypt, and it had steps leading down to its very bottom so that a man could walk all the way under the surface of the water and come back up again without ever bowing his head. It had only half as much water as it ought to have had, this pool, and there were many places where its walls were flaking or blackened and needed work. Joseph said we would bail out the water, and replaster the entire bath. The water from this pool was piped from one of the cisterns. And thanks to the heavy rains, the cisterns were full.

It was Old Sarah's grandfather who had built this pool, we were told, when he settled in Nazareth. This had been his house for him and his seven sons, and Joseph knew their names, every one, but I couldn't remember them, or all those who came down from them—only that my mother's father was descended from them, and also Joseph's mother's father, and so on it went with these stories. I was eager for us to get to work.

Brooms were at work everywhere by late afternoon; the women were beating the dust from rugs; and Cleopas went with the women to market to buy fresh food for supper, and the oven in the courtyard was working all day.

Bruria sat in the courtyard crying for her son who'd gone off with the rebels to Sepphoris. She believed that he was probably dead. We all knew this meant perhaps that he'd been nailed to one of the crosses on the road, but we didn't talk about this. No one was going to go down to Sepphoris, not yet. We worked in quiet.

By nightfall, the house had been divided up amongst the families: Alphaeus and his wife, and his two sons to one set of rooms, and Cleopas and Aunt Mary to their rooms with their little ones, and Joseph, my mother and James and I to others, though our rooms ran into Aunt Mary's rooms, and we had Old Sarah and Old Justus as well. Uncle Simon and Aunt Esther and Baby Esther had their rooms near the stable in the middle of the house.

Bruria and her slave Riba had their own room.

Then there was an old serving woman, a thin silent woman, named Ide, whom I hadn't seen the day before. She took care of Old Justus and Old Sarah, and she slept on the floor in their room. I didn't know for sure whether this woman could talk.

Again, our supper was very rich with the stew from the

night before, and the hot bread from the oven and more of the sweet figs and dates. Everyone was talking at once about what had to be done to the house and to the courtyard, and how eager they were to get out to the garden beyond the town, and see how it was there, and to see others, whom they had not yet seen.

We were lying back, taking our ease, not talking much, doing nothing, when a man came into the room from the courtyard. Joseph was on his feet at once. When he came back from the door, shutting it against the chill, he said:

"The Roman legions are gone out of Galilee. Only a small number of men are left with Herod's men to keep the peace until Archelaus comes home."

"Thanks be to the Lord on High," Cleopas said, and then everyone was saying it in one way or another. "And those who were crucified? Have they all been taken down?"

Everyone knew it could take two days or more for a man to die on a cross.

"I don't know," said Joseph.

Old Sarah bowed her head from her stool and chanted in Hebrew.

"The last of the soldiers passed on the main road over an hour ago," said Joseph.

"Pray they never have to come back," my mother said.

"A crucified man should be taken down before sunset!" said Cleopas. "It is a shameful thing, and it's been days since these men—."

"Cleopas, leave it," said Alphaeus. "We are here and we are alive!"

Cleopas was about to speak when my mother reached out and laid her hand on his knee.

"Please, brother," she said. "There are Jews in Sepphoris who know their duty. Leave it alone."

No one spoke after that. I didn't want to be sleepy, but I was.

When we went to bed, it was very strange to me to be in a room alone without Symeon and Joses, and the babies as well.

I'd always been with the women and the little ones. But the little ones were with their mothers. And my mother was with Old Sarah, and Old Justus, and Bruria and her slave, even though they had a separate room. I missed Little Salome. I even missed Baby Esther who woke up to start crying and only stopped when she went to sleep.

I felt very grown-up to be with Joseph and James, but I still asked Joseph if I could snuggle against him, and he said yes, that I could.

"If I wake up crying," I asked, "will you put me with my mother?"

"Is that what you want me to do," he asked, "to put you with your mother? You are little to be in here with us, but you're seven years old and you understand things. You will be eight years old soon. What do you want? You can be with your mother if you want."

I didn't answer. I turned over and closed my eyes.

I slept through the night.

14

IT WASN'T UNTIL THE THIRD DAY that we were allowed
to roam far and wide. By that time Cleopas had been down
the road a piece, and come back, and said that all the bodies
were taken down, and that the city was in order again, the
market was open, and with a laugh, he said, too, they needed
carpenters to rebuild what was burnt.

"We have enough here to do," said Joseph. "They'll be
building in Sepphoris from now until years from now after
we're all laid to rest." And we did have a great deal to do, bail-
ing out the mikvah first of all which took us children to get
down into the cold water, and to hand up the jars to the men.
And then the replastering had to be done, and when that was
finished, we would do the walls of the house.

I was happy because we could go outside the village, and
I went as soon as I could out into the woods. I saw children,
lots of them, and I wanted to talk to them, but first I wanted
to walk in the open and climb the slopes under the trees.

Alexandria had been a city of great wonders as everyone
was always saying, with its festivals and its processions and
its splendid temples and palaces, and houses such as Philo's
house with its marble floors. But here was the green grass.

It smelled good to me, better than any perfume, and when I passed under the branches of the trees, the ground became soft. A little wind was coming from down in the valley that I could see, and it caught the trees almost one at a time. I loved the rustling of the leaves above me. I walked on up the slope until I was out in the grass again, where the grass was thick, and there I lay down. It was damp there, because it had rained in the night, but it was good. I looked off towards the village. I could see men and women working in the vegetable gardens, and beyond that the farmers in the fields. People were picking weeds out of the earth. That's what it looked like to me.

But my mind was on the groves of trees here and there, and far away, and the blue of the sky.

I lost myself. I felt loose. I felt my skin. It was as if I was humming and the humming filled my ears, but I wasn't humming. And it was so sweet. It was the way I felt sometimes before I went to sleep. I wasn't drowsy. I wasn't sleeping. I lay still on the grass and I heard little tiny creatures around me in the grass. I even saw the flutter of little wings. I looked right before me, and there was a world of them, these tiny creatures, so very tiny, tumbling over the pieces of grass.

I let my eyes move slowly towards the trees. They had the wind in them again and were dancing back and forth. The leaves of the trees looked silver in the sunlight, and they never stopped moving even when the breeze died away.

My eyes went back to the closest thing I could see before me: the little creatures moving, running so fast over the broken bits of earth. It came to me that in lying down as I had done I had crushed some of these creatures, perhaps many many of them, and the longer I looked at them, the more little creatures I saw. Theirs was the world of the grass. That's all they knew. And what was I, coming to lie down here, feeling

the softness of the grass and loving the smell of it, and rob-
bing so many little creatures of life?

I was not sorry for it. I felt no sadness. My hand lay on
top of the blades of grass, and the creatures moved beneath it
faster and faster, until their world was all fluttering without a
sound that I could hear.

The earth was a bed under me. The cries of the birds were
a song. They streaked across the sky above me so fast I could
barely see them. Sparrows. And then beside me, I saw right in
front of me tiny flowers growing in the grass, so very little I
hadn't noticed them before, flowers with white petals and
yellow hearts.

The breeze grew strong and the branches above me
moved with it. Leaves came down in a shower, a silent rain.

But a man was coming. He came out of the grove of trees
down the hill, and made his way up towards me.

It was Joseph, with his head bowed as he walked up the
slope. His robe and its tassels blew in the breeze, and he was
thinner than when we'd left Alexandria. Perhaps all of us were
that way.

I knew I should get up out of respect for him, but I felt so
good here on the sweet grass and that humming was going on
as if I was doing it, all through me, and I only looked at him
as he came.

I didn't have sense enough to know it, but these moments
on the grass under the tree had been the first time in my
whole life that I'd ever been alone.

I only knew that this peace was broken, and had to be
broken. What was time that I could spend it here staring
until the world lost all its hard edges? Finally, I climbed to my
feet, and I felt as if I was waking up from deep sleep.

"I know," he said to me sadly. "It's just a little village, not
very much at all in this world, and nothing to rival the great

Alexandria, nothing, and you've probably thought a hundred times of your friend, Philo, and all your friends, and everything we left behind. I know. I know."

I couldn't answer. I tried. I wanted to tell him how I saw it, how soft and sweet it was, and how all of it was so good to me, and searching for the words I didn't have yet, I didn't speak quickly enough.

"But you see," he said, "nobody will ever look for you here. You're hidden, and that's how you'll remain."

Hidden.

"But why must I—?"

"No," he said. "No questions now. There will come a time. But listen. You must never tell people things." He stopped and looked at me to make sure I understood him. "You mustn't talk about what you hear at our fire. Never do you talk outside your house to anyone. You mustn't talk about where we've been or why, and you keep your questions in your heart, and when you're old enough, I'll tell you what you need to know."

I didn't say a word.

He took my hand. We walked back towards the village. We came to a little garden marked off with small stones, and near to a few trees. The plot was overgrown with weeds. But the trees were good. A great big tree stood by it, and the tree was full of knuckles and knots.

"My grandfather's grandfather planted this olive tree," Joseph said. "And there, you see that tree, that's the pomegranate, and wait till you see it come into bloom. It'll be covered with red blossoms."

He walked up and down looking at the garden plot. The others on the hill were neat and full of plantings.

"We'll harrow this tomorrow for the women," he said.

"It's not too late to plant a few vines, grapes, cucumbers, and plant some other things. We'll see what Old Sarah says."

He looked at me. "Are you sad?" he asked.

"No," I said quickly. "I like it!" I wanted so badly to find words, words like those in the Psalms.

He picked me up and he kissed me on both cheeks and he walked with me back home. He didn't believe me. He thought I was saying it to be kind. I wanted to run through the woods and climb the hills. I wanted to do all the things I'd never done in Alexandria. But we had our work waiting for us when we reached the courtyard, and more and more people were coming to pay their respects.

15

OLD SARAH SAID we were a whirlwind. Alphaeus with his sons, Levi and Silas, had the roof completely repaired in no time, and so well done that we could jump up and down on it, just to be sure. Our neighbors uphill to the right were happy about this, as they had a door out to this roof, and we welcomed them to use it as they had in the old days, to spread out their blankets in summer. There was plenty of roof left for us on the main part of the house and to the left side that looked out over the lower house downhill, and the houses in back which went down a slope as well.

There were women on the rooftops seated with their sewing and babies playing and every roof had a parapet like the ones in Jerusalem so that children would not fall. Some people even had plants in pots on their roofs, small fruit trees and plants I didn't know. But I loved to be up there and look out over the valley.

The winter cold was almost gone. A chill lingered, and I didn't like it but I knew the warm air was coming soon.

Cleopas and Little Joses, his eldest, who was still small, and Little Justus, a little older and very clever, though he was Simon's younger son, did the plastering of the mikvah with the waterproof plaster that we knew how to mix up from what we could get from the villages here. And soon the pool was white and ready for water from the cistern. There was a tiny drain in the bottom of the mikvah through which some water would be passing out at all times, and this would make it living water which the Law required for purification.

"It's living water because of that tiny drain?" Little Salome asked. "That makes it like the stream?"

"Yes," said Cleopas, her father. "The water moves. It's living. Enough."

The afternoon we finished refilling the pool we all gathered around it. It was bright and clear but cold. In the light of the lamps, it looked very fine.

Joseph and I rebuilt the frames for all the vines against the house and along the front of the courtyard, handling the green vines as carefully as we could so as not to break them too much. Some were lost and it was bad, but most of the vines were saved, and we tied up the thick parts with new rope.

James had set to work repairing the benches, taking what was good of some and putting it with what was good of others, to make a few that were sound.

Neighbors came to talk at the courtyard wall, men of few words who were on their way to work in the fields, or women who could stay for a while, with their market baskets, mostly the friends of Old Sarah, but seldom women as old as she was, and other boys came to help. James soon had a friend named Levi, who was kin to us, son of our cousins who owned farmland and rich olive groves, and Little Salome, near the end of the first few days, had a flock of little girls her own age to bring into the house for whispering and squealing and gathering together.

The women had more work to do than they ever had in

Alexandria where they could buy fresh bread and even pottage and vegetables every day. Here they were up early to bake the bread and no one brought the water here. They had to go to the spring outside the village and bring it back. And on top of that they were cleaning the upstairs rooms for which we had no use as yet, and scrubbing the benches as soon as James was finished with them, and mopping the courtyard, and sweeping the dirt floors inside.

The dirt floors were no different than those in Alexandria except that they were beaten harder and there wasn't so much dust. And the rugs here were much better, thicker and softer. When we lay down for the evening meal, with rugs and cushions, we felt good.

Finally, the Sabbath was upon us. It came so quick. But the women were ready, with all the food prepared ahead of time, and it was a feast of dried fish that had been plumped in wine and then roasted, together with dates, nuts I'd never tasted before, and fresh fruit from the farmland around us, as well as plenty of olives and other splendid things.

All this was set out, and then the Sabbath lamp was lighted to welcome the Sabbath into the house. This was the duty of my mother, and she spoke the prayer in a soft voice as she put the wick to the lamp.

We said our prayers of thanksgiving for our safe homecoming, and began our study, all together, singing, and talking and happy that it was our first Sabbath in our home.

I thought of what Joseph had said to Philo, as we studied. The Sabbath makes scholars of us all. It made philosophers of us all. I didn't know for sure what a philosopher was, but I'd heard the word before—and I connected it with scholars and those who studied the Law. The Teacher in Alexandria once said Philo was a philosopher. Yes.

And now we were all scholars and philosophers—in this

big room, all dusted and clean, with everyone fresh from washing, going deep into the mikvah and putting on fresh clean clothes afterwards, all this before the sunset, and Joseph reading by the lamplight, and the smell of the pure beaten olive oil of the lamp so sweet.

Why, we even had scrolls, like Philo did, though not as many, no, not as many. But some, and how many I didn't know for sure, because they came from chests in the house for which Joseph and Old Sarah kept the keys.

And even some scrolls were hidden, buried down in the tunnel, to which we children hadn't been allowed yet to go. If the house should be raided by the bandits, if it should burn, and it made me shiver to think of it, these scrolls would be saved.

Understand, I wanted to see the tunnel! But the men said that the tunnel needed repairing and no little ones were to go down there.

Now, Joseph had taken out and laid down some scrolls before the Sabbath began. Some of these were very old and cracking at the edges. But all were good.

"And now, we don't read from the Greek anymore," Joseph said, looking all around him, taking us all in. "We read only the Hebrew here in the Holy Land, and do I have to tell anyone why?"

We all laughed.

"But what shall I do with the book we love so much, which is in the Greek?" He held up the scroll. We knew it was The Book of Jonah. We clapped, and begged for him to read it.

He laughed. He loved nothing better than to have us gathered around him to listen, and we hadn't had a chance for this for so long.

"Tell me what I should do," he said. "Read it to you in the Greek, or tell it to you in our tongue."

Again we clapped our hands, all of us so happy. We loved the way Joseph told the story of Jonah. And he had never really read it in the Greek without putting down the book and telling most of it because he loved it so much.

At once, he went into the story with spirit—the Lord called the Prophet Jonah, the Lord told him to preach to Nineveh, "that great city!" said Joseph, and we all said it with him. But what did Jonah do? He tried to run from the Lord. Can anyone run from the Lord?

Down to the sea, he went and onto a ship to a foreign land. But a great storm overtook the little vessel. And all the Gentiles prayed to their gods to save them, but on raged the rain and the thunder and the dark clouds.

Then came the storm at sea, and the men cast lots to see the one who was the cause of it and the lot fell on Jonah, and where was Jonah? Fast asleep in the bottom of the ship. " 'What are you doing, Stranger, snoring in the bottom of this ship?' " Joseph said as he put on the face of the angry Captain. We laughed and clapped as he went on.

"And what did Jonah? Why, he told them he feared the Lord God of All Creation, and that they should cast him into the sea because he had run from the Lord and the Lord was angry, but did they do it, no. They rowed hard to bring the ship to land and—?"

We all cried, "The great storm went on."

"And they prayed unto the Lord, in fear of him, but what did they do?"

"They threw Jonah into the sea!"

Joseph grew grave, and narrowed his eyes.

"And the men feared the Lord and they sacrificed to him, and down in the depths of the sea, the Lord had made a great fish to—"

"Swallow up Jonah!" we cried.

"And he was three days and three nights in the belly of the whale!"

We grew quiet. And all together, as Joseph led us, we repeated Jonah's prayer to the Lord to save him, as we all knew it, in our tongue, as well as we knew it in Greek, and even the men were saying it with us and the women,

". . . I went down deep to the very bottoms of the mountains; the earth like a prison enclosed me. Yet you have brought up my life from corruption. O Lord my God."

I closed my eyes as we said it,

"When my soul was weak I remembered the Lord, and my prayer came to you, into your holy Temple. . . ."

I thought of the Temple. I thought not of the crowds inside it and the man dying on the spear, but of the great mass of shining limestone in the sun, with all its gold, and the songs of the faithful rising as if they were waves lapping as I'd seen the waves of the sea lapping over over and over as our ship drifted at anchor, waves without end. . . .

I was so deep in my thoughts, so deep in remembering the water lapping at the boat, and remembering the singing rising and falling, that when I looked up they had all gone on with the tale.

Jonah did now as the Lord commanded him. He went to "that great city of Nineveh," and he cried out: "Forty days and the city of Nineveh shall be destroyed!"

"All the people believed in the Lord!" said Joseph, raising his eyebrows. "They fasted, they put on sackcloth from the greatest among them to the least. Even the King stood up from his throne and covered himself with sackcloth and sat down in ashes!"

He put out his hands as if to say: Behold.

"The King!" he repeated and we nodded. "And a proclamation went out that no one, not man nor beast, herd or flock, must even taste a morsel, or drink a drop of water. And all of them, man and beast, were to be covered in sackcloth, and cry out to the Lord."

He stopped. He drew himself up. "Who can know if the Lord will turn and repent of his anger?"

He opened his hands for us to answer:

"And the Lord did repent of his anger," we said all together, "and Nineveh found grace with the Lord!"

Joseph waited, then he asked:

"But who was unhappy? Who was angry? Who stomped out of the city gates in a fit of temper!"

"Jonah!" we cried.

" 'Was this not the very thing I knew would happen?' " cried Jonah. " 'When I was in my own country! Was this not why I ran away on a ship to Tarshish?' "

As we laughed, Joseph held up his finger as he always did for patience, and softly he went on in the voice of the Prophet. " 'I knew that you were a gracious God, merciful, and slow to anger, of great kindness, and repenting of anger, did I not?' "

We all nodded.

" 'Now!' " Joseph went on as Jonah drawing himself up with great pride, " 'take my life, take it from me!' " He threw up his hands. " 'For it's better that I die than to live!' "

Laughter all around.

"Right by the gates of Nineveh, Jonah sat down. He was so tired and so angry that he sat right there. And made himself a booth with what he could and sat under it in the shade, just thinking, what may happen, what may happen yet . . .

"And the Lord had a design. The Lord made a great vine to grow up out of the ground and over Jonah so that it sheltered him as he sat there with his lip jutting out, and the shade of that vine made him very content.

"And so the night passed and the Prophet slept under that vine . . . and who knows? Perhaps the desert winds weren't too cold under that vine. What do you think?

"But before the morning came, the Lord made a worm, yes, an evil worm that ate the vine and the vine withered away."

He paused. He lifted his finger. "And the sun rose, and the Lord did make a strong wind, yes, we know it, a strong wind to blow against Jonah, and the sun beat down on his head.

"He fainted!" Joseph slapped his legs and nodded. "The Prophet fainted in the heat and the wind. And what did he say?"

We laughed but we waited for Joseph to throw up his hands and cry out in the voice of Jonah, "I want to die, Lord. It is better for me to die than to live!"

We all laughed easily, and Joseph waited for a moment and then he grew solemn yet smiling still and he spoke in the gentle voice of the Lord. " 'Do you do well to be so angry over the death of a vine?'

" 'Yes, Lord, I do well to be angry, even unto death!'

"Then the Lord said, 'So you had pity on a vine, did you, a vine which you did not plant, a vine which you did not labor over, a vine which came up in a night and was gone in a night. And should I not spare Nineveh, that great city, sixty thousand people, and cattle without number, and all those people who don't even know their left hand from their right!' "

We all smiled and we all nodded, and we all felt it as we always did, and the laughter warmed us as it always did.

After that, Cleopas read a little to us from The Book of Samuel in the story of David of which we never tired.

Some time late while the men were talking, disputing about the Law and about the Prophets, going back and forth over points I couldn't follow, I went to sleep. We all slept there in our clothes by the lamp as the lamp burned on.

When morning came it was still the Sabbath and would be until sundown.

And after everyone had eaten of the bread prepared before by hand, Old Sarah spoke up.

She was pushed back against the wall on a nest of pillows, and we hadn't heard a word from her all night.

Now she said,

"Is there no synagogue in this town now? Has it burned to the ground without my knowing it?"

No one spoke.

"Ah, so it's fallen down, has it?" she said.

No one spoke. I had not seen a synagogue. Yes, there was a synagogue but I didn't know where it was.

"Answer me, my nephew!" Old Sarah said. "Or have I lost my wits as well as my patience?"

"It's there," said Joseph.

"Then take these children to it," she said. "And I will go as well."

Joseph said nothing.

I had never heard a woman speak this way to a man before, but this was a woman with a great many gray hairs. This was Old Sarah.

Joseph looked at her. She looked at Joseph. She lifted her chin.

Joseph stood up and gestured for us to do the same.

The whole family, except for my mother, and Riba, and the littlest ones, who would be a nuisance in a House of Prayer, went up the hill, where I hadn't gone before.

Now I had been around the edges of the town to peek at

the spring, and thought it very beautiful, but I hadn't walked up over the hill and down.

The houses at the top of the hill were the same from the outside, whitewashed mud plaster mostly, but the courtyards were even bigger than ours and the fig trees and olive trees were very old. In one open doorway, two beautiful women stood smiling at us, clothed in the finest linen I'd seen in Nazareth, very white with gold embroidery along the edges of their veils. I liked to look at them. I saw a horse tethered in a stable and I had not seen a horse before in Nazareth, and we passed also a man at a cross-legged writing desk, with a cross legged stool beneath him, reading his scrolls out in the fresh air. He waved a greeting to Joseph as we passed.

People were in the street, nodding to us, some passing us because we were slow, others moving behind us. There was not a sign of work being done. All were observant of the Sabbath, but they were moving slowly about.

When we reached the very top of the slope, I saw my cousin Levi coming out, and his father Jehiel, and for the first time I saw their great house with its well-fitted doors and windows and freshly painted lattices and remembered that they owned a great piece of the nearby land.

They fell in behind us as we walked down the street and it now twisted and turned more than it had on the other side, and more and more people were headed the same way.

I saw a great clump of trees spread out before us and we followed a path through the trees and there was the spring, filling its two rock-cut basins to overflowing as it gushed and tumbled down the cliff.

The biggest of the rock-cut basins was overflowing and it was to this overflow that many went to wash their hands.

We did the same now, washing our hands and as much of our arms as we could without getting our clothes wet. It was cold. Really cold. But I liked it. I looked this way and that. The stream twisted and turned as did the road behind us, and I could see much of it in either direction.

I stood up. I pinched and squeezed my hands to make them not be cold.

There stood the House of Prayer, or the synagogue, to the left of the stream and back from the road, it was plain enough to see. It was a large building with a wide-open door, and even rooms above with a stair going up on one side, all very well tended with green grass clipped beside it.

We went towards it, and had to wait our turn as others went inside.

Something happened with us. Cleopas, Alphaeus, and Joseph and Simon and Old Sarah all moved in back of me. The others went on ahead, the women first except for Old Sarah. Cleopas took Old Sarah by the arm, and Silas and Levi went inside. James stood behind me too, with all my uncles and Joseph.

Gently Joseph pushed me towards the open door.

The men came up around me on either side.

I stood on the wood threshold. The place was a great deal bigger than the small synagogue in which we'd gathered in Alexandria, a place for just our own neighbors, as there were so many synagogues. And it had benches built along the walls, rising in steps, so that people sat as they did in a theater or the Great Synagogue of Alexandria to which I'd gone once.

The benches on the left side were filled with women. I saw my aunts and Bruria, our refugee, take their places. There were children on the floor, lots of them, all over, and on the right side in front of the men.

There was a row of posts, and at the end there stood a place for a man to stand and read.

I looked up as it was time to go inside now. There were

lots of people crowding behind me to come in. And no one was blocking my way.

But a tall man stood to the left, a man with a very long soft-looking black and gray beard and so much beard on his upper lip that I could hardly see his mouth. His eyes were dark, and his hair was long, to his shoulders, only a little gray, under his prayer shawl.

He put his hand out in front of me.

The man spoke in a very soft voice, looking at me as he did, but his words were for the others.

"I know James, yes, and Silas and Levi, I remember them, but this one? Who is this one?"

It was very quiet.

I saw that everyone in the synagogue was looking at us. I didn't like it. I was beginning to be scared of it.

Then Joseph spoke:

"He is my son," said Joseph. "Jesus bar Joseph bar Jacob."

Right when the words left Joseph's lips, I felt the men behind me draw in very close. Cleopas put his hand on my back, and so did my uncle Alphaeus. My uncle Simon stood close to me too and he put his hand on my shoulder too.

The bearded man kept his hand in my way, but his face was kind. He stared at me and then looked up at the others.

Then came the voice of Old Sarah, as clear as before. She stood behind all of us.

"You know who he is, Sherebiah bar Janneus," she said. "Need I say to you that this is the Sabbath? Let him in."

The Rabbi must have been looking at her. But I was not going to turn around to see. I looked ahead, and I saw nothing. Maybe I saw the dirt floor. Maybe I saw the light coming through the lattices. Maybe I saw all the faces turned towards us.

No matter where I looked, I knew that the Rabbi turned

around. I knew that one of the other Rabbis, and there were two of them on the bench, whispered something to him.

And next I knew we were going into the synagogue.

My uncles took the very end of the bench, with Cleopas sitting on the floor, and gesturing for me to do it too. James, who'd already been in, came and sat down by Cleopas. Then the other two boys got up and came over and sat with us. We had the inside corner.

Old Sarah made her way slowly with the help of Aunt Salome and Aunt Mary to the bench where the women sat. And for the first time I thought: my mother didn't come. She could have come. She could have left the children with Riba. But she didn't come.

The Rabbi greeted many other people, until the room was very full.

I didn't look up when the talking began. I knew the Rabbi was reciting from memory as he sang out in Hebrew:

"This is Solomon who speaks," he said, "the great King. 'Lord, Lord of our fathers, Lord of mercy, in wisdom you made man to rule over all creation, a steward to the world . . . to administer justice with a righteous heart. Give me wisdom, O Lord, wisdom who sits right by your throne, and don't refuse me a place with your servants." As he spoke these words, slowly the men and the boys began to repeat the words he was saying, and he slowed, so that we could repeat each phrase as he went on.

My fear was gone. The people had forgotten us. But I couldn't forget that the Rabbi had questioned us, that the Rabbi had wanted to stop us. I remembered my mother's strange words to me in Jerusalem. I remember her warnings. I knew that something was wrong.

We stayed for hours in the synagogue. There was reading.

There was talk. Some of the children went to sleep. After a while people left. Others came. It was warm there.

The Rabbi walked up and down asking questions and inviting answers. At times people were all laughing. We sang. Then came talk again, talk about the Law, and even arguments with the men raising their voices. But I grew sleepy and fell asleep against Joseph's knee.

When I woke up later, everyone was singing. It was full and pretty and not like the broken songs of the people at the River Jordan.

I slept.

I woke when Joseph told me we were going home.

"I can't carry you on the Sabbath!" he whispered. "Stand up."

And so I did. I walked out with my head down. I had not looked in the eye of anyone in the synagogue.

We came into the house. My mother looked up from where she sat against the wall, near to the brazier, with her blankets around her. She looked at Joseph and I saw the question in her eyes.

I went to her and went to sleep with my head on her knee.

Several times I woke up before sunset. We were never alone.

My uncles whispered in the light of the lamps that would never go out on the Sabbath.

Even if there had been a time when I could ask Joseph a question, what would I ask him? What would I ask him that he didn't want to tell me, that he had forbidden me to ask? I didn't want my mother to know that the Rabbi had stopped me at the door of the synagogue.

My memories became links in a chain. The death of

Eleazer in the street in Alexandria, and from all that happened after, link by link. What had they said that night in Alexandria about Bethlehem? What had happened in Bethlehem? I'd been born there but what had they been saying?

I saw the man dying in the Temple, the crowds frightened and trying to escape, the long journey, fire leaping against the sky. I heard the bandits. I shivered. I felt things to which I wouldn't attach words.

I thought of Cleopas, thinking he was going to die in Jerusalem and then my mother on the rooftop in Jerusalem. No matter what they say to you in Nazareth . . . an angel came . . . there was no man . . . a child who wove the fabric for the Temple until she was too old . . . an angel came.

Joseph said,

"Come now, Yeshua, how long am I to look at this troubled face? Tomorrow, we go into Sepphoris."

16

THE ROAD TO SEPPHORIS was crowded all the way from Nazareth, and other smaller villages lay along that way. And we bowed our heads when we passed the crosses, though all the bodies were gone from them. Blood had been shed in the land and we were sorrowful. We passed houses that were burnt, and even burnt stands of trees, and there were people begging, telling how they'd lost everything to the bandits, or to the soldiers who had "pillaged" their houses.

Over and over, we stopped and Joseph gave them money from the family purse. And my mother told them what words of comfort she had to give.

My teeth were chattering and my mother thought I was cold, but I wasn't. It was the sight of the burnt-out buildings of Sepphoris that I saw—even though most of the city was not burnt, and people were buying and selling in the market.

At once, my aunts sold the gold embroidered linen they'd brought from Egypt just for the purpose of selling, and pocketed more than they expected for it, and the same with all the bracelets and fine cups they'd brought to sell. The purse was bulging.

We went to the mourners who sat in the middle of the

burnt wooden beams and ashes, crying for those who were gone, or to those who were begging: "Did you see this one, or that one?" We gave to the widows from our purse. And for a while we were all crying—that is, I was and so was Little Salome and so were the women. The men had gone off and left us.

It was the very center of the city that had been burnt, people told us—the palace of Herod, the arsenal, and also the houses nearest it where the rebels had stayed with their men.

There were men already clearing the way for rebuilding at the top of the hill. There were soldiers of King Herod everywhere, looking people up and down, but the weepers and the mourners took no notice of them.

It was a sight, the weeping and the working, the howling and mourning, and the buying and selling. My teeth weren't chattering anymore. The sky was bright blue and the air was chilly but it felt clean.

I saw in one house nearby a few Roman soldiers who looked very ready to leave this place if they could, leaning against the door frames and staring off at nothing. The sun was shining on their helmets.

"Oh, yes," said a woman who saw me look at them. Her eyes were red, and her clothes covered with ashes and dust. "And days ago they massacred us, I tell you, and sold off anyone in sight to the filthy slave merchants who descended on us to put our loved ones in chains. They took my son, my only son, he's gone! And what had he done, but gone out to try to find his sister, and she too for what? That she was trying to go from my house to the house of her mother-in-law?"

Bruria began to sob for her lost son. She went off with her slave girl to write on a wall where others were writing a message to the lost ones. But she had little hope she'd ever see him again.

"Be careful in what you write on that wall," said my aunt Salome. The other women nodded.

Down out of the ruins came men asking people to work: "You want to stand here and weep all day? I'll pay you to come haul away the rubbage!" And another: "I need hands now to carry the buckets of dirt, who?" He held out coins to catch the light of the sun.

People cursed as they wept. They cursed the King; they cursed the bandits; they cursed the Roman soldiers. Some went to work and some didn't.

Pushing through the crowd came our men, with a new cart and it was full of fresh wood, and sacks of nails, Joseph told me, and even roof tiles.

In fact, the men were in a dispute over the roof tiles, with Cleopas saying they were a fine idea, and cheap enough, and Joseph saying the mud and branch roof was good enough, and Alphaeus agreeing with Joseph and saying we had far too much of a house to tile all of it. "And besides, with all this building going on, there won't be any roof tiles to be had in a day's time."

Men came up to them, offering them work.

"You're carpenters? I'll pay you double what you get from anyone else. Tell me. Now. I'll put you to work this minute."

Joseph bowed and said no. "We've just come from Alexandria," he said. "We do only skilled work—."

"But I have skilled work!" said a large well-dressed man. "I have a whole house to finish for my master. Everything was burned—I've nothing left but the foundations."

"We have so much to do in our own village," Joseph said, as we tried to go our way. The men surrounded us, on to us now, wanting to buy the wood in the cart and use us as a team. Joseph promised we'd come back as soon as we could. The name of the rich steward was Jannaeus. "I'll remember you," he said. "You're the Egyptians."

We laughed at that, and we did move on and back to the peace of the countryside.

But that was how we became known—as the Egyptians.

I looked back at the city from the road, where I could see all the busy people under the late sun. And my uncle Cleopas saw me looking. He said,

"You ever look at an anthill?"

"Yes."

"Ever step in one?"

"No, but I saw another boy step in one."

"What did the ants do? They all ran around all over the place, but they didn't leave the hill, and they rebuilt it. That's the way it is with war, little or great. People just go on. They get right up and they go on because they have to have water and bread and a roof, and they start again no matter what happens. And one day you can be grabbed by the soldiers and sold as a slave, and the next day they won't even see you pass by. Because it's over. Somebody said it was over."

"Why must you be the sage for my son?" Joseph asked.

We were walking at a slow pace behind the cart. The donkey was steady.

Cleopas laughed. "If I hadn't been snared by a woman," he said, "I would have been a prophet."

The whole family laughed at him. I even laughed before I could stop myself. And my aunt, his wife, said, "His talk is better than his singing. And if there's a psalm with an ant in it, he will sing it."

My uncle started to sing, and my aunt groaned, but soon

we were singing with him. There was no psalm with an ant in it that we knew.

When Cleopas had run out of singing, he said, "I should have been a prophet."

Even Joseph laughed at that.

His wife said, "Start now, tell us whether it's going to rain before we get home."

Cleopas took me by the shoulder.

"You're the only one who ever listens to me," he said, looking into my eyes. "Let me tell you: no one ever listens to a prophet in his own land!"

"I didn't listen to you in Egypt," said his wife.

After we had all laughed at that, even Cleopas, my mother said gently,

"I listen to you, brother. I always have."

"You do, sister, that's true," Cleopas said. "And you don't mind when I teach your son a thing or two, do you, because he has no grandfather living, and in my youth I was almost a scribe?"

"Were you almost a scribe?" I said. "I never heard this before."

Joseph waved his finger at me for my attention and grandly shook his head: No.

"And what would you know about it, brother?" asked Cleopas but his voice was friendly. "When we took Mary up to Jerusalem to commit her to the house where the veils were woven, I studied in the Temple for months. I studied with the Pharisees, I studied with the greatest of them. I sat at his feet." He tapped me on the shoulder to make sure of my attention. "There are many teachers in the Temple colonnades. The best in Jerusalem, and then, well, some of them not so good."

"And some of their students not so good either," said Alphaeus in a low voice that everyone could hear.

"Oh, what I might have been if I hadn't gone off to Egypt," said Cleopas.

"But why did you go?" I asked.

He looked at me. There was silence. We walked on in silence.

Then he smiled kindly. "I went because my kindred went—you, and my sister, and her husband and his brothers and my kin."

No answer to my question—no real answer. But I knew, and had known for some while, that it would be easier to learn things from my uncle Cleopas than from anyone else.

A low thunder rolled overhead.

We hurried, but a light rain caught us and we had to go off the road and into a grove of trees. The earth was thick with rotted leaves.

"All right, prophet," said my aunt Mary, "make the rain stop so we can go on home."

When we laughed, Joseph corrected us. "But you know a holy man can make the rain come and go," he said. "Mark my words. From Galilee, the holy one, Honi, the Circle Drawer, in my great-grandfather's time. He could make the rain come and he could make the rain go."

"And tell the children what became of him," said my aunt Salome. "You leave off at the best part."

"What did happen to him?" James asked.

"The Jews stoned him in the Temple," said Cleopas with a shrug. "They didn't like the prayer he said!" He laughed. Then he laughed more as if he thought this even funnier the more he thought about it.

But I couldn't see to laugh at it.

The rain was coming down harder now, and passing through the branches and we were getting wet.

A tiny thought came to me, so small I imagined it in my mind like a thought no bigger than my little finger. *I want this rain to stop.* Foolish of me to think such things. I thought of all the things that had happened . . . the sparrows, Eleazer—. I looked up.

The rain had stopped.

I was so amazed I stared up at the clouds, unable to do anything, even take a breath.

Everyone was very happy and we made our way out on the road and headed home.

I didn't say a word to anyone, but I was troubled, deeply troubled. And I knew I would never tell anyone what I had just done.

Nazareth was pretty to me when we came back. I loved the little street and the houses of white plaster and the vines that grew on our lattices even in the chill of spring. It seemed the fig tree had put out more leaves even in these few days.

And there was Old Sarah waiting for us. Little James was reading to Old Justus. And the little ones were playing in the courtyard and running through the rooms.

All the sadness and grief of Sepphoris was far off now.

So was the rain.

17

THAT NIGHT IT WAS DECIDED that I would stay and work with Joseph on the house, and Alphaeus and his sons, Levi and Silas, and also Cleopas, and perhaps Simon would go into Sepphoris, and there get up a team of laborers from the marketplace. The money was good. The weather was good.

It was further decided that no matter who worked where, we boys would go up to the synagogue where the school was taught, and we'd study with the three Rabbis. Only when they released us would we join the men, probably about mid-morning.

I didn't want to go up to the school. And when I realized that, once again, all the men of the family were walking up the hill with us, I felt afraid.

But then Cleopas had Little Symeon by the hand. And Uncle Alphaeus had Little Joses, and Uncle Simon had Silas and Levi. Maybe it was the way.

When we reached the school, there were three men whom I had seen in the synagogue, and we stood before the very oldest of the men who beckoned for us to come inside. This man hadn't spoken or taught on the Sabbath.

Now he was a very old man and I had not really looked at

him before because I was too afraid to do it in the synagogue.
But he was the teacher here.

Joseph said,

"These are our sons to be taught, Rabbi. What is it that
we can do for you?"

He offered the Rabbi a purse with his hand folded over it,
but the Rabbi didn't take it.

When I saw this, I felt sick.

Never had I seen a man refuse a purse. I looked up and
saw that the old man was looking directly at me. And at once
I looked down. I wanted to cry. I couldn't remember a single
word that my mother had said to me that night in Jerusalem.
I could remember only her face, and the way that she'd whispered to me. And the way Cleopas had looked on his sickbed
there, when he'd spoken and we all thought he was going
to die.

This old man had hair and beard that were pure white. I
could see even as I stared at the hem of his robes that they
were fine wool with their tassels sewn with the proper blue
thread.

Now he spoke in a soft and gentle voice.

"Yes, Joseph," he said. "James and Silas and Levi, I know,
but Jesus bar Joseph?"

Not a word came from the men behind me.

"Rabbi, you saw my son on the Sabbath," said Joseph.
"You know that he's my son."

I didn't have to look up at Joseph to know that he was not
himself.

I gathered all my strength. I looked at the old man. The
old man looked at Joseph.

I started to cry without making a sound. I couldn't help
it. No matter how steady my eyes were, the tears came. I
swallowed hard and quiet.

The old man said nothing. No one said a word.

Then Joseph spoke as if he was saying a prayer:

"Jesus bar Joseph bar Jacob bar Matthan bar Eleazar bar Eliud of the Tribe of David who came to Nazareth with a grant for land from the King to settle Galilee of the Gentiles. And son of Mary daughter of Anna daughter of Mattathias and Joachim bar Samuel bar Zakkai bar Eleazar bar Eliud of the Tribe of David—Mary of Anna and Joachim, one of those sent up to Jerusalem to be among the chosen of eighty-four maidens under the age of twelve and one month, to weave the two veils each year for the Temple which she did until she came of age and returned home. And so it's recorded in the Temple, her years of service, and this lineage, and was recorded on the day of the child's circumcision."

I closed my eyes and opened them. The Rabbi looked pleased and gentle and when he saw my eyes on him, he even smiled. Then he looked back to Joseph, above me.

"There's no one here who doesn't remember your betrothal," he said. "And there are other things which everyone remembers. Surely you understand."

Again there was a silence.

"I remember," said the Rabbi, his voice just as gentle as before, "the morning that your young betrothed came out of the house and made a cry in the village—."

"Rabbi, these are little children," said Joseph. "Is it not for the fathers of the children to tell them these things in time?"

"The fathers?" asked the Rabbi.

"I am the child's father by the Law," said Joseph.

"But where were you married to your betrothed and where was your son born?"

"In Judea."

"What city of Judea?"

"Close to Jerusalem."

"But not in Jerusalem?"

"Married in Bethany," said Joseph, "at the home of my wife's kinsmen there, priests of the Temple, her cousin Elizabeth and Elizabeth's husband Zechariah."

"Ah, yes, and there the child was born?"

Joseph didn't want to say it. But why?

"No," he said. "Not there."

"Then where?"

"In Bethlehem of Judea," he said at last.

The Rabbi stopped and looked to one side and the other, and the heads of those two Rabbis beside him turned towards him. But nothing was said.

"Bethlehem," said the Old Rabbi. "The city of David."

Joseph didn't answer.

"Why did you leave Nazareth and go there," asked the Rabbi, "when the parents of your bride, Joachim and Anna, were failing in age?"

"Because of the census," Joseph answered. "I had to go. I had still a piece of land left to me there in Bethlehem, to which our people returned after the Exile, and I had to claim that land or lose it. I went to register where my ancestors were born."

"Hmmm . . ." said the Rabbi. "And you claimed it."

"Yes. Claimed it and sold it. And the child was circumcised and his name was inscribed in the records of the Temple, as I've said, and such as they are."

"Such as they are, indeed," said the Rabbi, "until another King of the Jews chooses to burn them to hide his heritage."

At that the other men laughed softly and nodded, and some of the older boys in the room laughed and I saw them for the first time.

I didn't know what it meant. It seemed the bad doings of Old Herod, of which there were no end.

"And after that you went on to Egypt," said the Rabbi.

"We worked in Alexandria, my brothers, and my wife's brother and I," said Joseph.

"And you, Cleopas, you left your mother and father and took your sister to Bethany?"

"Our mother and father had servants," said Cleopas. "And Old Sarah daughter of Elias was with them, and Old Justus was not infirm."

"Ah, so I remember," said the Rabbi, "and you are so right. But how your parents wept for their son and their daughter."

"And we wept for them," said Cleopas.

"And you married an Egyptian woman."

"A Jewish woman," said Cleopas, "born and raised in the Jewish community in Alexandria. And of a good family who has sent you this."

Here came a surprise.

He stretched out his hand with two small scrolls in it, both of them in fine cases with bronze trimming on them.

"What is this?" asked the Old Rabbi.

"You're afraid to touch them, Rabbi?" asked Cleopas as he held out the gift. "Two short treatises from Philo of Alexandria, a scholar, a philosopher if you will, much admired by the Rabbis of Alexandria, and these purchased from published books in the market, and brought to you as a gift?"

The Rabbi stretched out his hand.

I took a deep breath as he took the scrolls.

I hadn't known my uncle had such scrolls. Philo's writings. I hadn't dreamt of such a thing. And to see the Rabbi receive them made me feel so glad that the tears came again but I was as quiet as before.

"And how many gray hairs has Philo of Alexandria?" asked the Rabbi.

Everyone laughed at that in their secret way.

But I was much better because they were not talking about me.

"If he had you for an accuser, he'd have gray hairs aplenty!" Cleopas said.

I heard Joseph rebuking him in a whisper, but the boys were laughing, and a great bright smile spread over the Rabbi's face.

Cleopas couldn't stop himself.

"We should take up a collection," he said, gesturing to the whole room, "and send the Rabbi to Alexandria. They are in dire need of Pharisees to straighten them out."

More laughter.

The old Rabbi laughed. Then the other two Rabbis laughed. They all laughed.

"I thank you for your gift," said the Old Rabbi. "Nothing's changed with you. And now that you are here, skilled craftsmen that you are, all of you, you can see there is work to be done in this synagogue, which the old carpenter, may God rest him, was unable to do while you were gone."

"I do see it," said Joseph, "and we are your servants, and will repair everything as you wish. A fresh coat of paint for this place, and lintels, that much I can see is needed, and we'll plaster the outside and see to the benches as you allow."

Silence.

I looked up. The three old men were again looking at me.

Why? What more could be asked? What more could be said? I felt my face on fire again. I blushed but I didn't know for what I was blushing. I blushed for all the eyes turned to me. The tears were wet on my face.

"Look at me, Jesus bar Joseph," said the Rabbi.

I did as he told me.

In Hebrew he asked,

"Why did the Phoenicians cut the hair of Samson?" he asked.

"I beg the Rabbi to forgive me, but it was not the Phoenicians," I answered in Hebrew. "It was the Philistines. And they cut his hair to make Samson weak."

He spoke to me in Aramaic,

"Where is Elisha who was taken up in the chariot?"

"I beg the Rabbi to forgive me," I said in Aramaic. "It was Elijah who was taken up, and Elijah is with the Lord."

In Greek he asked,

"Who is it that resides in the Garden of Eden, writing down all that takes place in this world?"

I didn't answer for a moment. Then I said in Greek:

"No one. There is no one in Eden."

The Rabbi sat back and looked to one side and then the other. The other Rabbis looked at him and all looked at me.

"No one is in Eden writing down the deeds of the world?" he asked.

I thought for a moment. I knew I had to say what I knew. But how I knew it, I couldn't tell. Was I remembering it? I answered in Greek,

"Men say it is Enoch, but Eden is empty until the Lord should say that all the world will be Eden once again."

The Rabbi spoke in Aramaic,

"Why did the Lord break his covenant with King David?"

"The Lord never broke it," I said. This I had always known as long as I knew any answer. I didn't even have to think about it. "The Lord does not break his covenants. The throne of David is there. . . ."

The Rabbi was quiet and so were the others. The old men didn't even look at each other.

"Why is there no King from the House of David on that throne?" the Rabbi asked, his voice getting louder. "Where is the King?"

"He will come," I said. "And his House will last forever."

His face was even more kind than before. He spoke softly.

"Will a carpenter build it?" he asked.

Laughter. The old men laughed first and then the boys who were seated on the floor. But the Old Rabbi didn't laugh. Just for a moment I saw sadness in his face, and then it was gone and he was waiting for me to answer, his eyes soft and wide.

My face burned.

"Yes, Rabbi," I said, "a carpenter will build the House of the King. There is always a carpenter. Even the Lord Himself is now and then a carpenter."

The Old Rabbi drew back in surprise. I could hear noises all around me. They didn't like this answer.

"Tell me how the Lord is a carpenter," said the Old Rabbi in Aramaic.

I thought of words Joseph had spoken to me many times:

"Did not the Lord Himself say to Noah how many cubits the ark was to be, and of what sort of wood? And that the wood should be pitched, and did the Lord not say how many stories the ark must be, and did the Lord not say that it should have a window finished to a cubit, and did the Lord not tell Noah where he was to build the door?" I stopped.

A smile came slowly to the face of the oldest man. I didn't look at anyone else. There was quiet again.

"And was it not so," I went on in our tongue, "that the Lord Himself brought the Prophet Ezekial to the vision of the new Temple, setting forth the measurement of the galleries and the pillars, and the gates, and the altar, saying how all things should be done?"

"Yes, it was," said the Old Rabbi, smiling.

"And my lord," I went on. "Was it not Wisdom who said that when the Lord made the world, Wisdom was there like a master craftsman, and if Wisdom is not the Lord, what is Wisdom?"

I stopped. I didn't know where I'd learned that part. But then I went on.

"My lord Rabbi," I said. "It was the carpenters that Nebuchadrezzar took to Babylon, instead of slaying them, because they knew how to build, and when Cyrus the Persian decreed that we could return, the carpenters came home to build the Temple as the Lord had said it should be built."

Quiet.

The Rabbi drew back. I couldn't read the meaning of his face. I looked down. What had I said?

I looked up again.

"Lord Rabbi," I said, "from the time of Sinai, where there is Israel there is a carpenter—a carpenter to build the tabernacle, and it was the Lord Himself who told out the measurements of the tabernacle, and—."

The Rabbi stopped me. He laughed and put up his hand for quiet.

"This is a good child," he said, looking at Joseph above me. "I like this child."

The other men nodded as the old one nodded. Again there was the laughter, not a loud laughter but a gentle laughter moving through the room.

He pointed to the floor right in front of him.

I sat down there on the mat.

There was more talk, friendly and easy, as the Rabbi received James and the other boys, but I didn't really hear it. I knew only that the worst was over. I felt my heart was beating so loud others could hear it. I still didn't wipe my tears, but they'd stopped.

At last, the men were gone. The school began.

The Old Rabbi recited the questions and the answers, and the boys repeated, and as the doors were closed the room grew warm.

No more was said to me that morning, and I didn't speak up, but I recited, and I sang with the others, and I looked at the Rabbi, and the Rabbi looked at me.

When we went home at last, there was the family meal, with no chance to ask anything, but I could tell by their faces that they would never tell me why the Old Rabbi had asked so much. It was their eyes when they looked at me, the way that they were trying to make me think that there was nothing wrong.

And my mother, my mother was very happy, and I knew she didn't know what had been said. She looked like a girl as she tended to the dishes and told us to eat more than we could.

I was as tired as if we'd laid marble pavers all day. I went into the women's room because I didn't know I was doing it, and I lay down on my mother's mat and slept.

When I woke, I could hear everyone talking and I smelled the porridge and the good smell of the baked bread. All the afternoon had passed and I'd slept like a baby, and it was time to eat again.

I went to the bath and washed my face and my hands in the cold water of the basin, and then I knelt and washed my hands in the mikvah. I came back to sit down and eat.

A bowl was given to me. In it were delicious curds with honey.

"What is this?" I asked.

"You eat it," said Cleopas. "Don't you know what it is?"

Then Joseph gave a little laugh and then my uncles all caught the laugh as if it were a breeze moving through the trees.

My mother looked at the bowl.

"You should eat it if your uncle gave it to you," she said.

Cleopas said under his breath for all to hear, " 'Butter and honey will he eat, so that he knows to refuse the evil, and choose the good.' "

"Do you know who spoke those words?" my mother asked.

I was eating the butter and the honey. I'd had enough and gave the bowl to James but he didn't want any. I gave it to Joseph who passed it on.

"I know it's Isaiah," I answered my mother, "but I don't remember any more than that."

That made them all laugh. And I laughed too.

And I didn't remember. Or think about it much again.

I wished for a little time, just a little, to ask a question of Cleopas alone, but the time never came. It was already evening. I'd slept too much. I hadn't done my work after school. I couldn't let that happen again.

18

As the days passed I came to love the morning study hours. The three Rabbis were known as "The Elders" and the oldest of the three was the great teacher, himself a priest now too old to go any longer to Jerusalem, and he told us the most wonderful stories I'd ever heard. His name was Rabbi Berekhaiah bar Phineas and he was always at home in the early evening if we wanted to visit him, any of us boys, near the very top of the hill in a spacious house because his wife was rich.

In the mornings, we repeated and learned to memory much of the holy books just as we had in Alexandria, but here it was always in Hebrew, and when we talked it was often in our tongue, and we could very often get Rabbi Berekhaiah to tell us about his adventures if we tried.

In the evenings, he sat in his library, with the doors open to the court, a modest room as he always said, smiling, and it was if one compared it to Philo's great library, but it was a warm and inviting place to me. He was there for any question, and no matter how tired I was from work, I went up there at least to sit at his feet for a little while. The servants were gentle, they served us cool water, and I could have stayed there for hours listening to him tell his tales, but I had to go home.

The youngest of the teachers, who did not speak up very much, was Rabbi Sherebiah, and he was also a priest, though no longer could he go to the Temple either, as he'd suffered a terrible mishap once on the road up from Jericho when robbers had attacked him as he went to fulfill his duties in the Temple. They had beat him and his brothers and he'd fallen from the cliff and in the fall his lower leg had been crushed, and was taken off by the physicians in Jerusalem.

He walked on a peg, but this could not be seen for his robes, and seemed a whole man with a quick healthy manner about him. But no priest with a missing limb could go before the Lord, and so he had become a Rabbi in the village school, and was sought out for his teachings by everyone. It was said he had become a Pharisee only after he could no longer go to the Temple. His brothers were also priests, but they lived in Capernaum which wasn't very far away.

The Rabbi between them, who made up the last of The Elders, the Rabbi who had received us in the synagogue, was Rabbi Jacimus, and he was a great Pharisee, though all three Rabbis wore blue tassels on their robes, and Rabbi Jacimus was very strict in all his habits which he tried to teach to us.

All of the family of Rabbi Jacimus, and there were many of his uncles, brothers and sisters and their husbands and their children, were Pharisees and they dined only with each other, as was the custom with Pharisees, and the customs of Nazareth were not always what they would have. But everyone went to them for judgements. And two of the brothers of Rabbi Jacimus were village scribes who wrote letters for people, and even read letters for the very old who couldn't read so well. These men wrote up other papers which had to be done, and they were often in their courtyards very busy with

such copying with a man or woman standing over them saying what had to be written. Or worse yet screaming and crying over what was being read to them.

These three teachers were the judges in disputes, but
there were other very old men, men who seldom left their
homes due to their age, who also came together with them if
something had to be done.

In fact, sometimes people came to ask Old Justus, our
uncle, his view of things. Now Old Justus couldn't speak, and
I could see plainly, as could all of us, that he didn't know
what was being said to him, yet people would come and pour
out their woe to him and he would nod. And his eyes would
bulge, and he'd smile. He loved people talking to him. And
this made the people happy and they went away thanking us
and thanking him.

My mother would shake her head. Old Sarah would
shake her head.

Now I should say a lot of people came to Old Sarah. Men
and women came to Old Sarah. Sometimes it seemed to me
that Old Sarah was so venerable as they said, by virtue of her
age and her cleverness and her quickness, that she was neither
man or woman to people anymore.

And it was by listening to some of this outpouring that I
learned a lot about the village, a lot I wanted to know and
some things I didn't want to know.

I learned a lot of things from the other children of the village, from Blind Marya who was always in her father's courtyard and full of laughter and ready talk, and from the boys
who came to play, Simon the Fool, who really wasn't a fool,
but who laughed all the time and was very kind, and Jason
the Fat, who was fat, and Round James and Tall James and
Bold Michael, and Daniel the Zealot, who was called that
because he went at everything "in a fury."

But from no one did I really learn the answers to the questions that were now eating at my heart. I struggled to remember the things my mother had said to me. I did this while I was working at something, like the slow polishing of a table leg or while we were walking up the hill and down to the school. But even then we were all talking or singing, and I couldn't really think. I did remember, really, what she'd said. I remembered it in pictures. An angel had come, an angel to my mother, and no man had been my father, but what did such a thing mean?

I thought when I could, but ours was a busy life.

What time there was from work, I went to the Rabbis. I didn't want to leave them at all. Rabbi Berekhaiah was curious about Alexandria and asked me many questions. He liked to hear me talk, and so did his wife Miriamne, who was the rich one and not so old, and her father, whose hair was white, was often in the room listening to us talk.

Rabbi Berekhaiah had read the scrolls of Philo given him by our family, and he had questions about Philo which I answered, saying always how kind Philo had been, and how he'd taken me to the Great Synagogue just to see it, and how Philo studied the Law and the Prophets and spoke on them as a Rabbi himself, though he was a bit too young perhaps, said some. And I told all about Philo's house and how beautiful it had been, insofar as it was proper to say so.

A carpenter had to be careful what he said about the houses of those for whom he worked. A house was a private place. I'd always been taught that. But Philo's house had been full of young pupils, and the Rabbis of Alexandria had come and gone there, and so it seemed all right to describe the patterns of the marble floors, and the racks of scrolls to the ceiling.

We talked too about the harbor of Alexandria, and about

the Great Lighthouse which I had seen most clearly when we'd sailed away. And I told of the temples, which even a good Jewish boy couldn't help seeing as they were everywhere and very fine, and of the marketplace where one could buy almost anything in the world, and one heard people speaking Latin as well as Greek, and so many other tongues.

I could speak some Latin, but not much.

They were happy to hear about the ships, too, and we had seen so many in Alexandria because it had not only the seafaring ships that went to Greece and Rome and Antioch and the Holy Land, but also the riverboats coming in from the Nile.

Sometimes I thought that I saw Alexandria more clearly than ever in these talks because in answers to the questions of Miriamne and the Old Rabbi, the father-in-law of Bere-khaiah, I had to remember so much. I spoke of the library, which had been rebuilt after Julius Caesar had been so foolish as to burn it. And I spoke about the special Festival of the Jews when we had celebrated the translation of the Law and the Prophets and all the sacred books into Greek.

Now here in Nazareth, no one was going to teach in Greek, but many spoke Greek, especially in Sepphoris where all the soldiers of the King spoke it, and most of the crafts-men, and these Rabbis spoke it and read it. They knew the Scripture in Greek. They had copies of it. They said so. But Hebrew was the language of our learning here, and our tongue, Aramaic, was the daily tongue. In the synagogue, the Scripture was read out in Hebrew, and then the Rabbi explained it in the common tongue. That way, if some-one didn't know the sacred language, he or she could still understand.

I could have spent all my time with my Rabbi Bere-khaiah. But it was not to be.

Very shortly after we started work on the house, Joseph and I had to go into Sepphoris because there was so much work to be had there, and people were in need of shelter due to the terrible war, and they had the means to pay. Joseph would not take the double wages they offered him, one after another, but held to what we had made for a day's work in Alexandria, and took those jobs where he thought what we knew would be used for the best.

He and his brothers, and my uncle Cleopas, could walk through the ruins of a house, talk to the owners about it, and then put it back the way it had been, even going to the painters and the plasterers and the masons, and taking care of all of it as they'd done in Egypt with ease. James and I knew how to go to the marketplace and pick the laborers from the men who stood around.

But no matter what we did, there was a lot of lifting and holding and carrying, and coughing in the dust and the ashes, and I was frightened by the talk of the trouble in Jerusalem where men said that in the Temple a full rebellion was going on. The land of Judea was full of fighting, and there were bandits hiding in the Galilean hills.

There was talk even of some young men, in spite of all that had happened in Galilee, going up to Jerusalem to fight in this war, that it was a holy cause.

Meanwhile the Romans tried everywhere in Judea to put down the rebellion, and they still had the Arabs marching with them, and the Arabs burned Judean villages. And the whole family of King Herod was still in Rome fighting and disputing before Augustus, as to who should be King.

My teeth no longer chattered in fear no matter what I heard, and our family didn't talk of it very much. All around us buildings for a King Herod, whoever he might be, were rising up. Men came from everywhere too, to mend rooftops, to fetch fresh water for those who worked, to mix and daub paint and lay mortar for stones, and our clan had many friends among those who had so much work they did not know how to say yes to all of it.

My uncle Cleopas looked around and said: "Now Sepphoris will be bigger than ever."

"But who will be King?" I asked.

He made a sound which showed his disgust for the family of Herod. But Joseph looked at him and he didn't say the words he wanted to say.

The Romans were still in the city, moving about to keep the peace, on the watch for the rebels out of the hills, and hearing the constant complaints of the people—their woes as to this son who was missing, or that house that should not have been burned, and sometimes the soldiers threw up their hands and cried for silence because they didn't know what to do about it.

The soldiers drank in open taverns, and at the street corners where they bought their food. They watched us at our work. The scribes were busy writing letters for them to their womenfolk and their children.

This was a Jewish city. I saw it by and by. There were no pagan temples here at all. There were few public women to hang around with soldiers, only the older tavern keeper women, and sometimes they had their own men. The soldiers yawned and threw a glance at our women as they came and went, but what could they see? Our women were always in their proper robes, and with their shawls and their veils.

Very different from Alexandria where there had been so many Greek and Roman women always in the crowds. They were veiled many of them, too, and modest, but there was another sort that hung about the public houses. We were never supposed to look at them, but we could not help it sometimes.

Here it was a different story.

When bad news came in of fighting in Jerusalem, people gathered in groups to talk about it, and they stared at the soldiers, and the soldiers became hard and they stopped being friendly and stood in bands on the streets. But nothing happened.

As for our family, and many many others, we went right on working no matter what the news. We prayed as we worked, under our breath. As we gathered to eat our little meal mid-day, we blessed the Lord and we blessed our food and drink. Then back to work we went.

I didn't mind all those times. But studying in Nazareth was better.

What I loved the most besides studying were our walks to and from Sepphoris because the air was warm and the harvest was almost finished, and the trees were full everywhere I looked. The blossoms were gone from the almond trees, but so many other trees were full of beautiful leaves. On every walk I saw new things.

I wanted to go off the road and wander in the woods, but we couldn't do this. So I'd run ahead sometimes and wander a little. Someday, I thought, there'll be time for wandering to the little villages everywhere in the little valleys, but for now life was full.

How could anyone ask for more than we had?

19

I DON'T KNOW how many days it was before I began to feel sick.

A fever came on me in the afternoon. Cleopas knew it before I did, and then James, too, said that he was sick, and Cleopas put his hand to my forehead and said we had to go back to Nazareth now.

Joseph carried me the last hour of the way. I woke up thirsty and my throat hurt, and my mother was frightened as she put me to bed. Little Salome was also sick. It turned out four of us, and then five were bedded down in the same room.

I could hear coughing everywhere around me, and my mother kept putting water to my lips. I heard my mother say to James, "You have to drink it! Wake up!" Little Salome was moaning and when I touched her, she was hot.

My mother was talking to me: "Who knows what it is," she said. "It could be from the Romans. They could have brought it. It could be that we've been away and now we're home. No one else in the village is sick—only our little ones."

But my aunt Mary was sick, too. Cleopas brought her in and laid her down. He said her name. He said it as if he was angry, but he wasn't. And she wouldn't answer him. These things I saw but I was half asleep. Old Sarah sang to us. When I couldn't see her clearly in the shadows, I could hear her voice.

My whole body hurt me—my shoulders, my hips, my knees—but I could sleep. I could dream.

For the first time it seemed to me that sleep was a place.

When I look back on it, I know that up to that point in my life, I always fought sleep. I never really wanted to run away into it. Even when I was afraid in the hills and the fires were burning, I wanted the fire to go away, the angry bandits to go away. I didn't want to flee into sleep. Flee into my mother's arms, yes. Flee to our own safe house, yes. But not to sleep.

But now, in this sickness, when my shoulders and legs were hurting me, it felt good to tumble down into deep sleep.

I dreamed while I was still awake. It was the most pleasant dream I'd ever had. I knew I was in Nazareth. I knew my mother was there and my aunt Mary was lying close by. I knew I was safe.

But at the same time I was walking in a palace. It was far larger than Philo's house in Alexandria, and when I came to the edge of the room, I saw the blue sea. The rocks went up on either side, and the coastline curved, and there were torches down below in the garden. So many torches. Columns held the roof over my head. I knew the style of the columns, the carved acanthus leaf capitals.

On a marble bench, there sat a being with wings. He looked like a man, a very comely man. I thought of Absolom, the son of David, who had been comely, and the strangest thing happened: this man on the bench grew longer, fuller hair.

"You're trying to look like Absolom," I said.

"Oh, you're very clever for your age, aren't you?" he said. "The Rabbi loves you." He had a soft musical voice. His eyes were blue like the sea. There was a shine to his eyes. There was green and red embroidery along his tunic, a vine full of the tiniest flowers. He smiled at me. "I knew you'd like that," he said. "What I want to know is . . . what do you think you're doing here?"

"Here? In this palace?" I asked. "I'm dreaming, of course." I laughed at him. I heard my laughter in the dream. I looked out over the sea and I saw the clouds piled high in the sky, and on the far limit of the sea, I saw ships moving. It seemed I could see the oars dipping, and the men at the helm. How clear was everything under the full moon.

All was beauty around me.

"Yes, it's a palace fit for an Emperor," he said. "Why don't you live in such a palace?"

"Why should I?" I asked.

"Well, certainly it's better than the dirt and filth of Nazareth," he said in his gracious tongue with his gracious smile.

"Are you certain of that?" I asked.

"I lived in both," he said. His face went dark. He looked at me with contempt.

I looked at the ships again, moving so fast, so smoothly out under the moon, sailing at night when night was a dangerous time for sailing, but so beautiful.

"Yes, they're coming out of Ostia," he said, "those beautiful galley ships. Your Archelaus is eager to be home. And so are his brothers and his sister."

"I know," I answered.

"Who are you!" he demanded. He was impatient. After all, this dream would shortly come to an end. All dreams came to an end.

I looked at him. He was angry and he was trying to hide it. He couldn't hide it. He made me think of my little brothers. But he was no child.

"And you're no child either!" he said.

"Oh, I see now," I said with the greatest satisfaction. "I didn't before. When you're with me like this, you don't know what's going to happen, do you? You don't know what's to come!" I laughed and I laughed. "That's your doom that you don't know how it will end."

He became so angry that he couldn't keep the smile on his face.

But as his smile broke up, he began to cry. He couldn't hold it back. It was a grown man's broken crying, which I'd almost never seen. "You know that I am what I am from love," he said. "This that I am is from love."

I felt sad for him. But I had to be careful. He had his hand to his face, and he was looking at me through his fingers. Crying, yes, but watching me, and it filled me with terrible misery to look at him. I didn't want to look at him. I could not do anything for him.

"Who are you!" he asked again. He became so angry that he stopped crying and he reached out for me. "I demand that you tell me!"

I moved back, away from him.

"Don't lay your hands on me," I said. I was not angry or excited, but I wanted him to understand. "Never, never lay your hands on me."

"Do you know what's happening in Jerusalem?" he asked. He was so angry that his face was red with it, and his eyes getting bigger and bigger.

I didn't answer him.

"Let me show you, angel child!" he said.

"Don't put yourself to the trouble," I said.

Before us, instead of the blue sea, I saw suddenly the great courtyard of the Temple. I didn't want to see it. I didn't want to think of the men fighting as they'd been when I was there. But this was far worse.

On top of the colonnades archers were shooting arrows down at the Roman soldiers, and others threw stones, and all manner of fighting went on until flames leapt out beneath the columns, flames, dread and terrible flames leaping up and catching the Jews unawares as the colonnades filled with fire, and the gold work on the outside of these places began to burn, and bodies fell down into the fire, and people screamed and cried for the Lord to save them.

The whole courtyard was girded with fire, yet some of the Jews threw down their armor and ran into the fire, roaring and hollering, and some Romans ran in where they could, and other Romans came out with arms loaded with treasure. Temple treasure, sacred treasure, treasure of the Lord. The screams of the suffering people were more than I could stand.

"Lord in Heaven, have mercy on them," I cried. I was so afraid. I was shivering. I was shaking. All my fear came back to me and was worse than it had ever been. One fire after another filled my mind, as though each fire were ignited from the one before it until the blaze reached to the stars. *Out of the depths, I cry unto thee, O Lord.*

"Is that all you can do?" this strange creature asked me. He stood very close to me, handsome in his rich clothing, his blue eyes full of anger even though he smiled.

I put my hands to my face. I wouldn't look. I heard his voice in my ear:

"I'm watching you, angel child!" he said. "I'm waiting to see what you mean to do. So go on: walk like a child, eat like a child, play like a child, work like a child. But I'm watching. And I may not know the future, no, but I know this: your mother's a whore, your father's a liar, and the floors of your house are dirt. Your cause is lost, I know it's lost, it's lost every day and every hour, and you know it is. You think your little miracles will help these foolish people? I tell you, chaos rules. And I am its Prince."

I looked at him. I knew that if I wanted to, I could answer him. The words would come easily and they would tell me things I didn't know now; they would draw this knowledge out of my mind, as surely as the sound would come out of my mouth. Everything would be there before me, all the answers, all the whole span of Time. But no, it wasn't to happen. No, not this way or any other way. I said nothing. His misery hurt me. His darkening face hurt me. His fury hurt me.

I woke up without a sound. I lay in the dark room, covered in sweat and thirsting.

The lamp was the only light. It seemed everywhere there were moans. I didn't know where I was, this room, this place—and my head ached. It hurt so badly I couldn't bear it. My mother was near but with someone else.

Cleopas was praying in a whisper. I could hear a strange voice, a woman's voice. "If this goes on like this, you don't want her to come back. . . ."

I closed my eyes. I dreamed. I saw the fields of wheat around Nazareth. I saw the flowering almond trees that we'd passed when we first came into the land. I saw the villages of white houses tumbling over the hills. Thin curling leaves flying in the gentle gusts of the wind. I dreamed of water. That creature wanted to come again, but I wouldn't let him come.

No, not the world of palaces and ships, no. "Stop," I said. "I will not."

My mother said, "You're dreaming, I'm holding you. You're safe." Safe.

It was days and nights before I came to myself. I found that out afterwards.

And even then I slept most of the time. Only the wailing woke me, the wailing and the crying, and I knew then that someone had died.

When I opened my eyes, I saw my mother feeding Little Symeon who was under the covers, and propped against a blanket roll. Little Salome slept nearby, her face very damp. But she wasn't really too sick anymore.

My mother looked at me and smiled. But her face was white and sad, and she'd been crying, and I knew it, and I knew that one of the people moaning and crying in the far room was Cleopas. I heard it, that broken grown man crying that I'd seen and heard in the dream.

"Tell me!" I whispered. The fear came, a grip on my throat.

"The children are better," she said. "Don't you remember? I told you all this last night."

"No, I want to know who?"

She wouldn't answer me.

"Is it Aunt Mary?" I asked. I turned to look. Aunt Mary had been lying right next to me and she was gone.

My mother closed her eyes and groaned. I turned towards her and put my hand on her knee, but I don't think she felt it through her robe. She rocked back and forth.

When next I woke up, it was the funeral feast that was happening. It must have been. I could hear the music of flutes that cut the air like wooden knives.

Joseph was with me and he made me drink some soup.

Little Salome was sitting straight up next to me, and she said with very wide eyes,

"Did you know my mother is dead?"

"I'm sorry for it," I said.

"And the baby too is dead because the baby was inside her."

"I'm sorry for it," I said.

"They already buried her. They put her in the cave."

I didn't say anything.

My aunts came in, Salome and Esther, and they made Little Salome drink soup and lie down. Little Salome wouldn't stop asking about her mother. "Was she covered up?" she asked. "Did she look white?"

They told her to be quiet.

"Did she cry when she died?"

I slept.

When I woke up, the room was still full of children sleeping, and my older cousins were there, sick, too.

It wasn't until the next morning that I got up.

At first I thought no one was awake in the house.

I went out into the courtyard.

The air was warm, and the leaves on the fig tree were big. There were white flowers all over the vines, and the sky was very blue yet full of clean clouds that didn't mean rain.

I was so hungry I could have eaten anything. I'd never been so hungry ever that I knew.

There were voices coming from one of the rooms that Cleopas and his family used on the other side of the court. I went in and saw my mother and my uncle seated there on the floor, talking together, before a meal of bread and sauce. The window had only a thin veil. The light fell on their shoulders.

I sat down beside my mother.

". . . and I'll take care of them, I'll gather them to me, and hold them to me, because I am their mother now, and they are my children." This is what she was saying to Cleopas. "You understand me? They are my children now. They are the brothers and sisters of Jesus and James. I can care for them. I want you to believe in me. Everyone has always treated me as if I were a girl. I'm not a girl. I'll care for all of them. We are all one family together."

Cleopas nodded but he had a faraway look.

He passed the bread to me, and whispered the blessing and I whispered it too. I gobbled the bread.

"No, not so fast," said my mother. "I mean it. You mustn't. And drink this." She gave me water. I wanted the bread.

My mother ran her hand over my hair. She kissed me. "You heard what I said to your uncle?"

"They're my brothers and sisters," I said, "as it's always been." I ate some more of the bread and sauce.

"That is enough," said my mother. She took all the bread and the sauce and got up and went out.

I sat there alone with my uncle. I drew up close to him.

His face was calm as if all the crying had gone away and left him empty.

He turned to me. He looked very serious.

"Do you think the Lord in Heaven had to take one of us?" he asked. "And when I was spared, he took her in my place?"

I was so surprised I could hardly breathe. I remembered all at once my prayer for him to live when he'd been praying in the Jordan River. I remember the power going out of me into him when I laid my hand on him as he sang in the river, and he hadn't even known.

I tried to say something but no words would come out.

What could I do but cry?

He gathered me in his arms, and rocked me. "Ah, my own," he said under his breath to me.

"O Lord of All Creation," he prayed, "you've restored me. It must have been for my good that I've known such bitterness . . . we who live thank you, as I do now, the father will tell the children of your faithfulness."

For weeks we didn't go outside the courtyard.

My eyes hurt in the light. Cleopas and I painted some of the rooms with fresh whitewash. But those who had to work in Sepphoris went to work.

Finally all had recovered from the illness, even Little Esther for whom we'd feared the worst just because she was little. But I knew she was all right because she was screaming her lungs out.

Rabbi Sherebiah, the priest with the wooden leg, came into our house with the Water of Purification so that we could be sprinkled one time and then again in the following days. This water he made up with the ashes of the red heifer, which had been slain and burnt at the Temple in accordance with the Law to make the ashes for this, and with the living water from the stream beyond the synagogue at the end of the village.

With this Water of Purification, not only were we sprinkled but also the entire house, and all the cooking vessels and the jars that held food or water or wine. Everything was sprinkled. The mikvah was sprinkled.

We bathed in the mikvah after each sprinkling; and after sundown on the last day of the sprinkling all of us and our house were clean.

This was from the impurity we had taken on from the death of our aunt Mary under our roof. And it was a solemn thing to us, especially to Cleopas, who had recited the passage from the Book of Numbers which told of this cleansing and how it was to be done.

My mind was much captured by this ritual; I made up my mind that I wanted to see the slaughter of the red heifer with my own eyes someday in Jerusalem.

Not now, when there was fighting, no. But someday when it would be peaceful and we could go there. The slaughter of the red heifer and the burning of the heifer, along with her skin and her flesh and her blood and her dung, to make these ashes of purification—what a sight it must be, I thought. There was so much to see at the Temple. And the Temple was now in the midst of fighting.

That was the only way I could remember it, full of dead bodies and people screaming, and that man killed before my eyes, and that soldier who on his horse had come in my memory to look like a horse and a man put together, with his long spear full of blood. That and then the fiery battle I'd seen in the dream, the strange dream. However could I have dreamed such a dream?

But that was far away, all of that.

It was peaceful here as we went through the purification.

Never in Alexandria could I remember such a thing being done, this sprinkling, and only dimly did I remember the death of a little child there, the infant son of my uncle Alphaeus. But here in the Land, it was the custom to do these things according to the Law. And everyone was happy to do it.

But I knew that my uncles had not waited on this ritual to go to work in Sepphoris. They could not have done that. Some of them had been working there all during the time of illness. And the women had been going out to the vegetable garden when they had to do it. I didn't ask any questions about it. I knew that we did what we could. And I trusted in what my uncles and Joseph said to do. People did what they could do.

Now, after that time, and not very long after at all, before I was even going out of the house yet, my uncles got into a big dispute.

There was so much work in Sepphoris that they could choose among the hardest jobs, and the jobs they most liked, and the jobs which most used all the skills of the family. But Joseph, upon whom everyone relied, would not charge any different for any one job over another. The uncles didn't think that was right, and neither did some of the other carpenters in Sepphoris. The uncles wanted double for the jobs of skill, and the other carpenters were for this, and Joseph would not charge this.

Finally, all of them went up the hill to Rabbi Berekhaiah, even though they wanted to see Rabbi Jacimus, the strictest Pharisee.

"We need a Pharisee to settle this," my uncle Cleopas had said. And everyone had agreed. Even Joseph. But no one was going to ask the younger Rabbi before asking the older Rabbi.

Rabbi Berekhaiah at once said to go to Rabbi Jacimus, the Pharisee, and do what he said to do.

We little boys couldn't crowd in and as it grew warmer and warmer outside, we went on home.

They were gone a long time, and when they came down they were all in good spirits. It seemed that Rabbi Jacimus had won the day with this argument: that if they charged double for the skilled jobs, they could let the boys go to school for a full half day. And Joseph had agreed to this!

We clapped our hands! This was wonderful news. James and I looked at each other. Even our cousins, Silas and Levi, were happy. Little Symeon was happy and he hardly knew what this was about.

We were to receive more education. And the house was to receive higher wages.

My mother was very pleased.

We had good wine with supper that night, and by the light of the lamps, Joseph read us one of the Greek stories we loved, from the scrolls we'd brought back from Alexandria, The Tale of Tobit.

Now everyone gathered round for this story, even the women, because we all enjoyed so much to hear of the angel coming to Tobias, the son of Tobit, and this angel, "in disguise," telling Tobias of cures he might work with the innards of the fish that tried to swallow his foot, and of how he must marry the young girl Sarah, daughter of Raguel, and of Tobias answering that wasn't it true that Sarah had had seven husbands already and each of them killed on the wedding night by a demon?

We roared with laughter as Joseph read this part in Tobias' innocent voice. And then Joseph became the angel Raphael again, "Now you listen to me and don't you worry about this demon!" On Joseph read in the voice of the angel, that Tobias would be wed to Sarah that very night and all he had to do was put the liver and heart of the dead fish on the fire in the wedding chamber and the smell would drive off the demon forever! "And who else do you think such a smell would drive off!" Cleopas asked. Even my mother was laughing.

Joseph went on as the helpful angel Raphael, his words in a rush. "Now before you get into your bed, stand and pray, asking that safety and mercy be granted you. Don't be afraid, the girl's set apart for you from before the beginning of the world, you'll save her, she'll go with you, I assume you'll have children and they will be brothers and sisters, and say no more to it." Again we were laughing so hard we could hardly keep from crying.

"That's the way it goes," said my aunt Esther, and all of them broke into laughing again looking at one another.

"Say no more to it!" cried my aunt Salome, and again they were all laughing as if they the mothers knew far more how funny it was even than we did.

"And an angel should know!" cried my aunt Esther.

They all went quiet. All the laughter stopped.

I saw they were looking at my mother and then looking away at each other.

My mother was looking off at nothing, and then she smiled. She laughed. She shook her head, and laughed, and they all broke into laughing again.

There were many funny parts in the story and we knew them all. From the stench of the fish, the demon fled, the angel bound him, Tobias loved Sarah, his father-in-law wouldn't let him go home he loved him so much, and the wedding feast went on for over fourteen days, and when he finally did go home, yes, he cured his father's blindness with the medicine of the fish who'd tried to swallow his foot, and another wedding feast went on for more days and everyone was happy. Then came the more serious part of the story, the long and beautiful prayers of Tobit, which we all knew in Greek and recited in Greek.

When we came to the end of the prayer, Joseph, who was leading us, spoke the words more slowly, as they had a meaning for us now that they hadn't had for us in Egypt.

" 'Jerusalem, our holy city, the Lord has scourged you for works of your hands, but He will have mercy on the children of the Righteous. Praise the Lord for He is Good, and bless the King of the ages, so that He will again pitch His tent in your midst. . . .' "

We were sad thinking of the fighting going on. And as the prayer went on, I made the memories of the fighting go away; I saw the Temple as it had been before I knew that men were going to fight with each other.

I saw the huge walls, and the hundreds of people gathered there to pray, crowding through the baths, through the tunnels into the Court of the Gentiles. I heard people crying out the Psalms.

We prayed now as Joseph led us:

" 'A great light will shine to all the ends of the Earth, and many nations will come to you from afar, the peoples of all the Earth, to dwell near to the name of the Lord, bearing in their hands gifts for the King of Heaven. . . .' "

I saw the light in my mind, and I grew sleepy in a beautiful soft sleep in which I could hear the words of the prayer as I lay on my mat, with my arm crooked under my head. " 'And they will call you The Chosen One through all ages forever.' "

And so it seemed the pestilence had left our house. Death had left it. Uncleanness had left it. And tears had left it. And though my dream of the strange creature with the wings and the beautiful eyes troubled me, and though it troubled me worse that I felt I could tell no one about it, I soon put the dream out of my mind as I put aside the picture of the Temple full of blood. And life began again. I was happy I knew it, because I had known what unhappiness was, and what fear was, and illness and sorrow, and these things were gone now.

2 O

AS SOON AS MY MOTHER SAID that I could, I bathed in
the mikvah which was very cold now, with the water so high
it went over my head, and I put on freshly washed clothes,
and I went up the hill to the house of the great Rabbi,
Berekhaiah. The servants told me he was at the synagogue so
I went there, careful to wash my hands in the stream for the
sake of anyone who didn't know I had bathed before coming.

I went in and sat down on the edge of the assembly, surprised to see so many there on this day of the week, but I
soon saw they were all listening not to the Rabbis but to a
man who had come to tell of events in Jerusalem. He was a
Pharisee and dressed in the finest clothes, with plenty of
white hairs beneath his shawl.

My brother James was there, and so was Joseph, and
Cleopas. My older cousins were there.

Rabbi Berekhaiah smiled when he saw me and gestured
for me to sit still as the man went on talking.

The man was speaking in Greek, and from time to time
he stopped and spoke in our tongue.

He was in the middle of his story:

"This Sabinus, this procurator of the Romans, he had his

men surround the Temple, and the Jews took to the roofs of the colonnades. They threw stones at the Romans. The arrows went like that through the air. And the Roman arrows couldn't reach the Jews because of their position. But this godless man, Sabinus, this man whose sole intent was, in everything he did, to find the treasure of the King in the King's absence, this greedy man, he set fire in secret to the colonnades, the very colonnades of the Temple with their gold work in wax, and the Jews were caught by the flames. The fire exploded as if from a mountain. The pitch in the roof of the Temple caught fire; the columns themselves were burning. And the gold was destroyed in the flames. And the men on the roofs were destroyed. How can we count the number of the dead?"

I felt my fear come back. Though it was warm, I felt cold as he went on.

". . . and the Romans, they went right through the flames to steal the treasures of the Lord before the eyes of those who watched helpless. They ran through the Great Courtyard right into the storehouses to steal in their greed, and they stole from the house of the Lord."

I saw it as I'd seen it in my dream. I bowed my head and closed my eyes. As he went on speaking, I could see what he was telling us.

Battle after battle, and the Roman legions coming, and the crosses going up along the road.

"Two thousand crucified," he said. "They went after those who had fled. They brought in those they suspected and executed them. Who knew if all these people were guilty? They can't tell the good from the bad among us! They don't know. And the Arabians, how many villages did they burn before General Varus finally sent them home, before he learned they couldn't be trusted as peacekeepers." Then came a string of names—places burned, families who had lost their homes. . . .

I couldn't open my eyes. I saw the flames against the night sky. I saw people running. Finally a hand came down on my shoulder and I heard Rabbi Berekhaiah whisper, "Pay heed."

"Yes, Rabbi," I whispered.

I looked at the man who walked back and forth before the assembly talking of the rebels—Simon, who burnt the palace of Jericho, had been chased by Gratus, the general of Herod who went over to the Romans. His rule was finished. But there were so many others. . . .

"They're in those caves to the north!" He gestured. "They'll never be wiped out."

People whispered, nodded.

"They're families, tribes of bandits. And now comes the word that Caesar has divided us amongst the children of Herod, and these princes, if that is what they are, are on the high seas bound for our ports."

I saw the nighttime sea under the moon. I felt my dream.

The messenger stopped as if he had a lot more to say, but couldn't say it.

"We await the ruler who is now put over us," he said.

A man spoke up from the back of the assembly.

"The priests of the Temple will rule!" he said.

And another: "The priests know the Law and we live by the Law. Why do we not have priests from the House of Zadok as the Law says we should have? I tell you, you purge the Temple of its impurities and the priests will rule again." Men stood up. Men shouted at each other. No one could be heard.

Rabbi Jacimus was on his feet.

Only when the old Rabbi Berekhaiah stood up did the men quiet down.

"Our embassy put its petitions before Caesar," said Rabbi Berekhaiah. "Caesar has made his decision and we will soon know the full words of it. Until then we wait." His eyes moved over the assembly. He turned this way and that as he looked into the faces of the men and the women gathered there.

"Who knows the lineage of the priest in the Temple at this hour?" he asked. "Who knows if there is even a High Priest?"

There was much nodding and approval of that. The men were taking their seats again.

The messenger went on to answer questions from the men.

But there was soon disputing and shouting all over again.

I got up and slipped out of the synagogue.

In the warm air I didn't shiver anymore. I went through the village and out and up the hill.

Women were tending the vegetable gardens. The farmers worked with their helpers in the fields.

The sky was big, and the clouds were moving as if they were ships at sea.

Wildflowers bloomed in the grass, some tall, and others small. And the trees were full of green olives.

I lay down on the grass, and felt of the wildflowers with my open hand. And I looked up through the branches of the olive tree. I wanted it that way—the sky in bits and pieces. I was happy. I could hear far away the pigeons and the doves of the village. I thought I could even hear the bees in their hives. I could hear something that was like the grass growing, but it wasn't that, I knew. It was all the sounds coming together, and being soft—so unlike the sounds of a city.

I thought of Alexandria. I thought of the great open Temple to Augustus Caesar by the port with all its gardens and its libraries. I had seen it many times as we passed it on our way to take supplies from the warehouses on the docks.

Yes, all that. And our procession, we, the Jews of Alexandria, the largest part of the population, celebrating the day the Scripture had been put into Greek. We had given the pagans something to look at, had we not? Or so the men said as we chanted the Psalms.

I saw the sea.

I did think of those things . . . but I loved this place. I knew love of it, love of the thick forests going up the slopes with the cypress and the sycamore, and the myrtle trees as Joseph taught me the names of them.

I prayed in my heart. "Father in Heaven, I thank you for this."

It wouldn't last, being alone here.

It was Cleopas who came to get me.

"Don't be unhappy," he said.

"I'm very happy," I said as I climbed to my feet. "I am not unhappy at all. I am not unhappy with anything."

"Oh, I see," he said in his usual tone. "I thought the talk in the synagogue had made you cry."

"No," I said, shaking my head. "This is a happy place, this," I said, looking back to where I'd been. "I come here and I think and my thoughts turn to prayers."

He liked this.

We walked down the slope together.

"Good," he said. "You mustn't worry about all those struggles, those defeats. The Romans will get every last one of those rebels in Judea. That fool, Simon, is just one of them. They'll catch Athronges, the shepherd King, and they'll catch his brothers. They'll hunt down these thieves in Galilee too. They're up there in the caves, at the Fountains of the Jordan.

They'll come out when they want something, and you'll hear them roaring through the village. Oh, not here, no, nothing much ever happens in Nazareth except—. Whoever is King here or in Judea, Archelaus or Antipas, Caesar is the judge to whom we can appeal. I'll tell you one thing about Caesar. He doesn't want trouble out here. And these Herods will rule as long as there's no trouble. We always have Caesar."

I stopped. I looked up at him.

"You want it this way, that we always have Caesar?"

"Why not?" he asked. "Who else is to keep the peace?"

I felt the fear so sharp that it hurt my belly. I didn't answer. "Will we never have another King for David's throne?" I asked.

He looked at me for a long time before he answered.

"I want peace," he said. "I want to build, and plaster and paint, and feed my little ones, and be with my kindred. That's what I want. And that's all the Romans want. You know they're not bad people, the Romans. They worship their gods. Their women are proper. They have their ways as we have ours. Here, you'd think that every pagan was a lawless fiend who burnt his children to Moloch and committed abominations every afternoon in his own house."

I laughed.

"But this is Galilee," he said. "Once one lives in a city like Alexandria, once one has been to Rome, you know these are illusions. Do you know what that word means?"

"Yes," I said. "Fancies. Dreams."

"Ah," he said. "You are the one who understands me."

I laughed and nodded.

"I'm your prophet," he said.

"Will you be my prophet?" I said.

"What? What is it you want me to do?"

"Tell me the answers. Why did they stop me at the door of the synagogue. Why didn't Joseph want to say that it was in—."

"No," he said. He shook his head. He put his hands up to his head. He looked down. "I can't do it because Joseph doesn't want me to do it."

"Joseph has forbidden me to ask questions of him, even to ask questions."

"You know why?" he asked.

"He doesn't want to know," I said. I shrugged. "What else could it be?"

He knelt down and took me by the shoulders. He looked into my eyes.

"He doesn't understand things himself," he said. "And when a man doesn't understand, he can't explain."

"Joseph? Not understand?"

"Yes, that's what I said. I said it for your ears only."

"You understand?" I asked.

"I try," he said. He raised his eyebrows and he smiled. "You know me. You know that I try. But Joseph's way is to wait, wait on the Lord himself. Joseph doesn't have to understand, because Joseph trusts in the Lord completely. There's something I can tell you and that you must remember. An angel has spoken to your mother. And angels have come to Joseph. But no angel has ever come to me."

"And not to me, but . . ." I broke off. I wasn't going to say it—about Eleazer in Egypt, and about the rain stopping, and least of all about Cleopas himself in the Jordan River, and my hand on his back. Or about that night on the banks of the Jordan when I'd thought there were others there, all around me in the darkness.

He was lost in his thoughts. He stood up and looked out

over the fields at the mountains rising to the east and the west.

"Tell me what happened!" I said. I kept my voice low. I pleaded. "Tell me everything."

"Let's talk about the battles, and the rebellion, and these Kings of the House of Herod. It's easier," he said. He was still looking off.

Then he looked down at me.

"I cannot tell you what you want to know. I don't know everything either. If I try to tell you things, your father will put me out of the house for it. You know he will. And I can't bring that trouble to our house. You're what, eight years old now?"

"Not yet," I said. "But soon!"

He smiled. "Yes, a man!" he said. "I see that. How could I not know you were a man? Listen to me, someday before I die, I'll tell you all I know. I promise you. . . ." He went into his thoughts again.

"What is it?"

His face was full of shadows.

"I will tell you this," he said. "Keep it in your heart. The day will come——." He shook his head. He looked away.

"Speak, go on, I'm listening to you."

When he turned back to me, he had a sharp smile again.

"Now to Caesar Augustus," he said. "What does it matter who is collecting the taxes or catching the thieves? What does it matter who stands at the city gates? You saw the Temple. How can the Temple be rebuilt and purified if the Romans don't bring order to Jerusalem? Herod Archelaus gives the order for slaughter in the very Temple. The thieves and the rebels stand on the cloisters and shoot their arrows in the very Temple. I'd have a Roman peace, yes, a peace such as we had in Alexandria. I'll tell you something about the Romans. Their cup is full, and it's good to be ruled by one whose cup is full."

I didn't answer him but I heard every word and remembered every word afterward.

"What did they do to Simon, the rebel whom they caught?"

"He was beheaded," said Cleopas. "He was let off easy, if you ask me. But then I didn't care that he burnt the two palaces of Herod. It's not that . . . it's all the rest of it, the lawlessness, the ruin."

He looked at me.

"Oh, you're too little to understand," he said.

"How many times have you said that to me?" I asked.

He laughed.

"But I do understand," I said. "We don't have a Jewish King who can rule over all of us, not a Jewish King whom men love."

He nodded. He looked around, at the sky, at the passing clouds.

"Nothing for us really changes," he said.

"I've heard this before."

"You'll hear it again. Tomorrow, you'll come with me to Sepphoris and help with the painting of the walls we're finishing. It's easy work. I've drawn the lines. I'll mix the color. You just fill in. You'll be working just as you did in Alexandria. That's what we want. Isn't it? That and to love the Lord with our whole hearts and minds, and to know his Law."

We walked back home together.

I didn't tell him what was in my heart. I couldn't. I wanted to tell him about the strange dream I'd had but I couldn't. And if I couldn't tell my uncle Cleopas, then I couldn't tell anyone what I'd dreamed. I'd never be able to ask the Old Rabbi about the man with wings, or the visions I saw, that I'd seen the colonnades of the Temple in flames.

And who would understand the night near the Jordan, the beings around me in the dark?

We were almost down the hill. There was a woman singing in her garden, and little ones playing.

I stopped.

"Was is it?" he asked. "Come," he gestured with his hand.

I didn't obey him.

"Uncle," I said. "What was it, up there, that you were going to tell me? Tell me now."

He looked at me and I looked at him.

In a small voice I said,

"I want to know."

He was quiet, and a change came over him, a softening, and then he spoke in a low voice as he answered me.

"You keep what I say in your heart," he said. "The day will come when you will have to give us the answers."

We looked at each other, and I was the one to look away. *I must give the answers!*

There came over me the remembrance of the Jordan River in the sunset, the fire in the water that was a beautiful fire, and the feeling of those others, those countless others all around me.

And there came in a flash to me a feeling of understanding everything, *everything!*

It was gone as soon as it had come. And I knew that I had let it go, this feeling. Yes, I had let it go.

My uncle was still looking at me.

He bent down and brushed my hair back from my forehead. He kissed me there.

"You smiling at me?" he asked.

"Yes," I said. "You spoke the truth," I said.

"What truth?"

"I'm too little to understand," I said.

He laughed. "You don't fool me," he said and he stood up and we walked down the hill together.

21

THE SUMMER had been so good.

The second crop of figs was pulling down our old tree in the courtyard, and the olive pickers beating the branches in the orchards, and I felt a happiness I'd never known, and I knew that I felt it.

It was the beginning of time for me—from the last days in Alexandria to the coming to this place.

As the months passed, we finished all the repairs on our house so that it was near to perfect for all of our families—that of my uncles, Simon and Alphaeus and Cleopas, and for Joseph and my mother, and for me.

The Greek slave, Riba, who had come with Bruria gave birth to a child.

There was much whispering and fussing about this matter, even among the children, with Little Salome whispering to me, "She didn't hide in that tunnel from the robbers far enough, did she?"

But the night of the baby's birth, I heard it crying, and I heard Riba singing to it in Greek, and then Bruria was singing to it, and my aunts were laughing and singing together, with the lamps lighted, and it was a happy night.

Joseph woke up and took the baby into his arms.

"That's no Arab child," said my aunt Salome, "that's a Jewish boy and you know it."

"Who said it was an Arab child!" cried Riba. "I told you—."

"Very well, very well," Joseph said quietly, as always, "we'll call him Ishmael. Does that make everyone happy?"

I liked the baby at once.

He had a good little chin and large black eyes. He didn't cry all the time like my aunt Salome's new baby, who fussed if you made a strange noise, and Little Salome loved to carry him around while his mother worked. And so there was Little Ishmael. Little John of Aunt Salome and Alphaeus was one of fifteen Johns in the village, along with seventeen Simons, and thirteen by the name of Judas, and more Marys than I had fingers on both hands—and these just in our kindred on this side of the hill.

But I go ahead of my story. These babies didn't come till winter.

Summer burned hot without the sea breeze of the coast, and bathing in the spring was great fun every night when we returned from Sepphoris, and the boys got into water fights with each other, while around the bend in the creek you could hear the girls laughing and talking amongst themselves. Upstream at the cistern cut in the rock where the women filled their jars there was much talking and laughing too, and my mother even sometimes came in the evening just to see the other women and walk with them.

As the summer wore on, there were weddings in the village, both of them long all-night celebrations at which it seemed everybody in Nazareth was drinking and dancing, the men dancing with the men wildly, and the women dancing with the women, and even the maidens, though they were fearful and stayed together always next to the canopy under which the bride sat, the bride covered in the most fine veils and shining gold bracelets.

Many in the village played the flutes; and several men the lyres and the women beat the tambourines over their heads, and old men hit the cymbals to make a steady time for the dancing. Even Old Justus was brought out and propped on pillows against the wall, and nodding, and smiling at the wedding, though the spit dripped down his chin and Old Sarah had to wipe it away.

The father of the bride sometimes did the wildest dance of joy, rocking and throwing up his arms, and turning fast in his brightly trimmed robes, and some of the people drank themselves drunk and their brothers or sons picked them up and took them into their houses without a whisper as was expected.

There was good food to eat, roasted lamb, and thick porridge of meat and lentils, and tears shed, and we little ones played out in the fields late, running and screaming and hooting and jumping, in the darkness, because nobody cared. I ran as far up into the forest as I dared to go and then up the hill and looked at the stars, and danced the way I'd seen the men dance.

More things happened that year than I can possibly tell.

There was one wedding of the rich farmer's daughter, Alexandra, a beauty, everyone said, and what a bride she was in her gold-threaded veils. When the canopy and the torches came to her door, everyone sang at the sight of her.

People came from other villages to share that feast, and when the Pharisees gathered to wish everyone well, and would not eat, the mother of Alexandra the beauty went and bowed to the ground to Rabbi Sherebiah and told him the food had been slaughtered and prepared as was perfect and clean, and if he would not partake of her food for this wedding of her daughter, she herself would not eat or drink at this wedding though it was her only daughter.

Rabbi Sherebiah called for his servant to bring him the water to wash his hands, as Pharisees always did that, washed their fingers right before they ate, even though they were clean, and then he ate from the banquet, holding up the morsel for all to see, and everyone cheered, and all the Pharisees did as he did, even Rabbi Jacimus, though Pharisees almost never dined with anyone but each other.

Then Rabbi Sherebiah danced in spite of his wooden leg, and all the men danced.

Our beloved Rabbi Berekhaiah came forward and danced a slow and wondrous dance that delighted all of us little ones who were his pupils. Moreover, after that his father-in-law, not to be outdone, had to dance, as did every old man in the village.

The mother of Alexandra went off to sit with the bride and the women and they were drinking happily that the Pharisees had come to the banquet.

Work went on.

Buildings went up in Sepphoris as if they were plants growing wild in a marsh. The burnt places were healed the way bruises are healed. The marketplace grew larger all the time, with more and more merchants there to sell to those furnishing their new houses. And there were laborers aplenty for us to hire for our work. And everyone called us the Egyptian Gang.

No one complained of our prices, and as Alphaeus and Simon directed the building of foundations and floors and new walls, Cleopas and Joseph were making the pretty banquet tables, and bookshelves, and Roman chairs we'd made in Alexandria.

I did learn to paint borders more cleverly than before. And even to paint some of the flowers and leaves, though pretty much I filled in what the skilled painters had outlined for us.

When we did stonework, it was of the richest kind, when matching the marble pavers took patience, and the plan took careful layout. We went to the village of Cana to do a floor there for a man who had come back from the Greek islands and wanted his library to be beautiful.

People came to hire us from other places as well. A merchant from Capernaum asked us to come there, and I really did want us to go because we would be near the Sea of Galilee if we went, but Joseph said those journeys were yet to come when the building stopped in Sepphoris.

And we took a lot of jobs home with us to Nazareth to be finished, especially the job of making couches or inlaid tables, and we learned of the best silversmiths and enamelers in Sepphoris and went to them for their finishing of the pieces.

If there was any bad thing, other than the talk of the soldiers chasing the rebels in Judea—which did go on without cease—it was that Little Salome and I couldn't be together much anymore at all.

She was busy all the time now with the women, much more so than she'd been in Alexandria, and it seemed to me that for all the work we had, and the money coming into our purses, that the women had a harder lot.

Food they had bought aplenty in Alexandria, but here they grew the vegetables, and had to pick them from the garden; and whereas one could always buy hot bread in Alexandria in the bakers' street, they baked all their bread here, after grinding the wheat themselves very early every morning.

Whenever I tried to talk to Little Salome, she put me off, and more and more she used the same voice to me that the women used to the children. She had grown up overnight, and was always tending to a baby. It was either Baby Esther who was beginning to keep quiet now and then for the first time, or the baby of some woman who had come to visit Old Sarah. This was no more the child who had whispered and laughed with me in Alexandria, or even the little girl who cried on the trip north from Jerusalem. She went to school with us now and then—there were a few young girls in the school who sat apart from the boys—but she was impatient with it, and wanted to get home to work, she said. Cleopas told her she had to learn to read and write Hebrew, but she didn't care for it.

I missed her.

Now what the women liked to do, however, was weaving, and when they set up their looms in the courtyard in the warm months, it caused talk from one end of Nazareth to the other.

It seemed that the women of this place used a loom with one pole to it, and one crosspiece at which they had to stand. But we had brought back from Alexandria bigger looms, with two sliding crosspieces, at which the woman could sit, and the women of the village all came to see this.

A woman could sit at this loom, as I said, which indeed, my mother did, and a woman could go much faster with her work, as my mother did, and make cloth to be sold in the marketplace, which my mother did—when she had time, that is, from Little Symeon and Little Judas with the help of Little Salome.

But my mother loved weaving. Her days of weaving the temple veils with the eighty-four young girls chosen for this, housed in Jerusalem, had given her great speed and skill, and she turned out cloth that was of the quality of the best in the marketplace, and she knew how to dye cloth as well, even to work in purple.

Now it was explained to us that those girls had been chosen to make the Temple veils because all things for the Temple had to be made by those in a state of purity. And only girls beneath the age of twelve were certain to be pure, and those chosen had a tradition, and my mother's family was part of it. But my mother didn't talk much of those days in Jerusalem. Only to say the veil had been very big and very elaborate, and two a year had to be made.

It was this veil that covered the entrance to the Holy of Holies: the place where the Lord himself was present.

No woman ever went to the Holy of Holies: only the High Priest. And so my mother had loved her work on the veil, and that the work of her hands had gone there.

Many women of the village came to talk to my mother and watch her with this loom. It was different after she began weaving in the open courtyard. She had more friends. Our kindred who had not come to talk were now coming often.

And ever after that summer they would call on her, and some of the young girls who did not have little ones underfoot would come to hold the babies on their knees. This was good for my mother because she was fearful.

In a village like Nazareth, all the women know everything. How cannot really be explained. But that is the way it is, and the way it was. And she almost surely knew of the hard questions put to Joseph when I was taken into the school. And it hurt her.

I knew this because I knew every little move of her face,

of her eyes and her lips, and I could see it. I could see her fearfulness of other women.

Of men, she had no fear, because no good man was going to look at her or talk to her or in any way disturb her. That was the way of the village. A man did not talk to a married woman unless he was her very near kin and even then, he never sought her out alone, unless he was her brother. So she had no real fear of men. But of women? She had been afraid, until the days of the loom, and the women coming to learn from her.

All this about my mother's fearfulness I hadn't really put together in my mind until it changed. My mother's fearfulness was her manner. But now as it changed, I was happy.

And another thought came to me, a secret thought, one of the many I couldn't tell anyone: my mother was innocent. She had to be. If she wasn't innocent, then she would have been afraid of men, wouldn't she? But she had no fear of men. No, and no fear of going to the stream for water, and no fear of going into Sepphoris now and then to sell the linen she had woven. Her eyes were more innocent than those of Little Salome. Yes, a secret thought.

Old Sarah was far too old to do any fancy work with a needle, or anything with a needle for that matter, or a loom, but she taught the young girls how to make embroidery, and they gathered around her often, talking and laughing and telling stories with my mother very nearby.

Now with all the hammering and polishing and fitting and sewing and weaving, the courtyard was a busy place. Add to that children screaming and crying and laughing, babies crawling on the stones, and the open stable where the men tended to the donkeys who carried our loads to Sepphoris, and the older boys going in and going out with loads of hay, and a pair of us rubbing the gold into a new banquet couch, one of eight for the same man, and the cooking over the fire in the brazier, and then the mats spread out on the stones for us to eat, and all of us gathered in prayer, trying to make the little ones be quiet for just a little while as we thanked the Lord for all our blessings; add all this, and you have a picture of our lives that first year in Nazareth which engraved itself upon my mind and which stayed with me over all the many years I was to live there.

"Hidden," Joseph had said. I was "hidden." And from what he wouldn't say. And I couldn't ask. But I was happily hidden. And when I thought of that, and of Cleopas' strange words to me, that someday I must answer the questions, I felt like I was someone else. I'd feel my skin all over and then I'd stop thinking about it.

My schooling went very well.

I learnt new words, words I'd always heard and said, but I came to know what they meant, and they were from the Psalms mostly. *Let the fields be joyful, yes, joyful, and all the trees of the wood rejoice. Make a joyful song to the Lord; sing praise.*

The darkness was gone; death was gone; fire was gone. And though people did talk of the boys who had run off to fight with the rebellion, and there was now and then a woman howling in her sorrow when she had news of her lost son, our life was full of sweet things.

In the long late light, I ran through groves of trees up and down the slopes until I couldn't see Nazareth. I found flowers so sweet that I wanted to pick them and make them grow at home. And at home, there was the sweetness of the wood shavings, and the nice smell of the oil that we rubbed into the wood. There was the smell of baking bread always, and we knew when the best sauce was there for dinner as soon as we came home.

We had good wine from the market of Sepphoris. We had delicious melons and cucumbers from our own soil.

In the synagogue, we clapped our hands and danced and sang as we learned our Scripture. It was a little harder in school, with the teachers making us write out our letters on our wax tablets, and making us repeat what we didn't do well. But even this was good and the time went fast.

Soon the men were harvesting the olives, batting the branches of the groves with their long sticks and gathering the berries. The olive press was busy, and I liked to pass there when I could and see the men at work, and the sweet-smelling oil pouring out.

The women of our house crushed olives in a small press for the purest oil at home.

The grapes in our gardens were ready for picking, and the figs, we had had all the figs we could want to be dried, to be made into cakes, to be eaten as they were. The later figs were so many from our courtyard and the garden that some were taken to the village market at the bottom of the hill.

The grapes we didn't eat were put out to dry as raisins; no wine was made from them as the land around Nazareth had no vineyards, but was for wheat and barley and sheep and the forests I loved.

As the air grew cooler, the early rains came with great force. Thunder roared over the rooftop, and everyone offered prayers of thanks. The cisterns of the house filled, and the freshwater poured into the mikvah.

In the synagogue, Rabbi Jacimus, who was our strictest Pharisee, told us that now the water from the gutters flowing into the mikvah was "living water," and that when we purified ourselves in "living water," this is what the Lord wanted of us. We must pray that the rains were enough not only for the fields and for the streams but to keep our cisterns full and our mikvah living as well.

Rabbi Sherebiah didn't completely agree with Rabbi Jacimus and they began to quote the sages on these points and to "dispute" in general, and finally the Old Rabbi called for us to offer our prayers of thanksgiving that the Windows of Heaven had been opened, and the fields would soon be ready for the planting to begin.

At night, over supper, as the rain came down on the roof high above, we talked about Rabbi Jacimus and this matter of "living water." It was troubling to James and to me too.

We'd come to Nazareth after the rains. And the mikvah was empty when we came. We'd replastered it, and then filled it from the cistern in which the water had been resting a long time. But this was rainwater, was it not? Had it been living water when we filled the mikvah?

"Wasn't this living water?" I asked.

"If it's not living water," said James, "then we were unclean after the mikvah."

"We bathe often in the stream, don't we?" Cleopas asked. "And as for the mikvah, it has a tiny hole in the very bottom, so the water continues to move always. And when the rain filled the cistern, it was living water. It's living water. So be it."

"But Rabbi Jacimus says that's not good enough," said James. "Why does he say this?"

"It is good enough," said Joseph, "but he's a Pharisee and Pharisees are careful. You have to understand: they think that if they take great care with each part of life, they'll be safer from transgressing the Law."

"But they can't say that our mikvah is not pure," said my uncle Alphaeus. "The women use the mikvah—."

"Look," said Joseph. "See two paths on a mountain ridge. One is close to the edge, the other is farther away. The one farther away is safer. That is the path of the Pharisee—to be farther from the edge of the cliff, farther from falling off the cliff and into sin, and so Rabbi Jacimus believes in his customs."

"But they aren't Laws," said my uncle Alphaeus. "Pharisees say all these things are Laws."

"The Rabbi Sherebiah said that it was the Law," said James timidly. "That Moses was given Laws that weren't written down, and these were passed down through the sages."

Joseph shrugged. "We do the best we can do. And now the rains have come. And the mikvah? It's full of freshwater!"

He threw up his hands as he said this and he smiled, and we all laughed at it, but we weren't laughing at the Rabbi. We were laughing as we always laughed at things we talked about for which there seemed no one answer.

Rabbi Jacimus was hard in his ways, but he was a gentle man, a wise man, and he told wonderful stories. Stories were our history, and who we were, and there were times when I liked nothing better than stories.

Yet I was coming to understand something of the greatest importance: all stories were part of one great story, the story of who we were. I hadn't seen it so clearly before, but now it was so clear that it thrilled me.

Often in the school and sometimes in the synagogue, Rabbi Berekhaiah stood up, though he was shaking on his bent legs and he raised his arms and with his head bent and his eyes cast upward he would cry out: "But who are we, children, tell me?"

And then we would sing it out after him:

We are the people of Abraham and Isaac. We went down into Egypt in the time of Joseph. We became slaves there. Egypt became the smelting forge and we suffered. But the Lord had redeemed us, the Lord raised up Moses to lead us, and the Lord brought us forth parting the waters of the Sea of Reeds, and into the Promised Land.

The Lord gave the Law to Moses on Sinai. And we are a holy people, a people of priests, a people of the Law. We are a people of great Kings—Saul, and David, and Solomon, and Josiah.

But Israel sinned in the eyes of the Lord. And the Lord sent Nebuchadrezzar of Babylon to lay waste to Jerusalem, even to the House of the Lord.

Yet Our Lord is a Lord slow to anger, and steadfast in his love, and full of mercy, and he sent a redeemer to end our captivity in Babylon, yea, this was Cyrus the Persian, and we returned to the Promised Land and rebuilt the Temple. Turn and look towards the Temple, for there every day the High Priest offers a sacrifice for the people of Israel to the Lord on High. All over the world there are Jews, a holy people, faithful to the Law and to the Lord, who look towards the Temple, and know no other gods but the Lord.

Hear, O Israel, the Lord our God is One.

And you will love the Lord your God with all your heart and all your soul, and with all your strength.

And these words, that I command you this day, will be in your heart:

And you will teach them diligently to your children, and you will talk of them when you sit in your houses, and you walk by the roads and when you lie down and when you get up.

We did not have to be at the Temple to keep the sacred Feasts. Jews all over the world kept the sacred Feasts.

It was not safe yet to travel to the Temple. But the news

came to us that the fighting had stopped in Jerusalem, and that the Temple had been purified. The fire signals coming from Jerusalem told us all was well.

And we went out at dawn before the Day of Atonement to watch for the first light because we knew that the High Priest was rising with that first light to begin his ceremonies in the Temple, his bathing which he would do again and again that day.

We hoped and prayed there would be no rebellion, no trouble.

Because on this day the High Priest would seek to atone for all the sins of the people of Israel. He would put on his finest vestments. The Rabbi Jacimus, the anointed priest himself, had described to us these holy garments, and we had learned how they were to be from the Scripture:

The long tunic of the High Priest was blue, and tied with a sash at the waist, and its hem was trimmed with tassels and small golden bells. One could hear these bells when the High Priest walked. Over this tunic the High Priest wore a second garment called the ephod which had much fine gold and fancy work on it, and a breastplate of twelve shining gems, one each for the tribes of Israel, so that when the High Priest went in before the Lord, he would have there the Twelve Tribes. And on the head of the High Priest was a great turban with a golden crown. It was a "glorious thing to behold."

But before the High Priest put on these beautiful vestments, these vestments as fine as those of any pagan priest in any Temple anywhere, he would dress in simple linen, pure and white, to perform the sacrifices.

On this day, the High Priest laid hands upon the bullock to be sacrificed for Israel. And he would lay hands upon the two goats.

Now one of these goats would be sacrificed, but the

other, the other would carry all the sins of the people of Israel out into the wilderness. It was the goat for Azazel.

And what was Azazel? We little boys wanted to know. But we already knew. Azazel was evil; it was the demons; it was the world "out there," without the Law, in the wilderness. And everyone knew what the word "wilderness" meant because all the people of Israel had once roamed through the wilderness before they entered the Promised Land. And the goat would carry the sins back to Azazel to show that the sins of Israel had been forgiven by the Lord, and evil could take back what was evil as we would have no more of it.

But the most important thing which the High Priest did was to enter the Holy of Holies of the Temple, the place where the Lord Himself was Present; the place where only the High Priest could go.

And all Israel prayed that the power of the Lord there would not break out upon the High Priest, but that his prayers of atonement would be heard for himself and for all of us, and that he would come out to the people having been in the Presence of the Lord.

In the late afternoon, we gathered in the synagogue where the Rabbi read the scroll that the High Priest was reading in the Court of the Women: "And on the tenth day of the seventh month there shall be a day of atonement . . . *and you shall afflict your souls.*"

The Rabbi told us what the High Priest was telling the crowd in the Temple Court: "More than what I've read out before you is written here."

At last darkness came. We stood on the rooftop barefoot waiting. Those on the highest places cried out. They could see the fire signals from the nearest villages south, and now they lighted the fires to spread the word north and east and west:

Everyone was shouting with joy. We were dancing. Our fast was ended. The wine was being poured. The food was put on lighted coals.

In a cleansed and renewed Temple, the High Priest had completed his task. He had come out of the Holy of Holies safely. His prayers for Israel had been complete. His sacrifices complete. His readings complete. And he was gone now as we were to a banquet among his kindred in his home.

The early rains had been good. The planting had started.

And hard on the Day of Atonement came the Feast of Booths where all Israel had to live for seven days in booths built of tree branches to remember the journey from Egypt into Canaan, and for the children this was special fun.

We gathered the finest branches we could from the forest, especially the willow branches from along the stream, and we lived in these booths, all of us, men, women, children as if they were our houses, and we sang the happy Psalms.

Finally, news came that Herod Archelaus and Herod Antipas had arrived home, along with all those who had gone to Caesar Augustus. We gathered in the synagogue to hear the announcement from a young priest who had just returned from Jerusalem and was charged with giving the word. He spoke Greek very well.

Herod Antipas, a son of the dreaded Herod the Great, was to be the ruler of Galilee and Perea. And Herod Archelaus whom everyone still hated very much would be the Ethnarch of Judea, and other children of Herod ruled other places beyond. One princess of Herod was given the palace of the Greek city of Ascalon. I thought that was a pretty name.

When I asked Joseph about the pretty city of Ascalon later, he told me there were Greek cities all through Israel and Perea, and even in Galilee—cities with temples to idols of marble and gold. There were ten Greek cities around the Sea of Galilee and they were called the Decapolis.

I was surprised to hear it. I had become so used to Sepphoris with its Jewish ways. I knew that Samaria was Samaria, yes, and we had no doings with Samaritans though they were very close to our borders. But I hadn't thought there were pagan cities in the land. Ascalon. I thought it beautiful. I formed a picture in my mind of Princess Salome, the daughter of Herod, wandering around her palace in Ascalon. What was a palace to me? I knew what a palace was, as surely as I knew what a pagan temple was.

"It's the way of the Empire," said my uncle Cleopas. "Don't be distressed over it, that we have all these Gentiles among us. Herod, King of the Jews," he said in a mean tone of voice, "built plenty of temples to the Emperor and to those pagan gods. That's our King of the Jews for you."

Joseph put his hand up for Cleopas to be quiet. "In this house we are in the Land of Israel," he said.

Everybody laughed.

"Yes," said Alphaeus, "and outside that door, it's the Empire."

We didn't know whether or not we could laugh at that, but Cleopas nodded to it.

"But where does Israel stop and start?" asked James, who sat with us.

"Here!" said Joseph, "and there!" He pointed. "And anywhere that there are Jews gathered together who keep to the Law."

"Will we ever see those Greek cities?" I asked.

"You saw Alexandria, you saw the best of them, the greatest," said Cleopas. "You saw a city second only to Rome."

We had to nod to that.

"And remember her and remember all of this," said

Cleopas. "Because in each of us, you must realize, is the full story of who we are. We were in Egypt, as were our people long ago, and as they did, we came home. We saw battle in the Temple, as our people did under Babylon, but the Temple is now restored. We suffered on our journey here, as our people suffered in the wilderness and under the scourge of the enemies, but we came home."

My mother looked up from her sewing.

"Ah, so that's why it happened this way," she said, like a child would say it. She shrugged her shoulder and shook her head, and went on picking at the embroidery. "Before I couldn't understand it—."

"What?" asked Cleopas.

"Well, why an angel would come to Joseph and tell him to come home through all the bloodshed and the terrors, but you just made sense of it, didn't you?"

She looked to Joseph.

He was smiling, but I think he was smiling because he hadn't thought of this before. And she had the bright eyes of a child, the trust of a child, my mother.

"Yes," he said. "Now it does seem that way. It was our journey through the wilderness."

My uncle Simon had been asleep on his mat, his head on his elbow, but he rose up now and said in a sleepy voice, "I think Jews can make sense of anything."

Silas laughed hard at that.

"No," said my mother, "it's true. It's a matter of seeing it. I remember, in Bethlehem, when I was asking the Lord, 'How, how . . . ?' and then—."

She looked at me, and ran her hand over my hair as she often did. I liked it as always, but I didn't cuddle close to her. I was too big for that.

"What happened in Bethlehem?" I asked. I blushed. I'd forgotten Joseph's order to me not to ask. I felt a sharp pain all through me. "I'm sorry that I said it," I whispered.

My mother looked at me, and I could see she knew that I was feeling bad. She looked at Joseph and then at me.

No one said a word.

My brother James had a hard look on his face as he stared at me.

"You were born there, you know that," said my mother, "in Bethlehem. The town was crowded." She spoke haltingly, looking at Joseph and then at me as she went on. "It was full of people that night, Bethlehem, and we couldn't find a place to stay—it was Cleopas and Joseph and James and I, and— the innkeeper put us in the stable. It was in the cave beside the place. It was good to be in there, because it was warm, and God had sent a snow."

"A snow!" I said. "I want to see snow."

"Well, maybe someday you will, " she said.

No one said a word. I looked at her. She wanted to go on. I knew she did. And she knew how much I wanted her to go on.

She started to talk again.

"You were born there in the stable," she said calmly. "And I wrapped you up and put you in the manger."

Everyone laughed the usual gentle family laugh.

"In the manger? The hay for the donkeys?" This was the secret of Bethlehem?

"Yes," said my mother, "and there you lay, probably in a softer bed than any newborn in Bethlehem that night. And the beasts kept us very warm, while the tenants froze in the rooms above."

Again, the family laughter.

The memory made them all happy, except for James. James looked almost dark. His thoughts were far away. He'd been by my reckoning maybe seven years old when this took place, the age I was now. How could I know what he thought?

He looked at me. Our eyes met, and something passed between us. He looked away.

I wanted my mother to tell me more.

But they had begun to talk of other things—of the good early rains, of the reports of peace coming from Judea, of the hope that we might go up to Jerusalem for the coming Passover if things continued to go well.

I got up and went out.

It was dark and chilly but it felt good after the close warmth of the house.

That couldn't be the whole story of Bethlehem! That couldn't be all that happened. My mind could not put all the pieces together, the questions, the moments and words spoken, and doubts.

I remembered my terrible dream. I remembered the winged man, and the mean things that he said. In the dream, they hadn't hurt me. But now they stung me.

Oh, if only I could talk to someone, but there was no one, no one to whom I could tell what was in my heart, and there never would be!

I heard steps behind me, soft, dragging steps, and then I felt a hand on my shoulder. I heard a breathing that I knew was from Old Sarah.

"You come inside, Jesus bar Joseph," she said, "it's too cold out here for you to be standing and looking at the stars."

I turned around and did what she said because she told me to, but I didn't want to. I went with her inside the house. And back to the warm gathering of the family and this time

I lay down like my uncles with my head on my arm and looked at the low brazier with its burning coals.

The little ones started fussing. My mother got up to tend to them, and then called for Joseph to help.

My uncles went off to bed in their rooms. Aunt Esther was in the other part of the house, with Baby Esther, who was howling as always.

Only Old Sarah sat on her bench because she was too old to sit on the floor, and James was there, and James was looking at me, and the fire was in both his eyes.

"What is it?" I asked him. "What's this thing you want to say?" I asked. But I said it low.

"What was that?" asked Old Sarah. She stood up. "Was that Old Justus?" she asked. She went off into the other room. It wasn't anything really bad. It was only Old Justus coughing because his throat was so weak that he couldn't swallow.

James and I were alone.

"Say it to me," I said.

"Men said they saw things," James said. "When you were born, they saw things."

"What?"

He looked away. He was angry, and hard.

At age twelve, a boy can take on the yoke of the Law. He was past that now.

"Men claimed to see things," he said. "But I can tell you what I saw, myself, with my eyes."

I waited.

His eyes came back to me, and his look was sharp.

"These men came. To the house in Bethlehem. We'd been in Bethlehem for a while. We'd found good lodgings. My father was tending to his affairs, finding our kindred, all of that. And then in the night, these men came. They were wise men, from the East, maybe from Persia. They were the men who read the stars and believe in magic, and advise the Kings of Persia as to what they should do and not do on account of the signs. They had servants with them. They were rich men, beautifully robed. They came asking to see you. They knelt in front of you. They brought gifts. They called you a King."

I was too surprised to speak.

"They said they had seen this great star in the Heavens," he said, "and they had followed that star to the house where we were. You were in a crib. And they laid their gifts before you."

I didn't dare to ask him anything.

"Everyone in Bethlehem saw those magi come, and their servants with them. They rode camels, those men. They spoke with authority. They bowed before you. And then they went away. It was the end of their journey, and they were satisfied."

I knew he was telling me the truth. No lie would ever pass the lips of my brother James.

And I knew that he knew I had caused that boy in Egypt to die, and that I'd brought him back to life. And he'd seen me bring clay sparrows to life, a thing I hardly remembered.

A King. *Son of David, Son of David, Son of David.*

The women were coming in now. And my older cousins had wandered in from where I didn't know.

My aunt Salome picked up the last of the bread and scraps from supper.

Old Sarah had taken her place on the bench.

"Pray that child sleeps till morning," said Old Sarah.

"Don't fret," said Aunt Salome. "Riba sleeps with one eye open for all of them."

"A blessing," said my mother, "that sweet girl."

"Poor Bruria would not be alive if it were not for that girl. That girl tends to her as if she were a child. Poor Bruria . . ."

"Poor Bruria . . ."

And so on it went.

My mother told me to go to bed.

The next day James wouldn't look at me. It was not a surprise. He hardly ever looked at me. And as the days passed, he never did.

The winter months grew colder and colder.

When it came time for the Feast of Lights, we had many lamps burning in our house, and from the rooftops one could see big fires from all the villages, and in our streets, the men danced with torches just as they would have if they had gone to Jerusalem.

On the morning at the end of the eighth day, as the Feast was ending, and I was sleeping, I heard shouts from outside. Soon everyone in the room was up and running.

Before I could ask what it was, I went with them.

The early morning light was perfectly gray. And the Lord had sent a snow!

All of Nazareth was beautifully covered with it, and it came down in big flakes, and the children ran out to gather the flakes as if they were leaves, but the flakes melted away.

Joseph looked at me with a secret smile, as everyone else went out into the silent snowfall.

"You prayed for a snow?" he asked. "Well, you have a snow."

"No!" I said. "I didn't do it. Did I?"

"Be careful what you pray for!" he whispered. "You understand?" His smile grew bigger, and he led me out to feel the snowflakes for myself. His laughter and happiness made me feel all right.

But James, who stood by himself, under the roof that jut-ted out over the courtyard stones, stared at me; and when Joseph went off, he crept up, and whispered in my ear:

"Why don't you pray for gold to drop from Heaven!"

I felt my face on fire.

But he was gone with the others. And we were almost never, never alone.

Later that day—the eight days of the Feast of Lights had ended at dawn—I sought out the grove of trees, the only place in the whole creation where I could be alone. The snow was thick. I wore heavy wool around my feet with thick san-dals, but the wool was wet by the time I got there and I was very cold. I couldn't stay long under the trees, but I stood there, thinking to myself and looking at the wonder of the snow covering the fields and making them look so very beau-tiful like a woman dressed in her finest robes.

How fresh, how clean it all looked.

I prayed. Father in Heaven, tell me what you want of me. Tell me what all these things mean? *Everything has a story to it.* And what is the story of all this?

I closed my eyes, and when I opened them, I saw the heavens had given us more snow, and it was making a veil over Nazareth. Slowly as I watched, the village disappeared. Yet I knew it was there.

"Father in Heaven, I won't pray for snow, Father in Heaven, I will never pray for what is not your will. Father in Heaven, I won't pray for this one to live or that one to die, oh, no, never for that one to die, and never, never will I try even to make it rain or stop rain, or to make it snow, never until I understand what it means, all of it. . . ." And there my prayer ran out into flashing memories, and the snow caught my eyes as I looked up into the trees and the snow came down softly on me as if it were kissing me.

I was hidden in the snow, I was hidden and safe, even from myself.

Far away someone called my name.

I woke from my prayer, I woke from the stillness, and the softness of the snow, and I ran down the hill, waving, and calling, and heading for the warm firelight and the family all around it.

22

My first year in the Promised Land came to an end as it had commenced: with the opening of the New Year for Israel.

Herod Archelaus and the Roman soldiers from Syria had made peace in Judea—at least enough peace—for us to pass through the land of Herod Archelaus, through the Jordan Valley, and up into the hill country to Jerusalem for the Feast of Passover.

To myself I was an older child since that sorrowful and frightening journey on the very same path to Nazareth. I knew many new words to think in my head about what I'd seen. And I loved it when we were in the open country. I loved the smiling and the laughter. And I loved the bathing in the Jordan River again.

Many other villagers had joined the men of our family, many wives had come along, and a great flock of young maidens under the eye of fathers and mothers, and all of my new friends from the village, most of them my kindred, and some not.

The little rains had been good this year, everyone said, and for a long time the land was green.

Old Sarah made the journey with us and she rode the

back of the donkey, and it was good to have her. We crowded around her. My mother came also, but Aunt Esther and Aunt Salome stayed behind to tend to the little ones and Little Salome remained with them.

Bruria, our refugee, came with us, and so did the Greek slave girl Riba, with her newborn in a sling, tending to everyone.

Now I should say one reason that Joseph brought Bruria was in the hope that when we passed the site of her farm Bruria would want to reclaim it. Bruria had many of her papers, which had been recovered from the burnt place, and surely, said Joseph, there were people there who knew it was her property.

But Bruria had no desire to do this. She wanted nothing. She worked as a woman in sleep, helping but wanting nothing for herself. And Joseph told us apart from her that we must never judge her or be unkind to her. If she wanted to remain with us forever, she could. We had all been strangers once in the Land of Egypt.

No one minded at all, and my mother said so. Riba was a joy to the women, said my aunt Salome. She was modest as a Jewish woman, and clean and helpful, and did as we all did in everything.

We had come to love Riba and Bruria. And when Bruria passed the site of her old farm and did not care, we were sad for her. That was her land and she ought to have it.

Now with us too on the road came the Pharisees, all in a group with their beasts for the women and the old men to ride, and their household. And there were other households from Nazareth as well, and from many other villages who joined the procession.

Our kindred from Capernaum, the fishermen and their wives and sons met us too—these were Zebedee, the beloved cousin of my mother and his wife, Mary Alexandra who was my mother's cousin, too, and both distantly cousins of Joseph, and many others, some of whom I remembered, some not.

Soon there was no end of people on the road, talking and singing the Psalms as we'd done that first day in Jerusalem so long ago. We sang those sweetest Psalms called the Psalms of Praise.

When we started to climb up from the Jordan towards the Holy City, through the steep mountains, I felt the old fear. I wanted my mother and I didn't want anyone to know it. It had been a long time since I'd had the bad dreams, but they came back. I slept close to Old Sarah when I could, and if I woke up crying, her voice would make the dream go away. I knew that James woke up at these times, and I didn't want for him to know this. I wanted to be strong, and with the men now.

It was not a hard journey; it was good to see the villages being rebuilt which had suffered fire; the city of Jericho was being rebuilt and all around it the beautiful date palms and the great forests of balsam were doing well.

Now the balsam was a tree that grew nowhere else in the world but here, and its perfume sold for a great deal, and the Romans were a big market for it.

The sun was shining on all this when I saw it this time, and before Jericho had been a city of the night in flames and made me cry in terror. Of course we had to see the foundations of the new palace and how the carpenters were proceeding. My uncles inspected everything from the piles of masonry on the site to the framing and the clearing of the land for the new rooms that would be built for Archelaus.

Now right after Jericho we came to the village where we'd left our cousin Elizabeth and Little John.

My mother was troubled as we approached, and so were Zebedee and his wife. It had been a long time since anyone had received a letter from Elizabeth.

When we arrived, we found the little house where we'd stayed shuttered and vacant. I thought my mother was going to suffer a terrible blow, and it did come but not as bad as I had feared.

Distant kindred there soon came to tell us that Elizabeth, wife of Zechariah the priest, had suffered a fall only a month before, and she'd been taken up to Bethany near Jerusalem. She could no longer speak, they told us, or move very much, and Little John had gone on to live with the Essenes in the desert. Several of the Essenes had come to take him out with them to a place near the edge of the mountains just above the Dead Sea.

Finally we had come up through the long winding mountain passes, to the Mount of Olives, from which we could see, over the Kidron Valley, the Holy City lying before us. There rose the white walls of the Temple, with its great trimmings of gold, and all the little houses spilling up and down the hills around it.

Everyone cried for joy and gave thanks at the sight of it. But the fear got a grip on me, and I didn't tell anyone. Joseph lifted me up but I was too big now to be on his shoulders. Some of the children were trying to squeeze to the front of the crowd. I didn't want to go.

Fear rose in me like a sickness in my throat, from which I couldn't escape. It didn't matter that there was the sun in the sky. I didn't see it. I didn't see anything but darkness. I think Old Sarah knew because she drew me close to her. I loved the smell of her wool robe, and the soft touch of her hand.

After the prayers were offered, people began to point out

where the colonnades had been burned, and where there was rebuilding. There was much pointing and trying to determine things.

"And you can be sure the carpenters and the stonemasons are happy," said my uncle Cleopas bitterly. "They burn it, we rebuild it." We laughed at the truth of that, but James gave Cleopas a sharp look as though he didn't want him to say this. My uncle Alphaeus spoke up, "Well, the carpenters and the stonemasons of Jerusalem are always happy. They've been working on the Temple since they were born, most of them!"

"They'll never finish," said Cleopas. "And why should they? We have kings with blood on their hands and in their guilt they build the great Temple as if this will make them righteous in the eyes of the Lord. Well, let them do it. Let them offer their sacrifices, the Prophets have spoken on their sacrifices—."

"That's enough talk against them," said Alphaeus. "We're going down into the city."

"And the Prophets have said it," Joseph added quietly with a smile.

Cleopas said under his breath the words of the Prophet, " 'Yea, I am the Lord and I do not change.' "

And more and more they talked of how this was the biggest Temple in all the world. But these things I heard through the fear I felt, remembering the bodies everywhere, and more than that a great terrible misery, a misery that said, you will know nothing but misery. This will never go away.

Again, I was lifted, this time by my uncle Alphaeus.

I looked at the Temple, fighting the fear, looking at its great size, and how the city appeared to grow up around it and hold on to it. The city was part of it. The city was nothing without it. There were no other temples in Jerusalem but the Temple. And the great glory of the Temple did seem beautiful—white and shining and full of gold—unspoilt—at least at this distance.

There were other big buildings, yes. Uncle Cleopas pointed out to me the great palace of Herod, and the fortress, the Antonio, which was right beside the Temple, and always full of soldiers. But these were nothing. The Temple *was* Jerusalem. I saw it. And the sunlight was shining, and the fear, the memories, the darkness, went away.

Now my mother wanted to go down into Bethany which was only a short distance from where we were, so that she could see to her cousin Elizabeth. But the kindred wanted to go down first into Jerusalem and find the place where we would stay. And so we went.

People were packed together, moving more and more tightly, and coming to stops when no one could move at all, and we all sang to keep up our spirits.

When at last we reached the city, it was very hard for us to get through the gates, the crowds were so thick, and all of us little ones were tired by that time. Some of the children were crying. Some had fallen asleep in their mothers' arms. I was far too old now, I thought, to ask anyone to carry me. And so I could not see where we were going or what we were doing.

Before we were very far inside the city, word reached us that all the synagogues were full, and that the houses had taken in all of the pilgrims that they could take, and Joseph decided we would go back out to Bethany where we had kindred near whom we could camp.

We had thought to come before so many people. We had hoped to have the rites of purification in the Temple, the same rite which we'd had in the village, yes, with the ashes and the living water, and the two sprinklings, but we had wanted it again in the Temple.

Now it was clear to us that too many other people had come for the same reasons, and the Feast had drawn all the world to it.

In such a crowd it was to be expected that people broke into arguments, and some even shouted at others, and when this happened, my teeth chattered. But as far as I could see, there was no fighting. High on the walls, the soldiers walked, and I tried not to look at them. My legs ached and I was hungry. But I knew it was the same for everyone else.

After the long struggle uphill away from the city and to the village, I was so tired I wanted to save all my joy and thanks for being near Jerusalem for tomorrow.

It was still daylight, but getting on towards dark. People were camped everywhere. And my mother and father took me by the hand and we went to see to Elizabeth right away.

It was a big house, a rich house, with fine pavers and painted walls, and rich curtains over the doors, and a young man received us who had a fine manner about him that marked him at once as rich. He was dressed completely in white linen and he wore fine tooled sandals. His black hair and his beard were shining with perfumed oil. He had a bright face, and he welcomed us with his arms out.

"This is your cousin Joseph," my mother said immediately. "Your cousin Joseph is a priest, and his father Caiaphas is a priest, and his father before him was a priest. Here is our son, Jesus." She laid her hand on my shoulder. "We come to find our cousin Elizabeth of Zechariah. We've been told she's not well, and is being kept here by your goodness and we're grateful for that."

"Elizabeth is my cousin, just as you are," said the young man in a soft voice. He had quick dark eyes, and he smiled at me in an open way that made me feel at ease. "You come into the house, please. I'd offer you a place to sleep here, but you see, we have people everywhere. The house is overflowing. . . ."

"Oh, no, we're not looking for that," Joseph said quickly to him, "only to see Elizabeth. And if we can camp outside. There, you see, there's quite a tribe of us from Nazareth and Capernaum and Cana."

"You're most welcome," he said. He beckoned for us to follow him. "You'll find Elizabeth peaceful but silent. I don't know whether or not she will know you. Don't hope for that."

I knew we were tracking the dust of the road through this house, but there was nothing to be done about it. There were pilgrims everywhere, on their blankets in every room, and people running here and there with jugs, and plenty of dust already. So all we could do was go on.

We came into a room that was as crowded as the others, but it had big latticed windows and the late sunlight was pouring in, and the air was nice and warm. Our cousin took us to a corner, where on a raised bed, propped on clean pillows, there lay Elizabeth, very wrapped up in white wool, with her eyes towards the window, and I think she was looking at the movement of the green leaves.

Out of respect, it seemed, people grew quiet, and our cousin bent down to her, and held her arm.

"Wife of Zechariah," he said gently, "there are kindred here to see you."

It was no good.

My mother bent low and kissed her and spoke to her, but there was no answer.

She lay still looking out the window. She looked far older than she had been last year. Her hands were tight and twisted at the wrists, so that they pointed sharply downward. She looked as old as our beloved Sarah. Like a withered flower ready to drop from the vine.

My mother turned to Joseph and cried against him, and our cousin Joseph shook his head, and said that everything was being done that could be done.

"She doesn't suffer, you see," he said. "She's dreaming."

My mother couldn't stop crying, so I went out with her while Joseph talked with our cousin who went over the ancestors and how they were connected, the familiar talk of the families and marriages, and my mother and I went out into the last of the afternoon light.

We found the uncles and Old Sarah gathered on the blankets, in a good campsite near the edge of the crowd of pilgrims, and not far from the well.

Several of the kindred from the house came out to us and offered us food and drink, and our cousin Joseph was with them. They were all in linen, all well spoken, and treated us kindly, more kindly maybe than they would have treated people like themselves.

The eldest of them, the father of Joseph, named Caiaphas, spoke to us and told us that we were near enough to Jerusalem that we could eat the Passover here. We must not worry that we weren't within the walls. What were the walls? We had come to Jerusalem and we were at Jerusalem and we would see the lights of the city as soon as it was dark.

The women came out and they offered us blankets, but we had our own.

Then Old Sarah and the uncles went in to see Elizabeth before it was too late. James went with them and came back.

When we were all gathered, and the rich cousins had gone down to Jerusalem for their duties in the Temple in the morning, Old Sarah said that she liked young Joseph bar Caiaphas, that he was a fine man.

"They're descendants of Zadok, and that's what matters," said Cleopas. "Not much else."

"Why are they rich?" I asked.

Everyone laughed.

"They're rich from the hides of the sacrifices which are theirs by right," said Joseph. He wasn't laughing. "And they come from rich families."

"Yes, and what else?" asked Cleopas.

"People never say good things of the rich," said Old Sarah.

"Do you have good things to say of them, old woman?" Cleopas asked.

"Ah, so I can speak in the assembly of the wise!" she answered. There was more laughter. "Yes, I have more to say. Who do you think would listen to them if they weren't rich?"

"There are plenty of poor priests," Cleopas said. "You know that as well as I do. The priests of our village are poor. Zechariah was poor."

"No, he was not poor," said Old Sarah. "He wasn't rich, no. But he was never poor. And yes, there are many who work with their hands, and they have to. And they go before the Lord, yes. But at the very top, those who protect the Temple? Who can do it but men whom other men fear?"

"Does it matter who they are?" asked Alphaeus, "as long as they perform their duties, as long as they don't defile the Sanctuary, as long as they take the sacrifices from our hands?"

"No, it doesn't matter," said Cleopas. "Old Herod chose Joazer as High Priest because that's who he wanted. And now Archelaus wants a different man. How long has it been since

Israel chose the High Priest? How long has it been since the Lord chose the High Priest?"

I raised my hand just as I would at school, and my uncle Cleopas turned to me.

"How do the people know," I asked, "that the priests do what the priests must do?"

"Everyone watches," said Joseph. "The other priests watch, the Levites watch, the scribes watch, the Pharisees watch."

"Oh, yes, the Pharisees watch!" said Cleopas.

And we did have a laugh at that. We loved our Pharisee Rabbi Jacimus. But he did watch all the rules.

"And you, James?" Cleopas asked. "You have no question?"

For the first time I saw that James was deep in his thoughts. He looked up and his face was dark.

"Old Herod murdered the High Priest once," he said in a low voice. He sounded like one of the men. "He murdered Aristobulos because he was beautiful when he went before the people, isn't that so?"

The men nodded, and Cleopas said, "That is so." He repeated the words. "He had him drowned on account of it, and everyone knew it. All because Aristobulos had gone before the people in his vestments and people had loved him."

James looked away.

"What kind of talk is this!" said Joseph. "We've come to the House of the Lord to offer sacrifice. We've come to be purified. We've come to eat the Passover. Let's put this talk out of our minds."

"Yes, let's put it away," said Old Sarah. "I say Joseph Caiaphas is a fine young man. And when he marries the daughter of Annas, he'll be closer to those in power."

My aunts, and Alexandra, agreed with this.

Cleopas was amazed.

"We haven't been here two hours and you women know who Joseph Caiaphas is going to marry! How do you find out these things!"

"Everyone knows this," said Salome. "If you weren't so busy quoting the Prophets, you'd know it too."

"Who knows?" asked Old Sarah. "Perhaps Joseph Caiaphas may be High Priest someday?"

I knew why she said it even though he was very young. He had a way about him, a way of moving and talking, an ease with everyone, a gentleness, and when he had greeted us he had cared about us, even though we were not rich, and behind his black eyes going on, there was a strong soul.

But now all my uncles and aunts were disputing on this, particularly the men, telling the women to be quiet, and they knew nothing about it, and some were insisting it hadn't happened yet, but all knew that Archelaus could change the High Priest any time he chose.

"Have you become a prophet, Sarah," asked Cleopas, "that you know this man will be High Priest?"

"Perhaps," she answered. "I know he'd be good as High Priest. He's clever and he's pious. He's our kindred. He . . . he touches my heart."

"Ah, well, give him time," said Cleopas. "And may our cousins who've received us here be blessed for their generosity."

Cleopas turned to Joseph, who was saying nothing.

"What do you think?" Cleopas asked Joseph. Joseph looked up, smiled, and rolled his eyes to make a playful show of thinking when he wasn't thinking, and then he said, "Joseph Caiaphas is a tall man. A very tall man. And he stands up tall, and he had long hands that move like birds flying slowly. And he's married to the daughter of Annas, our cousin, who is cousin to the House of Boethus. Yes, he'll be High Priest."

We all laughed. Even Old Sarah laughed.

I started to get up.

The fear was gone from me but I didn't know it then.

The full supper was ready and it was a good meal.

The House of Caiaphas brought us a thick porridge of lentils with lots of spice in it. And there was a paste of delicious salty olives in oil, and then sweet dates, which we seldom had at home, and lots of them. And as always there were cakes of dried figs but these were very rich and good. The bread was light and warm from the oven.

The wife of Caiaphas, the mother of Joseph Caiaphas, stood in the doorway of her house to see to the serving of the wine herself, her veils very proper, concealing all her hair, with only a little of her face peeping out. We could see her in the torchlight. She waved a greeting to everyone, and then went inside.

We talked of the Temple, our purification, and the Feast itself—the bitter herbs, the unleavened bread and the roast lamb, and all the prayers we would say. The men went over this so that we boys would understand, but the Rabbis in school had done the same, and we did know what to expect and what to do.

And we were eager for it because last year in the middle of the fighting and fear we'd not kept the Feast at all and we wanted to appear before the Lord this time as the Law required of us.

Now I must say that James was almost finished with school. He was thirteen years old now, and a man before the Lord. And Silas and Levi who were older than that didn't go to school anymore. They had both been very slow. The Rabbi didn't want them to leave but they begged off on account of work, which they wanted to do. So as we went over the rules of the Feast, I think they were glad of it.

As we were finishing our supper, some of the boys of the camps came up to meet with us. They were friendly enough. But I thought of my cousin John bar Zechariah who'd gone off with the Essenes. I wondered if he was content.

He was far away in the desert, they'd said, and how often I thought did he see his mother? Maybe she would have known her own son? But why think such things? Those old puzzling words came back, that he had been foretold. My mother had gone to them when she'd known I was to be born. I wanted so badly to see John. And when would I ever be able to do that?

Everybody knew the Essenes didn't come for the Feast. Essenes kept themselves apart in a life more strict even than Pharisees. Essenes dreamed of a renewed Temple. I'd seen a group of Essenes once in Sepphoris, all of them in their white garments. They were a people apart. They believed themselves to be the true Israel.

Finally I left the boys, even though I wanted to play, and I found Joseph. It was getting dark, and the city below was full of light. The lights of the Temple were great and beautiful. But I couldn't search the whole town and all the camps, and I couldn't even find my uncle Cleopas.

Joseph was looking at the city, and maybe he was listening to the music because there was music, and the beating of cymbals from somewhere close. He was sipping a bit of wine from a cup, and no one was near him for the moment.

I asked him right away,

"Will we ever see our cousin John again?"

"Who knows?" he asked. "The Essenes are beyond the Dead Sea, at the foot of the mountains."

"Do you believe they are good people?"

"They're Children of Abraham like the rest of us," he said. "A man could do worse than be an Essene." He waited a moment, then went on. "This is a way it is with Jews. You know that in our own village we have men who don't believe in the Resurrection on the Last Day. And we have Pharisees. And the Essenes, they believe in many things with their whole hearts, and they try very hard to please the Lord."

I nodded.

Now I knew that everyone in our village wanted to go to the Temple, and the keeping of every Feast in the right way was important to them. But I didn't say this. I didn't say it because there seemed truth in what he said, and I didn't have any more questions.

I was full of sadness. My mother loved her cousin so much. I could see them in my mind, the two women hugging each other when last we'd been together. And I had been so curious to talk to my cousin. There had been a seriousness in my cousin—that was the word, I found it at last—a seriousness, that drew me.

The other boys in the camp were very friendly, and the sons of the priests spoke well and said good things, but I didn't want to be with others.

I left Joseph. I was forbidden to ask him all the things that weighed down my heart. Forbidden.

I lay down on my mat, and wanted to sleep even though the sky was just filling with stars.

All around me the men were disputing, some of them saying the High Priest was not the right man, that Herod Archelaus had been wrong to put him in place, and others that the High Priest was acceptable, and we had to have peace, no more rebellion.

Their angry back-and-forth voices frightened me.

I got up, left my mat, to walk off alone, out of the camp,

and into the hillside under the stars. This was good to be away on the slope.

There were camps out there, too, but they were smaller—little gatherings covering the slopes and the fires giving off a little light while up above the moon shone very bright and beautiful over all, and I could see the stars broken and spread out in their fine patterns.

There was grass under my feet and it smelled sweet, and the air was not too cold now, and I was wondering if John saw these same stars tonight out in the desert.

James came up to me. He was crying.

"What's the matter with you?" I said. I sat up. I got to my feet. I took his hand.

I'd never seen my older brother like this.

"I have to tell you," he said, "I'm sorry. Sorry for the mean things I've said to you. Sorry for . . . being mean to you."

"Mean to me? James, what are you saying?" No one could hear us. It was dark. No one noticed us.

"I can't go into the Temple of the Lord tomorrow with this on my heart, that I've treated you so badly."

"But it's all right," I said. I put my hands out to hold him, but he drew back. "James, you never hurt me!"

"I had no right to tell you about the magi coming to Bethlehem."

"But I wanted you to," I said. "I wanted to know what happened when I was born. I want to know everything. James, if only you would tell me everything that happened—."

"I didn't do it because you wanted it. I did it to be strong over you!" he whispered. "I did it to know something that you didn't know!"

I knew this was the truth. It was the hard truth. It was just the kind of hard truth that James always said.

"But you told me what I wanted to know," I said. "It was good for me. I wanted it," I said.

He shook his head. He tears got worse. This was the sound of a man crying.

"James, you're sad about nothing. I'm telling you. I love you, my brother. Don't suffer for this."

"I have to tell you," he said in the same whisper, as if he needed to whisper. There was no one here but the two of us on the slope.

"I've hated you ever since you were born," he said. "I hated you before you were born. I hated you for coming!"

My face burned. I felt my skin all over.

I'd never heard anyone say something like this. It took me a moment and then I said:

"It doesn't hurt me."

He didn't answer.

"I didn't know," I said. "That's not right. I think I knew but I knew it would pass. I didn't think about it if I knew it."

"Listen to your own words," he said. He sounded so sad.

"What am I saying?"

"You're wiser than your years," he said, he who stood so tall at thirteen, a man. "You have a different face than you had when we left Egypt. You had a boy's face then, and your eyes were like your mother's eyes."

I knew what he meant. My mother always looked like a child. What I hadn't known was that I was any different.

I didn't know what to say to him.

"I'm sorry for hating you," he said. "Truly sorry. And I mean to love you and be loyal to you always."

I nodded. "I love you as well, my brother," I said.

Quiet.

He stood there wiping his tears.

"Will you let me put my arms around you?" I asked.

He nodded, and we held each other. And I hugged him tight and could feel him trembling. That was how bad he felt.

I drew back slowly. He didn't turn or go away.

"James," I said. "Why did you hate me?"

He shook his head. "Too many reasons," he said. "And I can't tell you all of it. Someday you'll learn."

"No, James, tell me now. I have to know. I'm begging you. Tell me."

He thought for a long time.

"I'm not the one to tell you the things that happened."

"But who is to tell me?" I asked. "James, tell me what made you hate me. Tell me that much. What was it?"

He looked at me and it seemed his face was full of hate. Or maybe it was just unhappiness. In the dark his eyes were burning.

"I'll tell you why I must love you," he said. "The angels came when you were born. That's why I have to love you!" He started to cry again.

"You mean the angel who came to my mother," I said.

"No." He shook his head. He smiled but it was a dark, bitter smile. "The angels came on the very night you were born. You know how it was, they told you. We were in the inn in Bethlehem, in the stable, with the beasts in the hay, all of us, it was the only place they had, and there were lots of people crowded in there that night. And your mother went through her pain in the back of the stable. She didn't cry at all. Aunt Salome was there to help her, and they lifted you up for my father to see, and I saw you. You were crying, but only as little babies cry because they can't talk. And they wrapped you up the way they wrap babies so they can't wriggle or move and hurt themselves, in swaddling clothes, and you were put in the manger, right on the soft hay there for a bed. And your mother lay in Aunt Salome's arms. And she began to cry for the first time, and it was terrible to hear her.

"My father went to her. She was all wrapped up and the rags from the birth had been taken away. He held her in his arms. 'Why here in this place?' she cried. 'Have we done some wrong? Are we being punished for it? Why here in this place? How can this be right?' That's what she asked him. And he had no answer.

"Don't you see? An angel had come to her and told of your birth, and here it had happened in a stable."

"I see," I said.

"It was terrible to hear her crying," he repeated, "and my father had nothing to say to her. But the door opened, and the cold air came in, a blast of it, and everybody huddled and groaned for the door to be shut. But these men were there, and a boy with them and a lantern. These were men in sheepskins with their feet wrapped against the winter, and their staffs, and anyone could see they were shepherds.

"Now you know shepherds never leave their flocks, not in the middle of the night, not in the snow, but there they were, and the looks on their faces were enough to make anyone get up from their beds in the hay and stare at them, and everyone did. I did.

"It was as if the fire from the lantern was burning in their faces! Never have I seen faces like their faces!

"They went right to the manger where you were lying and they looked down at you; and they knelt down, and they touched their heads to the ground with their hands up.

"They cried out: 'Glory to the Lord in the Highest; and peace on Earth, peace and goodwill to all!'

"Everyone was looking at them.

"Now your mother and my father said nothing but only looked at them; and the men climbed to their feet and they turned to the right and to the left telling everyone that an angel had come to them out in the field, in the snow where they'd been watching over their flocks. No one could have stopped them from their telling this, and now everyone lodged in the stable was gathered around.

"One of them cried out that the angel had said, 'Don't be afraid because I give you glad tidings of great joy; for today, to you, is born in the city of David a Savior: Christ the Lord!' "

He stopped.

His whole manner had changed.

He was no longer full of anger or tears.

His face had softened and his eyes were large.

"Christ the Lord," he said. He was not smiling. But he was back in Bethlehem, in that moment, and he was with the shepherds, and his voice was low and full of quiet.

"Christos Kyrios," he said in Greek. He and I had spoken Greek for most of my life. He went on in Greek. "They were so full of joy, those men. So elated. So full of conviction. No one could have doubted them. No one did." Then he went quiet. He seemed to drift into his memory altogether.

I was unable to speak.

So this is what they kept from me. Yes, and I knew why they kept it from me. But now I knew it, and it meant I had to know all the rest. I had to know what the angel had said who had come to my mother. I had to know all of it. I had to know why and how I had the power to take and give life, and the power to stop rain and bring snow, if I even had it, if, and what was I to do. I couldn't wait any longer. I had to know.

And it frightened me completely to think of what

Cleopas had said, that I must be the one to explain things to them.

It was too much to keep in my mind. It was too much even to frame the questions that remained unanswered.

And my James, my brother, it seemed he was becoming small and far away, even as he stood there—he was becoming a frail thing. I felt for a moment as if I wasn't part of this place, this grass, this slope, this mountainside above Jerusalem, the bits of music drifting towards us, the distant laughter, and yet it was so beautiful to me, all of it, and James, my brother, I loved him, I loved him and understood him and his sorrow with all my heart.

He began to speak again, his eyes moving as if he was seeing what he described.

"The shepherds, they said the Heavens had filled with angels. It was a host of angels in the Heavens. They threw up their arms as they said it, as if they were seeing the angels again. The angels sang: 'Glory to the Lord in the Highest! And on Earth, peace and goodwill to all.' "

He bowed his head. He had stopped crying, but he looked spent and sad.

"Picture it," he said in Greek. "The whole Heavens. And they'd seen this and come down into Bethlehem looking for the child in the manger as the angels had said to do."

I waited.

"How could I hate you for this?" he asked.

"You were just a little boy—a little boy younger than I am now," I said.

He shook his head.

"Don't offer me your kindness," he said. I could barely hear him. His head was down. "I don't deserve your kindness. I am mean to you."

"But you're my older brother," I said.

He lifted his tunic to wipe his tears.

"No," he said. "I have hated you," he said. "And it's a sin."

"Where did these men go, these shepherds who said these things?" I asked. "Where are they now? Who are they?"

"I don't know," he said. "They went out into the snow. They told everyone the same story. I don't know where they went. I never saw them again. They went back to their flocks. They had to go back." He looked at me. In the moonlight I could see he was better now. "But don't you see, your mother was happy. A sign had been given. She went to sleep with you tucked near her."

"And Joseph?"

"Call him Father."

"And Father?"

"He was as he always is, listening, and saying nothing. And when all the people in the stable questioned him, he gave them no answers. The people came one by one and knelt down to look at you, and they prayed, and they went away, back into the corners and under their blankets. The next day we found a new lodging. Everyone in the town knew about this. People kept coming to the door, asking to see you. Old men came, hobbling on their sticks. The other boys in the town knew. But we weren't going to stay there long, Joseph said. Only long enough for you to be circumcised and the sacrifice to be made at the Temple. And the magi from the East, they came to that house. If it hadn't been for the magi going to Herod—."

He stopped and turned.

"The magi going to Herod? What happened?"

But he couldn't say any more.

It was Joseph walking slowly up the slope.

I knew him in the dark by his walk. He stopped a little way away.

"You've been gone too long," he said. "Come back now. I don't want you this far from the camp."

He waited for us.

"I love you, my brother," I said in Hebrew.

"I love you, my brother," he said. "I will never hate you again. Never. I will never envy you. Envy is a terrible thing, a terrible sin. I will love you."

Joseph walked ahead.

"I love you, my brother," James said again, "and I love you, whoever you are."

Whoever I am! Christ the Lord . . . had never told Herod.

He put his arm around me. And I put my arm around him.

Now I knew as we walked back that I could not let Joseph know that James had told me these things. Joseph would never have wanted it. Joseph's way was to talk about nothing. Joseph's way was to go from day to day.

But I had to know the rest of this story! And if my brother could hate me all these years for this, if the Rabbi could stop me at the door of the school over questions to do with who I was, I had to know!

Were these strange happenings the reason we had gone to Egypt? No, it couldn't have been that way.

Even if the whole town of Bethlehem was talking about this, we could have gone to another town. We could have gone back to Nazareth. But what about the angel who appeared to my mother?

We had kindred here—in Bethany. And they weren't all chief priests who were rich. Why, Elizabeth had been here. Why hadn't we gone to her? But then Herod's men had killed

Zechariah! Had Zechariah died because of these stories! Stories of a child born who was Christ the Lord! Oh, if only I could remember more of what Elizabeth had told us on that terrible day last year, after the bandits had raided the village, about Zechariah being killed in the Temple.

Oh, how long would it be before I knew these things!

Later that night, as I lay on my blanket, I closed my eyes and prayed.

All the many lines of the Prophets drifted through my mind. I knew the Kings of Israel had been the Lord's anointed, but they had not been heralded by angels. No, they had not been born of a woman who had never been with a man.

Finally I couldn't think any longer. The struggle was too much.

I looked at the stars, and tried to see the hosts singing in the Heavens. I prayed for the angels to come to me as they would to anyone on the Earth.

A great sweetness came over me, a quiet in my heart. I thought to myself, All this World is the Temple of the Lord. All the Creation is his Temple.

And what we have built on the far hill is only a small place, a place through which we show our love for the Lord who has made everything. Father in Heaven, help me. When I slipped into sleep, a great song opened up, and when I woke, for a moment I didn't know where I was, and the dream was like a veil of gold being pulled away from me.

I was all right. It was early morning. The stars were still there.

23

I WASN'T A CHILD ANYMORE. According to the custom, a boy assumes the yoke of the Law when he's twelve, but that didn't matter. I wasn't a child. I knew it when I watched the other children that morning at play.

I knew it when we joined the pilgrims going to the Temple.

It was the same press as the day before, with hours passing in the singing, and the slow moving before we could reach the baths where we plunged naked into the cold water, and then put on the fresh garments we had brought in our bundles with us.

At last, we were in the tunnel moving upwards toward the Great Court. Here the voices of those who disputed echoed off the walls, and at times sounded angry, but I wasn't frightened anymore.

My mind was on the unfinished story that James had told.

Finally, the stream of singing pilgrims, full of the voices of all the world, poured out into the Court of the Temple and the clear sky was a welcome sight overhead. There was a spreading out, a freedom to take deep breaths, but we were soon in another crush to purchase the birds for our sacrifice. For James wanted to make a sin offering. And I soon realized this was why we had come.

For what sin James wanted to make this sacrifice I didn't know. Or I did know. But what did it matter to me? Cleopas said that I should see it, and that's why he had brought me along.

It wasn't until tomorrow that we would receive the first sprinkling of purification.

Now this puzzled me.

"How is it we'll go into the Sanctuary for the sacrifice if we haven't received the purification?" I asked.

"You know we are purified," said Cleopas. "We were purified before we left Nazareth in the mikvah. We bathed this morning in the stream beside the house of Caiaphas. We've just bathed in the bath. We go through the sprinkling because of Passover. It's the full purification in order to cleanse us if we've contracted any uncleanness of which we don't know." He shrugged. "And it's the custom. But there's no reason for James to wait. James is good. We're going into the Sanctuary now."

"Let the Greek Jews go through the purification before they enter," said my uncle Alphaeus who was with us. "All the Jews from other lands."

Joseph said nothing. He had his hand on James's shoulder as he guided him and us through the crowd.

Before we could purchase the birds, which were all selected as perfect for the Lord, we had to change our money for the proper shekels received by the Temple.

And above the busy tables of the money changers under the colonnade, I could see the burnt roof in either direction, and the men working on it, sweating under the sun, as they scraped and cleaned the stones that were left, and some fitting in new stones with mortar. I knew that job well.

But never had I seen such a great building, and I couldn't even see the end of the colonnade to the right or to the left of me. The capitals of the columns were beautiful, and a great deal of the gold work had been restored.

Voices grew angry in front of me. Men and women were disputing with the money changers. Cleopas was impatient.

"What is the point of their arguing?" he said in Greek to me. "Listen to them. Don't they know these people are robbers?" He used the same word in Greek that we all used for the robbers who lived in the hills, the rebels who'd come down and taken Sepphoris and brought the Romans out after them.

In our first visit, bloodshed had stopped us from ever getting this far. And now as we came up to the tables ourselves, it was a din of voices.

"Well, if you want to buy two birds, then you change to this!" a man said to a woman who stood over him, who seemed not to understand his Greek. She asked a question in an Aramaic that was different from ours. But I could follow what she said.

When Joseph offered to give her the right coins she needed, she put up her hand and would have none of it.

Joseph and Cleopas and all the men changed their coins without any words, but then Cleopas drew back and said, "You pack of thieves, are you proud of yourselves?" The money changers waved him away without much of a look, and Joseph pressed him to stop.

"Not in the House of the Lord," said Joseph.

"And why not?" Cleopas said. "The Lord knows they're thieves. They charge too much for the exchange."

"Leave it," said Uncle Alphaeus. "There hasn't been a riot yet today, has there? You want to start a riot?"

"But why do they charge too much, Father?" James asked.

"I don't know that they do. I accept it," Joseph said. "We've come with enough money for the sacrifice. Nothing's been taken from me that I haven't been prepared to give."

We were already in the place where the turtledoves were kept. The sun was hot. And the stones were hard under my feet, though they were beautiful stones. I could hear more anger, more disputing, along with the cluck and coo of the birds themselves. It was a long time before we reached the tables.

The stench of the cages was worse than any courtyard in Nazareth. The filth dripped from the cages.

Here even Joseph was surprised by the price that he had to pay, but the merchant was cross and pointed out how many people were waiting.

"Would you care to sit here and deal with these people!" the merchant demanded. "Or bring your own perfect birds from Galilee? That's where you come from, isn't it? I can tell by your speech."

Everywhere I heard the same quarreling. A family had returned with birds that the priests wouldn't accept. The merchant shouted in Greek that the birds had been unblemished when he sold them. Again, Joseph offered to pay for another sacrifice but the father said no, this time with thanks to him. The woman was crying.

"I've walked for fourteen days to get here to make this sacrifice."

"Listen, you have to let us pay for another pair of doves for you!" said Cleopas. "I don't give the money to you," he said to the woman. "I give it to this fellow here and then he gives you two more birds. That way, it's your sacrifice still. You understand? You don't take anything from me for it. He takes it."

The woman stopped crying. She looked at her husband. Her husband nodded.

Cleopas paid the money.

The merchant gave the women two fluttering little birds. Quickly, he shoved the others into an empty cage.

"You miserable thief!" said Cleopas under his breath.

The merchant nodded. "Yes, yes, yes."

James made his purchase quickly.

Thoughts came into my mind that frightened me, not memories of the battle or the man who'd died here, but other thoughts—that this was not a place of prayer, that it was not the beautiful place of Yahweh to which all would come to worship Him. It seemed so simple, the laws of sacrifice when we recited the Scripture, but here it was a huge marketplace full of noise and anger and disappointment.

There were Gentiles all around us in this great ever moving crowd and I blushed secretly for what they saw and heard. Yet I could see that many did not mind it. They had come to see the Temple, and they seemed happier perhaps than the Jews around me, who were the ones who would go on into the Court of Women, where the Gentiles couldn't enter.

Of course Gentiles had their own temples, their own merchants selling animals for sacrifice. I'd seen them plenty enough in Alexandria. Perhaps they fought and argued just as much.

But our Lord was the Lord who had created all things, our Lord was invisible, our Lord was the Lord of all places and all things. Our Lord dwelt only in this Temple, and we were all his holy people, every one.

When we reached the Court of Women, Old Sarah, my mother, and the other women stopped here as this was as far as women were allowed to go. The crowd was not bad here. The Gentiles couldn't enter under pain of death. We were really in the Temple now, though the noise of the animals for sacrifice was still with us, as the men brought their cows, sheep, and birds with them.

The terrible fires had not harmed this place. Everywhere around us was silver and gold. The columns were Greek and as beautiful as any in Alexandria. Many of the women went up into the gallery from which they could see the sacrifice in the Inner Court, but Old Sarah could not climb any more stairs, and our women remained with her.

As we left her, we agreed to meet again in the southeastern corner of the Great Court. I worried as to how we would find each other.

My legs were aching as we climbed the steps. But I was filled with a new happiness, and for the first time my painful memories, my confusion, left me.

I was in the House of the Lord. I could hear the singing of the Levites.

As we reached the gate, the Levite on duty stopped us.

"This is a little boy," he said. "Why not leave him with your women?"

"He's older than his years and he knows the Law," said Joseph. "He's prepared," said Joseph.

The Levite nodded and let us go in.

Once again, the crowd grew thick. The sound of the animals was loud, and the turtledoves fluttered in James' grip.

But the music, the music was all around us. I could hear the pipes and the cymbals and the deep blended voices of the singers. Never had I heard such rich music, such full music as that of the Levites singing. It wasn't the gay, broken, and high song of the Psalms we sang on the road, or the happy fast-paced songs of the weddings. It was a dark and almost sad sound that flowed on and on with great power. The Hebrew words melted in the chorus. There was no beginning or end to any part of it.

It caught me up so completely that only slowly did I see what was happening in front of me, in front of the railing.

The priests in their pure white linen with white turbans on their heads moved back and forth with the animals from the crowd in which we stood to the great altar. I saw the little lambs and the goats going to the sacrifice. I saw the birds being carried.

The priests were so thick around the altar I couldn't see what they did, but only now and then see the splashes of blood high and low. The hands of the priests were covered in blood. Their beautiful linen robes were splashed with blood. A great fire burned on the altar. And the smell of roasting meat was strong beyond words. I smelled it with every breath that I took.

Though Joseph pointed to the altar of incense and I saw that too, I couldn't smell the incense.

"Look, the singers, do you see them?" asked Cleopas, bending down close to my ear.

"Yes," I said. "James, look." I made them out through the goings and comings of the priests.

They were on the steps going up to the Inner Sanctuary, a great number, bearded men with long locks, all with scrolls in their hands, and I saw the lyres from which came the delicate sounds I hadn't picked out from the great blended beauty of their music.

Their singing grew louder in my ears when I saw them. It was so beautiful I felt myself floating with it. It drowned out the sounds of the crowd completely.

All my troubles went away as I stood here, as I prayed, my words becoming no words—only worship of the Lord who had created all things as I listened to the music and looked on all that was happening.

Lord. Lord, whoever I am, whatever I am, whatever I am meant to be, I am part of this, this world that is all of a flowing wonder—like this music. And you are with us. You are here. You have pitched your tent here, among us. This music is your song. This is your house.

I started to cry, but it was quiet. Nobody saw it.

James closed his eyes in prayer as he held the two birds, waiting for the priest to come. There were so many priests I couldn't count them. They received the lambs that bleated and the goats that cried until the last moment. The blood was caught in basins according to the Law. Then taken to be dashed on the stones of the altar.

"Now, you know," said Cleopas to us in a clear whisper, "this is not the Altar of the Presence. The Altar of the Presence. That's up, past the singers, in the Sanctuary, and beyond the great veil. And these things you'll never see. Your mother was among those who wove those veils, two a year. Ah, it was such gorgeous embroidery. Only the High Priest goes into the Holy of Holies. And when he enters, it is filled with a cloud of incense."

I thought of Joseph Caiaphas. I pictured him in my mind entering that sacred place. Then I thought of the young Aristobulos, the high priest whom Old Herod had murdered. *If only the magi had not told Herod . . .*

My mother's words came back to me. "You are not the son of an angel." What a little boy I'd been when she said that to me. I hadn't thought of those words since the night she spoke them to me on the roof here in Jerusalem. I hadn't let myself think of them. But I did now, and all the strange pictures which James had painted for me in his tale were fired in my mind with color.

But I didn't want these thoughts, these fragments of something that I couldn't complete.

I wanted the peace and happiness that I'd felt only moments ago. And it did come back to me.

Such a peace and happiness took hold of me that I was scarcely a boy standing there among others. I was my soul, my mind, as if it could grow beyond the size of my body, as if it could move outward from me, carried on the waves of music, as if I had no weight or size and in this way, in this moment, I could go into the Holy of Holies, and I did, passing through gate, and wall, and veil, and moving yet even farther outward. *They called you Christos Kyrios. Christ the Lord.*

Lord, tell me who I am. Tell me what I am to do.

The sound of crying brought me back to myself. A little sound amid the music and the Hebrew prayers whispered all around.

James cried. He was shaking.

I looked once more at the great stone altar of sacrifice, and the priests dashing the blood against the stones. The blood belonged to the Lord. It belonged to the Lord when it was in the animal, and it belonged to the Lord now. The blood was the life of the animal. Never could an Israelite eat blood. The stones of the altar were drenched in blood.

It was a dark and beautiful thing like the music rising, and the prayers spoken everywhere in Hebrew. Even the priests going back and forth seemed like the movement of a dance.

No, I'm not a child anymore. I'm not.

I thought of the men killed on that day last year. I thought of the men burned in the rebellion within this very

Temple. I thought of blood on the stones of this Temple. Blood. And blood.

James held the two birds tightly as they tried to escape from his hands, his fingers a cage around them.

"I confess my sins," he whispered in Hebrew. "That I am guilty of envy, of spite."

He choked back his crying. At thirteen he was a man crying. I didn't know that anyone else but me knew he was crying. Then I saw Joseph's hand pressing his shoulder, rubbing it, and comforting him. Joseph kissed his cheek. Joseph loved James. He loved him so much. He loved me. He loved each person in a different way.

James held the birds, and he bowed his head as the priest came down the line towards us.

" 'For a child has been born to us,' " James recited from Isaiah, " 'a son is given us, and dominion shall rest on his shoulders.' " He tried to stop his tears. He went on, " 'And the name he has been given is Wonder-Counsellor, Mighty God, Eternal-Father, Prince of Peace.' "

I turned and looked at James. Why this prayer?

"May the Lord forgive me my envy. May the Lord forgive my sins, and may I be cleansed. Let me not be afraid. Let me understand. I repent of all."

The priest was suddenly standing tall in front of us, and the blood spatters were on his beard and on his face. But he was beautiful in his white linen and his miter. The Levite stood beside him. The priest held the golden basin. With very narrow eyes he looked at James, and James nodded and gave over to him the two birds.

"This is an offering for sin," said James.

I was pushed forward and bent over to see, but the priest was soon lost among the other priests and I couldn't see what they did at the altar. I knew from the Scriptures what they did. They would wring the neck of one bird and pour out its blood. That was the sin offering. And the body of the second bird would be burnt.

We were not there very long.

It was finished. Paid in full.

We made our way back, pushing and almost shoving, and soon into the mob of the Court of the Gentiles. This time we walked not in the very middle of everything but along the colonnade called Solomon's Portico.

Teachers sat back under the porch, with many young men gathered around them. Women stopped to listen as well. I heard one teaching in Aramaic and the next one who had a very large crowd was answering a question in Greek for one of a great gathering.

I wanted to stop, but the family kept moving, and every time I went slow to look at the teachers, to catch a single word perhaps, someone took my hand and led me on.

Finally, I saw the great stoa coming up ahead. The crowd was easy now.

We passed the stairs for leaving and then I saw why.

Old Sarah was under the roof, seated beside one of the columns in the shade, with Bruria, our sad refugee, and also Riba playing with her little baby. My mother and my aunts were there.

I'd forgotten all about them. I hadn't even known we were to find them. Old Sarah at once received James in her arms and kissed him.

As we were all very tired, we sat down there with them. And I soon saw that many people were doing the same, even though the stonemasons were working not far off on the back wall of the colonnade. We kept very close together so as not to be stepped on by others.

Many were leaving the Temple. Even two or more of the

merchants had packed up their birds in their cages and were
going down the stairs. But still there were others complaining and even shouting at each other, and some people were
backed up at the tables of the money changers.

The Levites who sold the oil and flour for sacrifice were
folding up their tables. And then I saw the guards, perhaps
the men who are called the Temple Police, coming near to
the stairway to watch the flow of those leaving.

The evening sacrifice of the lamb would very soon be
over. I didn't know for certain. There was so much to learn. It
would all come in time. I wasn't worried about it.

Nearby I saw a blind man seated on a stool, a man with a
very long gray beard, and he was talking in Greek to no one,
his arms out, or maybe he was talking to everyone. People
threw coins in his lap. Some listened for a moment and then
moved on. I couldn't hear him too well over the noise. Finally
I asked Joseph if I might give him something and go listen to
him.

Joseph considered and then gave me a denarius, which
was quite a lot. I took it and ran at once to sit down at the
feet of the man.

It was beautiful Greek he was speaking, smooth as Philo
would have spoken it. He was reciting from the Psalm:

" 'Let my cry of joy come to you, Lord, give me understanding as you promised. Let my plea for favor reach you;
rescue me as you've promised. . . .' " He stopped to feel the
coin I'd laid in his lap. I touched the back of his hand. His
eyes were pale gray, covered with film.

"And who is this who gives me so much, and comes to sit
at my feet?" he asked. "A Son of Israel or one seeking the
Lord of All?"

"A Son of Israel, Teacher," I said in Greek. "A student
who seeks the wisdom of your gray hairs."

"And what would you learn, child?" he asked, staring forward. He slipped the coin into his girdle beneath the fold of his woolen robe.

"Teacher, tell me please who is Christos Kyrios?"

"Ah, child, there are many anointed ones," he said. "But the anointed one who is Lord? Who do you think it would be, if it would not be the Son of David, the anointed King come from the root of Jesse to rule over Israel and bring peace to the Land?"

"But what if angels sang when the anointed one was born, Rabbi," I asked, "and what if magi came following a star in the sky to give him gifts?"

"Oh, that old story, child," he said. "The story from Bethlehem, the story of the babe born in the manger. So you know it. Almost no one talks about it anymore. It's too sad. I'd thought it was forgotten."

I was speechless.

"People say 'Here is the Messiah,' and 'There is the Messiah,'" he went on, saying the word "Messiah" in Hebrew. "We will know when the Messiah comes, how can we not know?"

I was too excited to think what to say.

"Tell me the words, child, from Daniel. . . . 'One like the Son of Man coming.' Are you there, child."

"Yes, Rabbi, but what is the story, Rabbi, of the child in the manger, in Bethlehem?" I asked.

"That was too dreadful, and who knows what really happened? It was so quick and so terrible. Only Herod could have done such a thing, a bloodthirsty and evil man! But I mustn't say these things. His son is King."

"But Rabbi, what did he do? We're alone here, there's no one near us."

He took my hand.

"How old are you, child? Your hand is small and rough from work."

I didn't want to tell him. I knew he would be surprised.

"Rabbi, I must find out what happened in Bethlehem. I beg you, tell me."

He shook his head. "Unspeakable things," he said. "How did we come to be ruled by such a family? These men, given to rages, murdering their own children? How many of his own children did Herod destroy? Five? And Caesar Augustus, what did he say of Herod after the man had slain his two sons? 'I'd sooner be Herod's pig than his son.' " He laughed.

So did I out of respect for him, but my mind was racing with thoughts.

"Child, answer for me," he said. "In my blindness I can no longer read my books and my books were all to me, my consolation, and it costs for me to have someone to read to me, and my books are my treasure. I will not give them up to pay for a boy to read to me what is left of them. I cannot give up those I copied myself, or those copied so carefully according to the Law. Tell me, Zechariah: 'On that day . . . On that day . . .' the last line, child . . . ?"

" 'On that day there will no longer be any traders in the house of the Lord,' " I said.

He nodded.

"You hear them?" he asked.

He meant the money changers, and the people who disputed with them.

"Yes, I hear them, Rabbi."

"On that day!" he said. "On that day."

I looked at his eyes, at the thickness of the film. It was milk over his eyes. If only, but I had promised. If only I knew that it was right, if only, but I had promised.

His fingers tightened on mine, dusty, soft.

And I held tight to him and I prayed in my heart for him. *All merciful God, only if it is your will, grant him consolation, grant him some relief.* . . .

Joseph stood beside me. He said, "Come, Yeshua."

"May God bless you, Rabbi," I said, and I kissed his hand. He was waving to me, though I was gone.

As soon as Old Sarah was on her feet, and Riba had the baby securely tied up to her, we started on our journey out.

At the top of the stairs into the tunnel, Joseph stopped. He held my hand. James had gone on.

The blind man ran towards us, his eyes dark and fierce with light. He squinted, looking to left and right and back at Joseph. It couldn't have been more startling to see a dead man back to life.

My heart pounded.

"There was a child here!" the man said. "A child!" He glanced over me and down the stairs and over the crowd. "A boy of twelve or thirteen," he said. "I heard his voice just now again. Where did he go?"

Joseph shook his head, and picking me up with a strong right arm, he swung me up against his shoulder and carried me down and through the tunnel and away.

Not one word did he say to me on the way home.

I wanted to tell him the words of my prayer, that my prayer had come from my heart, that I had not meant to do what was not right, that I had prayed, and put it in the hands of the Lord.

24

THE FOLLOWING DAYS were cheerful and rich days for the family. We went to the sprinkling in the Temple, and bathed after the second time as was required. And during the period of waiting, we wandered the streets of Jerusalem in the day, marveling over the jewels, and books, and fabrics for sale in the marketplace, and Cleopas even bought a little bound book in Latin, and for my mother, Joseph bought some fine embroidery which she could sew to a veil to wear to the village weddings.

At night there was much music and even dancing in Bethany among the camps.

And the Feast of Passover itself was a great marvel.

It was Joseph who slit the throat of the lamb before the priest and the Levite who caught the blood. And after it was roasted, we dined according to the custom with unleavened bread, and the bitter herbs, telling the story of our captivity in the land of Egypt, and how the Lord had ransomed us from Egypt and brought us through the Red Sea and to the Promised Land.

The unleavened bread we ate because we had had no

time in fleeing Egypt to make bread with leaven; the bitter herbs we ate because our captivity had been bitter; the lamb we ate because we were free now and could feast for the Lord had saved us; and it was the blood of the lamb on the lintels of the Israelites that had caused the Angel of Death to pass over us when that Angel had slain the firstborn of Egypt because Pharaoh wouldn't let us go.

And who among us, in our little gathering, could not attach a special meaning to all of this, since we had a year ago come from Egypt, through war and suffering, and found a peaceful Promised Land in Nazareth from which we'd come joyfully to the Temple of the Lord?

The day after the Feast, when many were leaving Jerusalem, and the family was talking about when to go, and what should we do, and was Old Sarah ready to make the journey, and thus and so, I looked for Joseph and couldn't find him.

Cleopas told me he'd gone back into Jerusalem with my mother, to the marketplace, now that the crowds were gone, so that she might buy some thread.

"I want to go back to the Temple, to hear the Teachers in the portico," I said to Cleopas. "We won't be leaving today, will we?"

"No, not at all," he said. "Find someone to go with you," he said. "It's good for you to see it when it's not so full of people. But you can't go alone." He went back to talking to the men.

Now all this time Joseph had not said one word to me about the blind man. What had happened with the blind man had made him afraid. I hadn't known it when we hurried down the stairs that evening, but I knew it now.

And I didn't know whether he could see the change in me or not. But I was changed.

I knew that my mother saw it. She marked it, but she didn't worry. After all, I wasn't sad. I had only given up running with the other boys. And because I saw things with different eyes, I was quiet but not at all unhappy. I listened to the men when they talked. I paid attention to things that before I would not have noticed. And I kept to myself most of the time.

Now and then I knew the temptation to be angry, angry with those who wouldn't tell me all the things I wanted to know. But when I remembered the blind man's unwillingness to say these "terrible things," I understood why I wasn't told. My mother and Joseph were trying to protect me from something. But I couldn't be protected any longer. I had to know.

I had to know all that others knew.

I went to the road now that led down to the Temple. Joseph Caiaphas was on his way down with several members of his close family, and he nodded to me and smiled.

I fell in behind him.

He looked back once or twice, calling me by name, which surprised me, and motioned for me to come up beside his party, and I did do it but still kept a little behind. After all, I was very dusty from the camp, and he was in his usual fine linen, and so were those with him who must have been priests as well.

But I was doing what Cleopas had told me to do. I was going with someone. I was not alone.

When we reached the Temple Mount, I slipped away.

The crowds in the Court of the Gentiles were loose and free, and for the first time I could really see the great size of the Temple, and the scale of the adornments. It was just as Cleopas had said.

But it was not this that I wanted to see.

I went to Solomon's Portico to hear the Teachers.

There were many there, some with larger crowds than others. But I was looking for a very old man, a man who was frail with years as well as white hair.

Finally I came upon the very oldest, a man who was gaunt, with deep glowing eyes, and no hair on the top of his head beneath his shawl, but gray hair flowing down over his ears. He was well dressed and he had his blue threads sewn in his tassels. He had a fair crowd of young boys around him, some much older than me.

I watched him and I listened to him.

He threw out questions to the eager boys. He looked carefully into the face of each boy who answered him. He had a quick laugh that was friendly and kind; but there was a sharp authority in him. He said what he had to say. There were no wasted words with him. And his voice had the quickness of a young man.

His questions were questions our own Rabbis might have asked us. I came in close and I gave back answers. He was pleased with my answers. He gestured for me to come closer. The boys made room for me to sit at his feet. I didn't even think about James. I offered answer after answer to the questions. Rabbi Berekhaiah had trained me well. And soon, the Rabbi passed me over with a smile, to let the other boys have a turn instead of me.

When the horn was blown for the evening sacrifice, we stopped to say the prayers.

Then came the moment for which I'd been waiting, and I hadn't even known I was waiting for it. My heart was beating fast. The boys went their way into the rooms where they slept, or to their homes in Jerusalem. And the Rabbi was making his way into the library in the Temple, and I followed him, along with one or two of the other boys.

The library was very big, bigger than that of Philo, and full of scrolls. There were scribes at work there, at tables, copying, with their heads bent, and they rose out of respect for the old man.

But the Rabbi passed through these rooms into his own place of study, and he let us come with him, one of the other boys talking to him, questioning him on the Law.

I heard all this, but it didn't go deep into my mind. I had but one purpose.

At last I stood alone before the Rabbi. He had taken his seat at the desk, and a cup of wine had been brought to him. The lamps were lighted, and all around him were the scrolls. The scents of the room were of the parchment, the papyrus, and the burning oil. If my heart had not been pounding in my chest, I would have loved this place.

"What is it you want of me?" he asked. "You've waited a long time for this. Say what it is."

I waited for a moment, but no thought came to me, no design. I matched his words with my own.

"Eight years ago, a child was born in Bethlehem. Angels sang to shepherds when he was born. The angels called him Christ the Lord. Days after that three men from the East came, Persian magi who offered him gifts. They claimed a star had led them to this child."

"Yes?" he said. "I know this tale."

"What happened to this child?"

"Why must you know this? Why do you care about this at all?"

"I beg you to tell me. I can't think of anything but this night or day. I can't eat or drink until I find out about this child."

He thought about this. He took a drink of his wine.

"I'll tell you," he said. "So that you may put it out of your mind and be done with it. And study as you should."

"Yes," I said.

"These magi, as you call them, these wise men, they came to Jerusalem. They came to Herod's palace just south of Bethlehem. They claimed to have been following a star. They said they had seen signs in the Heavens that told of the birth of a new King." He stopped for a moment, then went on. "These were men of wealth, richly dressed, with a caravan and servants, advisors to their rulers. They had gifts to present to this child. But now close to Jerusalem, the star hovered over a vast collection of settlements. They could find no one place where the child might be. Herod had received these men, pretended that he wanted to know who this King might be himself." He smiled a bitter smile. He took another drink of his wine.

I waited.

"He called us together, the elders, the scribes, those who knew the Scriptures as to where the true King of Israel would be born. The Christ. He was full of pretense as he always was in such matters, putting on quite the show for these magi, begging that we tell him what the Scriptures foretold."

He shook his head. And he looked away, his eyes moving up the walls and then slowly back to me.

"We told him Bethlehem would be the birthplace of the Messiah. It was the truth, no more than that. Would we had told him nothing at all. But we didn't know then that a child had been born in Bethlehem surrounded by miraculous signs! We hadn't heard the stories yet because the child was only a few days old. We didn't know yet the talk of angels, or the virgin mother. All that we learned later, much later. We knew only the Scripture, and we thought these men from the East were Gentiles on a foolish quest, really. So we answered, not with cunning, but with the truth. As for Herod, we understood perfectly that the very last thing the man would ever want was to find the true King, the Christ."

He bowed his head.

When he said nothing, I couldn't bear it.

"Rabbi, what happened?" I asked.

"The magi went there. We learned that afterwards. They found the child. They presented their gifts. But they didn't return to Herod as he'd asked of them. They went away, homeward, by some unknown road. And when Herod discovered this deception, he went into a rage. Early in the morning, while it was still dark, he sent the soldiers down from his fortress and while he watched from the parapet, they went through every house in Bethlehem and slaughtered every child under two years of age!"

I put my hands up. I felt the sob rise in my throat.

"They dragged the children from the arms of their mothers. They bashed their heads against the stones. They slit their throats. They killed them all. Not a single little one escaped."

"No, this couldn't have happened!" I cried out under my breath, the words almost strangled. "No, they didn't do that!"

"Oh, but yes they did," he said.

The sob in me rose higher and higher. I couldn't move. I tried to cover my face but I couldn't move.

I began to shake and to cry with all my body and my soul.

The Rabbi's hands tightened on my shoulders.

"My son," he said, "my son."

But I couldn't stop.

I couldn't stop and I couldn't tell him. I couldn't tell anyone! *This had happened because of my birth!* I began to scream. I screamed as I had that night when I saw Jericho burning and this horror that gripped me now was a thousand times that fear, a thousand times. I couldn't stand upright.

People held me. The Rabbi spoke gentle words to me. But the words were lost in my terror.

I saw the babies. I saw them dashed on the stones. I saw the throats slit. I saw the throats of the lambs slit in the Temple at Passover. I saw the blood. I saw the mothers screaming. I couldn't stop crying.

Around me, people whispered. Hands lifted me.

I was put down on a bed. I felt a cool rag against my forehead. I was choking in my sobs. I couldn't open my eyes. I couldn't stop seeing the babies dying, I couldn't stop seeing the lambs slaughtered, the blood on the altar, the blood of the babies. I saw the man, our man, in the Temple with the spear through his chest. I saw him turn over. I saw Baby Esther, Baby Esther bleeding. Babies on the stones. Lord in Heaven, no. Not because of me. No.

"No, no . . ." I said this word over and over if I said any word.

"Sit up, I want you to drink this!"

I was lifted.

"Open your mouth, drink this!"

I choked on the liquid, the honey, the wine. I tried to swallow. "But they're dead, they're dead, they're dead!"

I don't know how long it went on until it became an easy crying, a full-throated crying, and I said, "I don't want to sleep. I'll see them when I dream."

25

I WAS SICK. I was thirsty. The voices and hands were so kind. I was given the wine and the honey to drink. I slept, and the cold rags on my head felt good. If there were dreams, I didn't remember them. I heard music—the deep smooth voices of the Levites. I drifted. Only now and then did I see the babies, the murdered innocent ones, and I cried. I turned my head into the pillow and cried.

I have to wake up, I thought, but I couldn't wake up. And once when I did, it was dark, and the old Rabbi was asleep in his chair. It was like a dream, this, and I slid back into sleep without being able to stop it.

Finally, there came a moment when I opened my eyes, and I knew I was well.

I thought at once of the murdered children, but I could see it without crying. I sat up and looked about. The old Rabbi was there and at once got up from his table. Another man was there and he came to me as well.

The younger man felt of my forehead and looked into my eyes.

"Ah, it's over," he said. "Little nameless one. You're yourself again. I want to hear you speak."

"I thank you," I said. My throat hurt but I knew it was only from not talking. "I thank you for tending to me. I didn't want to be sick."

"Come, I have fresh clothes for you," said the younger man. "I'll help you."

I saw as I got up that I was in a new tunic and that kindness touched my heart.

When I'd returned from the bath, much refreshed and dressed, the old Rabbi dismissed the man and told me to sit down opposite him.

There was a stool there. I don't think I'd ever sat on a stool before. I did as I was told.

"You're a little boy," he said, "and I forgot that you were a little boy. A little boy with a heart."

"I wanted to know the answers to my questions, Rabbi. I had to know the answers. I would never have stopped asking."

"But why?" he asked. "The child born in Bethlehem has been dead for eight years, as you said yourself. Now don't begin to cry again."

"No, I won't."

"And the virgin mother, who could believe such a thing."

"I believe it, Rabbi," I said. "And the child's not dead. The child escaped."

For a long moment, he looked at me.

And in that moment, I felt all my sadness, all my separation from those around me. I felt it so bitterly.

I felt that he was about to dismiss what I had said, about to say that even if the child had somehow escaped Bethlehem, it was all just a story, and Herod's butchery was all the more a horrid thing.

Before he could speak, however, I heard voices that I knew very close by.

My mother and Joseph were there.

My mother called my name.

I stood at once and turned to greet them as they came in, quickly saying to the scribe that yes, I was their son.

My mother put her arms around me.

Joseph kissed the hands of the old Rabbi.

Much was said quickly. I couldn't follow all of it. Joseph and my mother had been looking for me for three days.

The Rabbi praised my answers to his questions, when I had been with the other boys. As far as I could tell, he was saying nothing about our talk of Bethlehem, and nothing about my being ill.

I went to him and I kissed his hands and thanked him for all the time he had spent with me, and he said,

"You go now with your mother and father."

Joseph wanted to pay for my keep, but the Rabbi refused this.

When we were out in the bright light of the Great Court, my mother took me by the shoulders:

"Why have you done this?" she asked. "We've been in misery searching for you!"

"Mother, I must know things now," I said. "Things I'm forbidden to ask you or Joseph. I must be about what it is that I have to do!"

It was a blow to her. I could hardly bear to see it in her face.

"I'm sorry for it," I said. "I'm so sorry for it. But it's the truth."

She looked at Joseph and he nodded.

We went together out of the Temple and down into the old city, and through the narrow streets until we came to the Synagogue of the Nazarenes, and there up to a small room. It was there that they had been staying as they looked for me.

There was a window in the room, covered by a lattice and the light was good. The room was clean.

My mother sat against the wall, with her legs crossed. And Joseph quietly went out.

I waited, but he didn't come back.

"Sit here and listen to me," my mother said.

I sat down across from her.

The light was full on her face.

"I've never told this story," she said. "I want to tell it one time."

I nodded.

"Don't say anything to me as I tell it."

I nodded.

She looked away as she spoke.

"I was thirteen years old," she said. "I was betrothed to Joseph, my kinsman, as was always the custom with us, distantly related, yet part of the same tribe. Old Sarah had given her approval to my mother and father of him even before I came down from Jerusalem where I'd worked on the Temple veils. I hardly remembered him. I met him. He was a good man.

"I was strictly brought up. I never went out of the house. The servants went to the well. Cleopas taught me what little I know of reading. What little I know of the world. I was to be married in Nazareth, as my parents had come there from Sepphoris to live with Old Sarah. And it was the big house in which you live now.

"Now one morning, I'd awakened early and I didn't know why. It wasn't light yet. I was up and standing in the room. My first thought was that my mother needed me. But I went in to her and she was asleep and well.

"I came back into my room. The room completely filled with light. It happened instantly. It happened silently. The light was everywhere. Everything that was in the room was still there but it was filled with the light. It was a light that didn't hurt my eyes but it was absolutely bright. If you can imagine looking at the sun and the sun not hurting your eyes, you can imagine this light.

"I wasn't afraid. I stood there and I saw a figure in the light, the figure of a man only it was much bigger than a man and it didn't move. I knew it wasn't a man.

"It spoke to me. It said that I had found favor with the Lord. It said that I was blessed among women. And that from my womb would come a son named Jesus, that he would be great and he would be the Son of the Most High. It said that the Lord God would give him the throne of his father David and that he would reign over the House of Jacob forever. I spoke to the voice. I said I'd never been with a man. The voice said the Holy Spirit would come over me. It said the Holy Child born from me would be the Son of God."

My mother looked at me for the first time.

"This voice, this being, this angel wanted an answer from me and I said, 'I'm the servant of the Lord. Let it be done.'

"Almost at once, I felt life inside me. Oh, not the weight of the baby that comes later, or the movement, no. But the change. I knew it was happening. I knew! I knew as the light completely disappeared.

"I ran out into the street. I didn't mean to do it. I didn't know what I was doing. I cried out. I cried out that an angel had come to me, that an angel had appeared to me and spoken to me, that a child was coming."

She stopped.

"And that has earned me the everlasting ridicule of some in Nazareth, hasn't it?" she asked. "Though in time many forget."

I waited.

"The hardest part was to tell Joseph bar Jacob," she said. "But my parents, they waited. They believed me, yes, yet they waited. And when they saw that their virgin daughter had a child within her, when there was no denying it, then and only then did they talk to Joseph. And what they'd seen, others came to know as well.

"But an angel had come to Joseph in a dream. He didn't cry out in the streets about this as I had. And it wasn't the angel who came to me, who filled the room with light, no. But it was an angel and the angel had told him to take me as his wife. He didn't care that the whole village was talking. He had to go to Bethlehem for the census and he spoke to Cleopas and it was decided we would all travel together to Bethany, where Cleopas and I could lodge with Elizabeth and there Joseph and I would be married, and it would be over and done with, in that way. It was a winter journey and a hard journey, but we went together, all of us, and Joseph's brothers went with us, as you know now, and so did little James, our beloved James."

She went, speaking slowly.

She told me now the story that James had told—of the crowded stable and the shepherds coming, of their faces so full of happiness, and of the angels they'd seen. She told of the magi coming, and of their gifts.

I listened to her as if I hadn't heard these things.

"I knew we had to leave Bethlehem," she said. "There was too much talk there. The shepherds and then the magi. People came to the door night and day. Then Joseph awoke one morning and said we had to go right away. We packed up everything, and left within the hour. He wouldn't tell me why—only that an angel had come to him again in a dream. I didn't know we were going south to Egypt until it was evening, and we pushed on late into the night."

Her face became troubled. She looked away again.

"We wandered, all of us," she said. "We lived in many a small town in Egypt. The men took work when they could, and we did well. Carpenters can always work. People were kind. You were my delight. I didn't think of anything but you. You were the sweet child every woman wants. And all this while I didn't know why we were running. Then finally we went back north up to Alexandria and settled in the Street of the Carpenters. I loved it there. Salome and Esther loved it. So did Cleopas.

"Only after a while I heard stories, stories of what had happened in Bethlehem. Tales of a Messiah born there had caused a jealous rage to come from King Herod. He'd sent soldiers down from his fortress only a few miles away. They'd killed every little child in the village! Some two hundred children murdered in the darkness before dawn."

She watched me.

I struggled not to cry, not to fear, not to tremble—only to wait.

She bowed her head, and her face tightened.

When she looked up, her eyes were moist with tears.

"I said to Joseph, 'Did you know that was going to happen? Did the angel who came to you tell you?' He said, 'No, I knew nothing about it.' I said, 'How could the Lord let such a thing happen as the murder of those innocent children!' " She bit her lower lip. "I couldn't understand it. I felt, 'We have blood on our hands!' "

I thought for a moment I would give way to tears, but I used all my strength not to do it.

"Joseph said to me, 'No, the blood is not on our hands. Shepherds came to worship this child. Gentiles came to worship him. An evil King has sought to kill him because the darkness cannot abide the light, but the light can't be quenched by the darkness. The darkness always tries to swallow the light. But the light will shine. Don't you see? We must protect him and that we will do, and the Lord will show how.' "

Her eyes settled on mine.

She stared intently at me.

She reached out and took me by the shoulders.

"You weren't born of a man," she said.

I said nothing.

"You are the begotten of God!" she whispered. "Not the Son of God as Caesar calls himself the Son of God; not the Son of God as a good man calls himself the Son of God. Not the Son of God as an anointed King is called the Son of God! You are the begotten of God!"

She waited, staring at me, but she asked nothing of me. Her hands remained firm on my shoulders. Her eyes never changed.

When she spoke again, her voice was lower, softer.

"You are the son of the Lord God!" she said. "That's why you can kill and bring back to life, that's why you can heal a blind man as Joseph saw you do, that's why you can pray for snow and there will be snow, that's why you can dispute with your uncle Cleopas when he forgets you're a boy, that's why you make sparrows from clay and bring them to life. Keep your power inside you. Guard it until your Father in Heaven shows you the time to use it. If he's made you a child, then he's made you a child to grow in wisdom as well as in everything else."

Slowly I nodded.

"And now you come home with us to Nazareth. Not back to the Temple. Oh, I know how much you want to stay at the Temple. I know. But no. The Lord in Heaven did not send you to the house of a Teacher in the Temple or a priest in the Temple or a scribe or a rich Pharisee. He sent you to Joseph bar Jacob, the carpenter, and his betrothed, Mary of the Tribe of David in Nazareth. And you come home to Nazareth with us."

26

FROM THE MOUNT OF OLIVES, we took the last look back on the city of Jerusalem.

Joseph told me what I knew, that three times a year we would come up to Jerusalem for the great Feasts, and that I would come to know the great city very well.

Our journey was a quick one back to Nazareth, as we didn't have the whole family with us, but we were never hurried, and we fell into easy conversation about the beauty of the land around us, and the little things of our daily lives.

When we finally came over the ridge, and the village was clearly in sight, I told both my parents that I would never do again what I had done—that is, leave them as I'd left them. I didn't try to explain what had happened. I simply told them that they need never worry that I would go off on my own away from the family again.

I could see that they were pleased but they didn't want to talk about what had happened. They had already let it slip deep and away from the current of everyday thoughts. At once my mother talked simple things to do with the household and Joseph was nodding to what she said.

A stillness came over me.

I walked with them, but I was alone.

I thought about what my mother had said—her quotation of Joseph, that the darkness tries to swallow the light and the darkness never succeeds in swallowing it. These were beautiful words, but they were words.

In my mind, without feeling, without crying, without shivering, I saw the dead man in the Temple, I saw the Passover lamb bleeding into the basin, I saw the children I'd never seen killed in Bethlehem. I saw the fire in the night leaping up to the sky from Jericho. My mind went over and over these things.

When we entered the house, I sat down and rested.

Little Salome came up and stood before me. I didn't say anything, because I thought she would set down a bowl or a cup and then go away as she always did, the busy little woman that she was.

But she didn't do this. She stood there.

Finally I looked up.

"What?" I asked.

She knelt down and she put her hand on the side of my face. I looked at her and it was as if she'd never left me to be busy with the women. She looked into my eyes.

"What is it, Yeshua?" she asked.

I swallowed. I felt my voice would be too big for me if I tried to say it, yet say it I did.

"Only what everyone has to learn," I said. "I don't know why I didn't see it before." The man on the stones. The lamb. The children. I looked her.

"Tell me," she said.

"Yes!" I whispered. "Why didn't I see it?"

"Tell me," she said.

"It's so simple. It won't mean anything to you until it comes to you, no matter who you are."

"I want to know," she said.

"It's this. That whatever is born into this world, no matter how, and for whatever reason, *is born to die.*"

She didn't answer.

I stood up. I went outside. It was getting dark. I walked through the street and out to the hillside and up to where the grass was soft and undisturbed. This was my favorite place, just short of the grove of trees near which I loved so to rest.

I looked up at the first few stars coming through the twilight.

Born to die, I thought. Yes, born to die. Why else would I be born of a woman? Why else would I be flesh and blood if it wasn't to die? The pain was so terrible I didn't think I could bear it. I would go home crying if I didn't stop thinking of it. But no, that must not happen. No, never again.

And when will the angels come to me with such bright light that I am not afraid of it? When will the angels fill up the sky with singing so that I can see them? When will angels come to me in my dreams?

A quiet fell over me, just when I thought my heart would burst.

The answer came as if from the earth itself, as if from the stars, and the soft grass, and the nearby trees, and the purring of the evening.

I wasn't sent here to find angels! I wasn't sent here to dream of them. I wasn't sent here to hear them sing! *I was sent here to be alive.* To breathe and sweat and thirst and sometimes cry.

And everything that happened to me, everything both great and small, was something I had to learn! There was room for it in the infinite mind of the Lord and I had to seek the lesson in it, no matter how hard it was to find.

I almost laughed.

It was so simple, so beautiful. If only I could keep it in my mind, this understanding, this moment—never forget it as one day followed another, never forget it no matter what happened, never forget it no matter what came to pass.

Oh, yes, I would grow up, and there would come a time when I would leave Nazareth, surely. I would go out into the world and do what it was I was meant to do. Yes. But for now? All was clear. My fear was gone.

It seemed the whole world was holding me. Why had I ever thought I was alone? I was in the embrace of the earth, of those who loved me no matter what they thought or understood, of the very stars.

"Father," I said. "I am your child."

AUTHOR'S NOTE

EVERY NOVEL I've ever written since 1974 involved historical research. It's been my delight that no matter how many supernatural elements were involved in the story, and no matter how imaginative the plot and characters, the background would be thoroughly historically accurate. And over the years, I've become known for that accuracy. If one of my novels is set in Venice in the eighteenth century, one can be certain that the details as to the opera, the dress, the milieu, the values of the people—all of this is correct.

Without ever planning it, I've moved slowly backwards in history, from the nineteenth century, where I felt at home in my first two novels, to the first century, where I sought the answers to enormous questions that became an obsession with me that simply couldn't be ignored.

Ultimately, the figure of Jesus Christ was at the heart of this obsession. More generally, it was the birth of Christianity and the fall of the ancient world. I wanted to know desperately what happened in the first century, and why people in general never talked about it.

Understand, I had experienced an old-fashioned, strict Roman Catholic childhood in the 1940s and 1950s, in an

Irish American parish that would now be called a Catholic ghetto, where we attended daily Mass and Communion in an enormous and magnificently decorated church, which had been built by our forefathers, some with their own hands. Classes were segregated, boys from girls. We learned Catechism and Bible history, and the lives of the saints. Stained-glass windows, the Latin Mass, the detailed answers to complex questions on good and evil—these things were imprinted on my soul forever, along with a great deal of church history that existed as a great chain of events triumphing over schism and reformation to culminate in the papacy of Pius XII.

I left this church at age eighteen, because I stopped believing it was "the one true church established by Christ to give grace." No personal event precipitated this loss of faith. It happened on a secular college campus; there was intense sexual pressure; but more than that there was the world itself, without Catholicism, filled with good people and people who read books that were strictly speaking forbidden to me. I wanted to read Kierkegaard, Sartre, and Camus. I wanted to know why so many seemingly good people didn't believe in any organized religion yet cared passionately about their behavior and the value of their lives. As the rigid Catholic I was, I had no options for exploration. I broke with the Church. And I broke with my belief in God.

When I married two years later, it was to a passionate atheist, Stan Rice, who not only didn't believe in God, he felt he had had something akin to a vision which had given him a certainty that God didn't exist. He was one of the most honorable and conscience-driven people I ever knew. For him and for me, our writing was our lives.

In 1974, I became a published writer. The novel reflected my guilt and my misery in being cut off from God and from

salvation; my being lost in a world without light. It was set in
the nineteenth century, a context I'd researched heavily in
trying to answer questions about New Orleans, where I was
born and no longer lived.

After that, I wrote many novels without my being aware
that they reflected my quest for meaning in a world without
God. As I said before, I was working my way backwards in
history, answering questions for myself about whole historical developments—why certain revolutions happened, why
Queen Elizabeth I was the way she was, who really wrote
Shakespeare's plays (this I never used in a novel), what the
Italian Renaissance really was, and what had the Black Death
been like before it. And how had feudalism come about.

In the 1990s, living in New Orleans again, living among
adults who were churchgoers and believers, flexible Catholics
of some sophistication, I no doubt imbibed some influence
from them.

But I also inevitably plunged into researching the first
century because I wanted to know about Ancient Rome. I
had novels to write with Roman characters. Just maybe, I
might discover something I'd wanted to know all my life and
never had known:

How did Christianity actually "happen"? Why did Rome
actually fall?

To me these were the ultimate questions and always had
been. They had to do with who we were today.

I remember in the 1960s, being at a party in a lovely
house in San Francisco, given in honor of a famous poet. A
European scholar was there, I found myself alone with him,
seated on a couch. I asked him, "Why did Rome fall?" For
the next two hours he explained it to me.

I couldn't absorb most of what he said. But I never forgot
what I did understand—about all the grain for the city hav-

ing to come from Egypt, and the land around the city being taken up with villas, and the crowds being fed the dole.

It was a wonderful evening, but I didn't leave with a feeling that I had the true grasp of what had happened.

Catholic Church history had given me an awareness of our cultural heritage, although it was presented to me early and quite without context. And I wanted to know the context, why things were the way they were.

When I was a little child, maybe eleven or younger, I was lying on my mother's bed, reading or trying to read one of her books. I read a sentence that said the Protestant Reformation split Europe culturally in half. I thought that was absurd and I asked her, was this true? She said it was. I never forgot that. All my life I wanted to know what that meant.

In 1993, I dug into this early period, and of course went earlier, into the history of Sumer and Babylon and the whole Middle East, and back to Egypt, which I'd studied in college, and I struggled with it all. I read specialized archaeological texts like detective novels searching for patterns, enthralled with the Gilgamesh story, and details such as the masonry tool which the ancient kings (statues) held in their hands.

I wrote two novels during this period that reflect what I was doing. But something happened to me that may not be recorded in any book.

I stumbled upon a mystery without a solution, a mystery so immense that I gave up trying to find an explanation because the whole mystery defied belief. The mystery was the survival of the Jews.

As I sat on the floor of my office surrounded by books about Sumer, Egypt, Rome, etc., and some skeptical material about Jesus that had come into my hands, I couldn't understand how these people had endured as the great people who they were.

It was this mystery that drew me back to God. It set into motion the idea that there may in fact be God. And when that happened there grew in me for whatever reason an immense desire to return to the banquet table. In 1998 I went back to the Catholic Church.

But even then I had not closed in on the question of Jesus Christ and Christianity. I did read the Bible in a state of utter amazement at its variety, its poetry, its startling portraits of women, its inclusion of bizarre and often bloody and violent details. When I was depressed, which was often, someone read the Bible to me, often literary translations of the New Testament—that is, translations by Richard Lattimore that are wondrously literal and beautiful and revealing and that open the text anew.

In 2002 I put aside everything else and decided to focus entirely on answering the questions that had dogged me all my life. The decision came in July of that year. I had been reading the Bible constantly, reading parts of it out loud to my sister, and poring over the Tanach (Old Testament), and I decided that I would give myself utterly to the task of trying to understand Jesus himself and how Christianity emerged.

I wanted to write the life of Jesus Christ. I had known that years ago. But now I was ready. I was ready to do violence to my career. I wanted to write the book in the first person. Nothing else mattered. I consecrated the book to Christ.

I consecrated myself and my work to Christ. I didn't know exactly how I was going to do it.

Even then I did not know what my character of Jesus would be like.

I had taken in a lot of fashionable notions about Jesus— that he'd been oversold, that the Gospels were "late" documents, that we really didn't know anything about him, that violence and quarreling marked the movement of Christianity from its start. I'd acquired many books on Jesus, and they filled the shelves of my office.

But the true investigation began in July of 2002.

In August, I went to my beach apartment, to write the book. Such naiveté. I had no idea I was entering a field of research where no one agreed on anything—whether we are talking about the size of Nazareth, the economic level of Jesus' family, the Jewish attitudes of Galileans in general, the reason Jesus rose to fame, the reason he was executed, or why his followers went out into the world.

As to the size of the field, it was virtually without end. New Testament scholarship included books of every conceivable kind from skeptical books that sought to disprove Jesus had any real value to theology or an enduring church, to books that conscientiously met every objection of the skeptics with footnotes halfway up the page.

Bibliographies were endless. Disputes sometimes produced rancor.

And the primary source material for the first century was a matter of continuous controversy in which the Gospels were called secondary sources by some, and primary sources by others, and the history of Josephus and the works of Philo were subject to exhaustive examination and contentions as to their relevance or validity or whether they had any truth.

Then there was the question of the Rabbis. Could the Mishnah, the Tosefta, and the Talmuds be trusted to give an accurate picture of the first century? Did they actually mention Jesus? And if not, so what, because they didn't mention Herod, who built the Temple, either.

Oh, what lay in store.

But let me backtrack. In 1999, I had received in the mail from my editor and longtime mentor a copy of Paula Fredriksen's *Jesus of Nazareth, King of the Jews*. I had read a substantial part of this book in which Fredriksen re-created beautifully the Jewish milieu in which the boy Jesus might have lived in Nazareth and in which he might have gone to the Temple for Passover along with his family. Fredriksen made the point strongly that Jesus was a Jew. And that this had to be addressed when one wrote about him or thought about him, or so it seems to me.

Now six years later, I have produced a book which is obviously inspired by that scene which Fredriksen wrote, and I can only offer my humble thanks to her and acknowledge her influence.

Of course my beliefs are the polar opposite of Fredriksen's as the book *Christ the Lord* reveals. But it was Fredriksen who steered me in the right direction as to exploring Jesus as a Jew, and there my serious research of him began.

But to return to the year 2002. As I began my serious work, a call came from my husband. He was experiencing the first symptoms of a brain tumor from which he died in less than four months.

We had been married for forty-one years. After my return to the Church, he had consented to marry me in the great old church of my childhood with a priest who was my cousin saying the words. This was a marvelous concession coming from a committed atheist. But out of love for me, my husband did it. Forty-one years. And he was gone.

Was I given the gift of purpose before this tragedy so that it would sustain me through it? I don't know. I do know that during his last weeks, my husband when he was conscious became a saint. He expressed love for those around him, understanding of people he hadn't understood before. He wanted gifts given to those who helped him in his illness. Before that he had managed, though half paralyzed, to create three amazing paintings. I must not neglect to say that. Then after that period of love and understanding, he slowly lapsed into a coma, and was gone.

He left more than three hundred paintings, all done in fifteen years, and many books of poetry, most published during the same period, and thousands of unpublished poems. His memorial gallery will soon move from New Orleans to Dallas, Texas, where he was born.

I went on with my quest right through his illness and his death. My books sustained me. I told him about what I was writing. He thought it was wonderful. He gave me glowing praise.

From that time on, December 2002 when he died, until 2005, I have studied the New Testament period, and I continue to study. I read constantly, night and day.

I have covered an enormous amount of skeptical criticism, violent arguments, and I have read voraciously in the primary sources of Philo and Josephus which I deeply enjoy.

Having started with the skeptical critics, those who take their cue from the earliest skeptical New Testament scholars of the Enlightenment, I expected to discover that their arguments would be frighteningly strong, and that Christianity was, at heart, a kind of fraud. I'd have to end up compartmentalizing my mind with faith in one part of it, and truth in another. And what would I write about my Jesus? I had no idea. But the prospects were interesting. Surely he was a liberal, married, had children, was a homosexual, and who knew what? But I must do my research before I wrote one word.

These skeptical scholars seemed so very sure of themselves. They built their books on certain assertions without even examining these assertions. How could they be wrong? The Jewish scholars presented their case with such care. Certainly Jesus was simply an observant Jew or a Hasid who got crucified. End of story.

I read and I read and I read. Sometimes I thought I was walking through the valley of the shadow of Death, as I read. But I went on, ready to risk everything. I had to know who Jesus was—that is, if anyone knew, I had to know what that person knew.

Now, I couldn't read the ancient languages, but as a scholar I can certainly follow the logic of an argument; I can check the footnotes, and the bibliographical references; I can go to the biblical text in English. I can check all the translations I have and I have every one of which I know from Wycliffe to Lamsa, including the New Annotated Oxford Bible and the old English King James which I love. I have the old Catholic translation, and every literary translation I can find. I have offbeat translations scholars don't mention, such as that by Barnstone and Schonfield. I acquired every single translation for the light it might shed on an obscure line.

What gradually came clear to me was that many of the skeptical arguments—arguments that insisted most of the Gospels were suspect, for instance, or written too late to be eyewitness accounts—lacked coherence. They were not elegant. Arguments about Jesus himself were full of conjecture. Some books were no more than assumptions piled upon assumptions. Absurd conclusions were reached on the basis of little or no data at all.

In sum, the whole case for the nondivine Jesus who stumbled into Jerusalem and somehow got crucified by nobody and had nothing to do with the founding of Christianity and would be horrified by it if he knew about it—that whole picture which had floated in the liberal circles I frequented as an atheist for thirty years—that case was not made. Not only was it not made, I discovered in this field some of the worst and most biased scholarship I'd ever read.

I saw almost no skeptical scholarship that was convincing, and the Gospels, shredded by critics, lost all intensity when reconstructed by various theorists. They were in no way compelling when treated as composites and records of later "communities."

I was unconvinced by the wild postulations of those who claimed to be children of the Enlightenment. And I had also sensed something else. Many of these scholars, scholars who apparently devoted their life to New Testament scholarship, disliked Jesus Christ. Some pitied him as a hopeless failure. Others sneered at him, and some felt an outright contempt. This came between the lines of the books. This emerged in the personality of the texts.

I'd never come across this kind of emotion in any other field of research, at least not to this extent. It was puzzling.

The people who go into Elizabethan studies don't set out to prove that Queen Elizabeth I was a fool. They don't personally dislike her. They don't make snickering remarks about her, or spend their careers trying to pick apart her historical reputation. They approach her in other ways. They don't even apply this sort of dislike or suspicion or contempt to other Elizabethan figures. If they do, the person is usually not the focus of the study. Occasionally a scholar studies a villain, yes. But even then, the author generally ends up arguing for the good points of a villain or for his or her place in history, or for some mitigating circumstance, that redeems the study itself. People studying disasters in history may be highly critical of the rulers or the milieu at the time, yes. But in general scholars don't spend their lives in the company of historical figures whom they openly despise.

But there are New Testament scholars who detest and despise Jesus Christ. Of course, we all benefit from freedom in the academic community; we benefit from the enormous size of biblical studies today and the great range of contributions that are being made. I'm not arguing for censorship. But maybe I'm arguing for sensitivity—on the part of those who read these books. Maybe I'm arguing for a little wariness when it comes to the field in general. What looks like solid ground might not be solid ground at all.

Another point bothered me a great deal.

All these skeptics insisted that the Gospels were late documents, that the prophesies in them had been written after the Fall of Jerusalem. But the more I read about the Fall of Jerusalem, the more I couldn't understand this.

The Fall of Jerusalem was horrific, and involved an enormous and cataclysmic war, a war that went on and on for years in Palestine, followed by other revolts and persecutions, and punitive laws. As I read about this in the pages of S. G. F. Brandon, and in Josephus, I found myself amazed by the details of this appalling disaster in which the greatest Temple of the ancient world was forever destroyed.

I had never truly confronted these events before, never tried to comprehend them. And now I found it absolutely impossible that the Gospel writers could not have included the Fall of the Temple in their work had they written after it as critics insist.

It simply didn't and doesn't make sense.

These Gospel writers were in a Judeo-Christian cult. That's what Christianity was. And the core story of Judaism has to do with redemption from Egypt, and redemption from Babylon. And before redemption from Babylon there was a Fall of Jerusalem in which the Jews were taken to Babylon. And here we have this horrible war. Would Christian writers not have written about it had they seen it? Would they not have seen in the Fall of Jerusalem some echo of the Babylonian conquest? Of course they would have. They were writing for Jews and Gentiles.

The way the skeptics put this issue aside, they simply assumed the Gospels were late documents because of these prophesies in the Gospels. This does not begin to convince.

Before I leave this question of the Jewish War and the Fall of the Temple, let me make this suggestion. When Jewish and Christian scholars begin to take this war seriously, when they begin to really study what happened during the terrible years of the siege of Jerusalem, the destruction of the Temple, and the revolts that continued in Palestine right up through Bar Kokhba, when they focus upon the persecution of Christians in Palestine by Jews; upon the civil war in Rome in the 60s which Kenneth L. Gentry so well describes in his work *Before Jerusalem Fell;* as well as the persecution of Jews in the Diaspora during this period—in sum, when all of this dark era is brought into the light of examination—Bible studies will change.

Right now, scholars neglect or ignore the realities of this period. To some it seems a two-thousand-year-old embarrassment and I'm not sure I understand why.

But I am convinced that the key to understanding the Gospels is that they were written before all this ever happened. That's why they were preserved without question though they contradicted one another. They came from a time that was, for later Christians, catastrophically lost forever.

As I continued my quest, I discovered a scholarship quite different from that of the skeptics—that of John A. T. Robinson, in *The Priority of John.* In reading his descriptions, which took seriously the words of the Gospel itself, I saw what was happening to Jesus in the text of John.

It was a turning point. I was able to enter the Fourth Gospel, and see Jesus alive and moving. And what eventually emerged for me from the Gospels was their unique coherence, their personalities—the inevitable stamp of individual authorship.

Of course John A. T. Robinson made the case for an early date for the Gospels far better than I ever could. He made it brilliantly in 1975, and he took to task the liberal scholars for their assumptions then in *Redating the New Testament,* but what he said is as true now as it was when he wrote those words.

After Robinson I made many great discoveries, among them Richard Bauckham who in *The Gospels for All Christians* soundly refutes the idea that isolated communities produced the Gospels and shows what is obvious, that they were written to be circulated and read by all.

The work of Martin Hengel is brilliant in clearing away assumptions, and his achievements are enormous. I continue to study him.

The scholarship of Jacob Neusner cannot be praised enough. His translations of the Mishnah and the Tosefta are of inestimable value, and his essays are brilliant. He is a giant. Among the Jewish scholars Géza Vermès and David Flusser certainly ought to be read. David Flusser drew my attention to things in Luke's Gospel which I hadn't seen before.

General books I found important that cover the entire development of Jesus in the arts include a great survey book by Charlotte Allen called *The Human Christ,* which discusses how the early quest for the historical Jesus influenced the

motion-picture images of Jesus and Jesus in novels. The work
of Luke Timothy Johnson has always been helpful, and so
also the scholarship of Raymond E. Brown, and John P.
Meier. The work of Seán Freyne on Galilee is extremely
important as is the work of Eric M. Meyers.

Let me mention Larry Hurtado's *Lord Jesus Christ,* and
Craig L. Blomberg's *The Historical Reliability of John's Gospel,*
and the work of Craig S. Keener which I've only begun to
read. I greatly admire Kenneth L. Gentry, Jr.

Roger Aus always teaches me something though I dis-
agree with his conclusions completely. Mary S. Thompson's
work is wonderful.

Highly recommended are the works of Robert Alter and
Frank Kermode on the Bible as literature, and *Mimesis* by
Erich Auerbach. In general, I must praise the work of Ellis
Rivkin, Lee I. Levine, Martin Goodman, Claude Tresmon-
tant, Jonathan Reed, Bruce J. Malina, Kenneth Bailey,
D. Moody Smith, C. H. Dodd, D. A. Carson, Leon Morris,
R. Alan Culpepper, and the great Joachim Jeremias. My spe-
cial thanks to BibleGateway.com.

I learned something from every single book I examined.

The scholar who has given me perhaps some of my most
important insights and who continues to do so through his
enormous output is N. T. Wright. N. T. Wright is one of the
most brilliant writers I've ever read, and his generosity in
embracing the skeptics and commenting on their arguments
is an inspiration. His faith is immense, and his knowledge
vast.

In his book *The Resurrection of the Son of God,* he answers
solidly the question that has haunted me all my life. Christianity achieved what it did, according to N. T. Wright,
because Jesus rose from the dead.

It was the fact of the resurrection that sent the apostles

out into the world with the force necessary to create Christianity. Nothing else would have done it but that.

Wright does a great deal more to put the entire question into historical perspective. How can I do justice to him here? I can only recommend him without reservation, and go on studying him.

Of course my quest is not over. There are thousands of pages of the above-mentioned scholars to be read and reread.

There is so much of Josephus and Philo and Tacitus and Cicero and Julius Caesar that I have yet to cover. And there are so many texts on archaeology—I must go back to Freyne and Eric Meyers in Galilee, and things are being dug up in Palestine, and new books on the Gospels are being printed as I write.

But I see now a great coherence to the life of Christ and the beginning of Christianity that eluded me before, and I see also the subtle transformation of the ancient world because of its economic stagnation and the assault upon it of the values of monotheism, Jewish values melded with Christian values, for which it was not perhaps prepared.

There are also theologians who must be studied, more of Teilhard de Chardin, and Rahner, and St. Augustine.

Now somewhere during my journey through all of this, as I became disillusioned with the skeptics and with the flimsy evidence for their conclusions, I realized something about my book.

It was this. The challenge was to write about the Jesus of the Gospels, of course!

Anybody could write about a liberal Jesus, a married Jesus, a gay Jesus, a Jesus who was a rebel. The "Quest for the Historical Jesus" had become a joke because of all the many definitions it had ascribed to Jesus.

The true challenge was to take the Jesus of the Gospels,

the Gospels which were becoming ever more coherent to me, the Gospels which appealed to me as elegant first-person witness, dictated to scribes no doubt, but definitely early, the Gospels produced before Jerusalem fell—to take the Jesus of the Gospels, and try to get inside him and imagine what he felt.

Then there were the legends—the Apocrypha—including the tantalizing tales in the Infancy Gospel of Thomas describing a boy Jesus who could strike a child dead, bring another to life, turn clay birds into living creatures, and perform other miracles. I'd stumbled on them very early in my research, in multiple editions, and never forgotten them. And neither had the world. They were fanciful, some of them humorous, extreme to be sure, but they had lived on into the Middle Ages, and beyond. I couldn't get these legends out of my mind.

Ultimately I chose to embrace this material, to enclose it within the canonical framework as best I could. I felt there was a deep truth in it, and I wanted to preserve that truth as it spoke to me. Of course that is an assumption. But I made it. And perhaps in assuming that Jesus did manifest supernatural powers at an early age I am somehow being true to the declaration of the Council of Chalcedon, that Jesus was God and Man at all times.

I am certainly trying to be true to Paul when he said that Our Lord emptied himself for us, in that my character has emptied himself of his Divine awareness in order to suffer as a human being.

This is a book I offer to all Christians—to the fundamentalists, to the Roman Catholics, to the most liberal Christians in the hope that my embrace of more conservative doctrines will have some coherence for them in the here and now of the book. I offer it to scholars in the hope that they will perhaps enjoy seeing the evidence of the research that's gone into it, and of course I offer it to those whom I so greatly admire who have been my teachers though I've never met them and probably never will.

I offer this book to those who know nothing of Jesus Christ in the hope that you will see him in these pages in some form. I offer this novel with love to my readers who've followed me through one strange turn after another in the hope that Jesus will be as real to you as any other character I've ever launched into the world we share.

After all, is Christ Our Lord not the ultimate supernatural hero, the ultimate outsider, the ultimate immortal of them all?

If you've followed me this far, I thank you. I could append to this a bibliography of stifling length but I will not.

Let me in conclusion thank several people who have been my support and inspiration throughout these years:

Fr. Dennis Hayes, my spiritual director, who has answered my theological questions with patience always.

Fr. Joseph Callipare, whose sermons on the Gospel of John were brilliant and wonderful. My time spent in his parish in Florida was one of the most beautiful periods of my research and work.

Fr. Joseph Cocucci, whose letters and discussions on theology with me have been inspiring and truly great.

The Redemptorist Fathers, the priests of my parish in New Orleans, whose sermons have sustained me, and whose example has been a shining light. I leave them with regret. My father's education in the Redemptorist Seminary at Kirkwood, Missouri, no doubt changed the course of his life. My debt to the Redemptorists can never be paid.

Fr. Dean Robins and Fr. Curtis Thomas of the Nativity of Our Lord Parish, who have been welcoming to me as a new parishioner. I leave them with regret.

Br. Becket Ghioto, whose letters have been patient, wise, and full of wonderful insights and answers.

And last, but hardly least, Amy Troxler, my friend and companion, who has answered so many fundamental questions for me, and listened to my endless ravings, who has been with me to Mass, and brought me Communion when I couldn't go, who has been more of a help to me than I can ever say. It was Amy who was there for me on the afternoon in 1998 when I asked if she knew a priest who could hear my confession, who could help me go back to the Church. It was Amy who found the priest and took me to see him. It was Amy's example during those early months of attending the Mass in English that helped me so much to adjust to a liturgy that was wholly different from that which I'd left behind. I leave Amy as I leave New Orleans with the deepest regret.

My beloved staff, my dearest friends, my editor Vicky Wilson who read and commented on this manuscript much to its benefit, my family, I thank them all. I live in the environment of their nourishing love. I am blessed.

As for my son, this novel is dedicated to him. That says it all.

6 a.m., February 24, 2005